The Strawberry Field

The Strawberry Field

by Barbara Jean Ruther

Published by
Torrid Books
An imprint of Whiskey Creek Press LLC
Torridbooks.com

Cover Artist: Kelly Martin
Editor: Dave Field
Printed in the United States of America

Print ISBN: 978-1-63596-661-9

In Appreciation

My heartfelt thanks for the time-consuming contributions from Millie
Evans and Jerry Ruther.
BJR ~ Author

PREFACE

The character of Alyssa, in this story, is derived from studies about siblings with totally opposite physical, mental, emotional, and social characteristics. I imposed the trait of sadomasochism to Alyssa's nature after reading about people with those tendencies. Research into the subject brought to light individuals and cults who derive pleasure, especially sexual, through inflicting or receiving pain. You can imagine how it stirred my curiosity, especially since I dread the needle prick of a blood test.

The Strawberry Field is the story of two sisters—Beth, outwardly a ray of sunshine, repressing sadness and fear. Hopelessly yearning for a child, she is married to the narcissistic, deceitful, too handsome Raymond James. Alyssa, with a wickedly mean personality, was born unhappy, challenging the patience of everyone unfortunate enough to be near her. Alyssa is the uncontrollable mold that suffocates the basket of fresh fruit.

At nine years old, in fourth grade, an overweight classmate, angry with the incessant, teasing insults from Alyssa, stabbed her in the shoulder with sharp scissors from the Art Room. She laughed loudly, enjoying the injury. Later, she discovered there was a name for the pleasure of pain—sadomasochism. She spent her life cultivating the craft.

We meet them at the memorial service for Elizabeth Alexander, widow, mother of Beth and Alyssa.

The death of Elizabeth sends three people on new paths in their lives. BJR ~ *Author*

Chapter 1

The solemn dark-clad mourners filled the gazebo and spilled out the arched door, leaning inward to hear Elizabeth's old neighbor, Charles, tearfully give the eulogy she had requested of him and written herself.

The clouds were dark and low, seeming to push the air into the ground. The heat and humidity combined forces, causing shoulders to droop like wilting petals. People couldn't be sure of their next breath.

It was a proper day for a funeral.

The white wood gazebo, sides flush with climbing roses, stood in the center of a carefully tended garden where Elizabeth Alexander usually had her afternoon tea, either alone or with her friend, Charles Sullivan. Her Siamese cat, Sam Number Two, had always been nearby, napping in a shaded spot, preferably on the cushioned circular bench. Elizabeth's white toy poodle, Sugarfoot, fifteen years old, slow and quiet, had been happy to lie at her feet, biding his time until offered a little piece of banana bread.

Today, Charles supported a tired back against the frame of the gazebo, let his head hang until his chin rested on the red suede vest, tight over his broad chest, and blocked the mourners from his mind as vivid memories went back to his afternoons in Elizabeth's garden. "These flowers are my reward for the years of protecting and watching over them," Elizabeth had said to Charles every day during the short blooming season.

"And having tea with you, my dear Elizabeth, is my reward for living past my expiration date," he had answered.

After tea, she would walk with him on the flagstone path that wound through the garden, holding his arm as he stepped carefully, haltingly. He leaned heavily on the thick, carved cane he had picked up in some exotic country as a souvenir, never thinking he would someday need it. She praised the perfection of the roses and bent down to inhale their scent, pointed out the newly opened daylilies and the paper-thin petals of the graceful poppies. Then she led him to the back of the yard where her husband, Christopher, had planted six Viking apple trees, six Reliance peach trees, and six Bartlett pear trees, all recommended by the nursery to survive the cold Chicago-area winters. She picked two plump, almost yellow, but not quite ripe pears and rubbed them on the leg of her khaki pants. She and Charles then sat on the white wrought-iron bench and ate the crispy fruit.

He'd laughed at her cleaning method and said, "I hope the birds haven't pooped on these pears."

Indignantly she had answered, "Do you know why so many children have allergies today? Their mothers want them to live in a sterile world. Everything they eat has been disinfected. If a piece of bread falls on the floor, it is thrown in the garbage. Kids are fed over-washed organic fruits and vegetables. They have built up no resistance to germs. A little dirt is good for you." She took another bite of the greenish-yellow pear. "In two more weeks, these pears will be so perfectly ripe, the juice will drip from our chins."

He'd smiled, thinking of her allergy theory and knowing he was eating a green pear, not yet ripe, simply because she had handed it to him. Why would he refuse? He loved her and thought, *Maybe there's some truth to that mysterious thing called fate...the circumstances that led me to a friendship at this late stage in my life, filling an old banged-up tin can with flowers.*

The setting could have been a picture from *Better Homes and Gardens* come to life, as was the town of Clarington Hills, a horsey suburb an hour out of Chicago, where each ample house boasted a swimming pool or a tennis court or a paddock, or any combination of the three. But Elizabeth had opted for a floriferous display with an orchard, and her centerpiece gazebo. It was a surprise every spring when the snow piles finally thawed and the recurrent flora sprouted up in a celebration of green, as if to boldly defy the colorless winter that had kept them imprisoned in the frozen ground. And then to prove its audacity, the greenery produced abundant color. The garden covered half an acre in the back of the two-story, white-columned amber-brick house where Elizabeth and Christopher had raised their two daughters. A thick hedge of peonies bloomed in a profusion of cherry pink and snow white. The blooms, as big as mixing bowls, grew across the front yard, leaving two openings for the circular driveway, then continuing down both sides and into the back of the huge yard. Elizabeth had spent hours in her garden working alongside her helper. "Diego, I love the feel of earth on my hands," she often told him. "It's like we're taking part in the miracle of growth." She had designed the layout on graph paper according to scale, labeled the desired flowers, carefully drawn the flagstone walkway, and placed the gazebo in the center. *I will call this little part of paradise Contentment, a place to relax with a sigh and a cup of Earl Grey tea.*

Elizabeth had felt she and Christopher didn't need a tennis court. They belonged to the Green Hills of Clarington Country Club and "a swimming pool is too dangerous with lots of babies running around." Lots of babies that never arrived. But one baby had come, Beth, then five years later, Alyssa. Christopher had consoled her. "I know you want lots of children. I'm sorry that hasn't happened for us."

"I'm happy to have our two girls," the ever-optimistic Elizabeth had replied.

Now, on this gloomiest of days, Charles mentally prepared himself to read the poem Elizabeth had given him only two weeks ago. The pain from pancreatic cancer had confined her to bed, and the morphine had given her the relief of a drowsy state. Still, as Charles had sat by her bedside in an uncomfortable French boudoir chair, she'd put her hand on his arm and in a raspy, hushed voice had said, "Charles, on my desk is a poem for my daughter, Beth, but she will not be able to read it out loud. I want friends to hear it, to let them know I have accepted death. I don't want a religious service, but invite my friends to walk in my garden. My spirit will be lingering there. Then read the poem and scatter my ashes around my lovely garden that gave me such pleasure."

As he'd kissed her damp, warm forehead, she had whispered, almost out of breath, "Thank you for your short but cherished friendship, Charles."

Charles knew both daughters and also knew they had opposite personalities. Elizabeth had shared her innermost thoughts and feelings with him, and he was a most attentive listener, providing compassion and sympathy. Beth had been the joy in Elizabeth's life, and Alyssa the pain she'd endured. Two daughters, five years apart in age, eons apart emotionally—the rose and the thorn.

Inside the gazebo, Charles Sullivan, actor extraordinaire, straightened to his full six feet two inches and said, "Ladies and gentlemen."

To himself he said, *My dear Elizabeth, I shall summon the strength to carry out your request and give my final soliloquy for you, for you have taken my heart with you.*

The group turned toward the trained, smooth, stage voice, to the aged but still distinguished-looking actor. His thick white hair swayed as he talked, as if a slight breeze had seeped into the screened, circular structure and uplifted him for his difficult task. His head dipped like a symphony conductor's with the weight of his grief but back up with the beat of his words. He showed a barely visible smile for Elizabeth, as if she was watching and he was letting her know he would complete her bidding. "I give you the writing of Elizabeth Alexander as she composed for this most grievous day."

He wiped his teary eyes with his knuckles, took his reading glasses from the inside pocket of his navy blazer, cleared his throat, and read Elizabeth's farewell with poise and dignity, as though he was giving a serious reading on the New York stage.

The Cycle of Life

I have listened to the lonely wind
as he whispered to me through tall pines,
and have known the warmth
of the sun's glow, encircling my shoulders
like comforting arms of a friend.
I plucked each petal of the dewy, soft pink rose,
dismantling her like a dancer in seven veils,
searching for her mystery.
One day I cupped a baby bird in my hands,
felt his tiny heart beat with fear
as I placed him back in his twig-home.
I have cried the unbearable joy—
my newborn asleep on my breast,
our hearts intertwined, locked into
impenetrable force of Mother/Daughter.

The end of my time may bring some sadness,
as in the passing of summer,
but be renewed when gentle snowflakes
touch your cheek, refreshing your mind
to continue your own journey.

Let my ashes float free so some small speck of me
may join soil in the valley
and accompany apple blossoms into fruit,
or perhaps nourish a field of sweet strawberries,
my memorial, to soothe your sorrow.
In remembrance of me lift your face to the breeze
and let it ruffle your hair.
Watch young birds, challenged by bravery,
take flight and learn from their courage.
Inhale the scent of fresh velvety roses
and close your eyes, so the memory
of them, and me, will linger in your soul.

As my ashes scatter,
think of laughter we shared
and know you overflowed my heart with joy,
like snow thaw fills the mountain creek
to sate the thirst of new fawns.
All life must end
as even luminescent green hummingbirds,
who delight us with their return in Spring,
one May fail to show up.
As sure as one life ends, another begins,
and someday your Spirit will join mine.
Together we will watch your children's children,
choosing their own path,
continuing their own cycle.

The sobs that overcame Beth added to the sorrow of bowed heads of Elizabeth's friends who were spilling out of the gazebo. Beth's husband, Raymond, a Cary Grant–looking, too-handsome type, put an arm around her shoulders and led her to the wide, stone-paved terrace where a caterer was setting out a buffet lunch on oblong white-clothed tables.

* * * *

Beth was the elder of Elizabeth's two daughters, a pregnancy that was yearned for but had taken five years to accomplish. When Beth was finally born, the overjoyed Elizabeth held the pink-bundled child close to her breast and whispered, "Little clone from my body, I will give you my heart and my name. I will protect you like the mother bird holds her young under her wing until you fly off into your own world." The newborn looked into her mother's eyes as if she understood the promise.

* * * *

Now, after greeting Elizabeth's friends, and the reading by Charles Sullivan, Beth sat with Raymond and Alyssa at the ornate wrought-iron and glass-top table on the covered terrace overlooking the screened-in gazebo and the carefully tended backyard. Elizabeth's friends had eaten and left but their sad smiles stayed behind, hanging in the air like a gray atmosphere of depression. Beth was quiet, sullen, grievous, staring through the humid haze to the small orchard of fruit trees at the far back, sunk in the deep thought of her loss—her mother, her best friend. Alyssa interrupted the silence. "I think it's bizarre that Mother wrote her own eulogy. It was embarrassing. I have never heard of anyone doing that, and why did she leave the service to that rickety old man? People should just die and certainly forget ridiculous recitations or ceremonies."

An anger long suppressed in Beth finally boiled to the top. She had always ignored her sister's nasty comments, excusing her with, "Oh, that's Alyssa," but this time the criticism of their mother enraged Beth. It seemed to her that Alyssa wasn't feeling any sadness, wasn't even mourning.

Of course Alyssa wasn't mourning. She felt no grief, no sorrow, no loss. To Alyssa, her mother was an inconvenience, a ridiculous obligation to acknowledge a person in charge of one's life, even if only financially. She thought, *Thankfully, that's over. How annoying that my inane sister can't realize she is now released from a suffocating bond.*

Raymond turned as Beth uncharacteristically screamed at Alyssa, "Stop, stop—right this instant. You have been rude to our mother all your life. She and Dad let you get away with your harsh, cruel behavior because they thought you would become a nicer person as you got older, but you became even more discourteous, especially toward Mom. You are mean and spiteful. She never deserved your criticism, and it caused her great pain. Now it shall end. You are never to talk unkindly about her or dishonor her character in my presence. From this day on, her memory will be held with high respect."

Tears filled Beth's eyes. She had never been bold enough to defy her sister, had never confronted her, mostly because she was afraid of Alyssa, who had been a constant threat all her life. Now grief empowered Beth, but Alyssa merely sloughed off the comments as though she hadn't even heard. Beth inhaled deeply, calmly stood up. It had helped her to finally speak what was on her mind. She walked into the house and up the stairs to her old room, where the memories of growing up were stored in every corner, stashed away for rainy days of remembering. The bedroom had changed through the stages in her life—the canopied white crib replaced with the adolescent youth bed, pink and green floral wallpaper became stark-white walls with travel posters—the old train station clock at Musée d'Orsay, the Great Wall of China, the Taj Mahal—all places she'd hoped to visit with a handsome husband, never to happen. Her favorite reading space was at a large bay window, a cushioned window seat strewn with pillows of pinks, purples, greens, violet. It was an inviting private nook, a place to avoid the sinister eyes of her sister, a place to snuggle under a cozy afghan by the frosted window and read from the piles of books stacked around her room. She sat in her window seat looking down at the garden, the gazebo, the shriveling leaves of the pear trees revealing intricate bird's nests, and the memories of her childhood kept flashing in her mind like slides being projected on the wall. She remembered holding the ladder when her mother wanted to put a fallen baby bird back into its nest. That was her mother, deeply concerned about life, even little creatures. She saw her father carrying an early-morning breakfast tray for her mother to the gazebo, both in robes, hushed voices, but then laughter; always when they were together, there had been laughter. Beth remembered thinking she would marry a man exactly like her father, who would love her completely, as her father loved.

She looked around her room and thought of her mother's advice: "Read, read, read, it will take you wherever you want to go." She escaped into the lives of other people—Marie Curie, Helen Keller, Amelia Earhart, Anne Frank, Mother Teresa, Rosa Parks. *So many escapes, it wasn't normal, I shouldn't have had to avoid Alyssa, but I truly feared her. I was older, bigger, but I still considered her dangerous. She had an evil look on her face that made me cower.*

Beth's thoughts went back to when she was five years old and her parents had brought her baby sister home from the hospital. They had promised a sister who would look to her for help, depend on her, adore her. The baby cried day and night for three months, only giving all a relief when she finally fell into an exhausted sleep. "Colic," they explained. In a daze of fatigue, their mother finally gave in to her husband's insistence to hire a nurse. Beth watched, longing to hold her sister, yearning to feed, kiss, talk. As a little girl, Alyssa had been prone to temper tantrums and throwing herself on the floor, screaming and pounding her fists. When Elizabeth tried to pick her up, Alyssa would kick and bite her. "She will grow out of it," Elizabeth would announce hopefully. Later, Beth would think, *She's never grown out of it. She's still the same dreadful child. Mom could never do enough for her, and she was horribly disrespectful to our kind and loving father, refusing to acknowledge his thoughtful gifts or even his compassionate words.* Elizabeth would try to explain the rude behavior to her exasperated husband. "She is just going through a stage. It will be over soon."

Elizabeth and Christopher were rewarded for their patience but not with a mellowing of Alyssa. No gentleness or loving kindness came with age and maturity. Their compensation was the continuous efforts of young Beth to put the joy of a child into their life. She would draw pictures, glue flower petals and leaves to the artwork, add messages of her love and present them to her parents, often including a rose from her mother's garden. Because Beth couldn't bear to increase their burden, she never related to her parents Alyssa's mean antics or nasty words—"Be careful what you eat, I plan to poison you." "You're so stupid, your brain is made from jellyfish." "My friends laugh at the way you dress, dorky."

As Alyssa got older, the reports from the school principal and her teachers caused Elizabeth and Christopher to seek advice from psychologists, but Alyssa refused to keep appointments. When she was grounded for her malicious behavior, she would simply sneak out through her bedroom window. When she lost the privilege of using her phone, she would take Beth's phone, knowing Beth wouldn't tell. Beth was careful to keep distance, at least some space, between herself and Alyssa. She not only wanted to avoid confrontations, but she was afraid of Alyssa, who would hit her with a book or whatever she was carrying as they passed in the hallway outside their bedrooms. Many times she held scissors high like a dagger and smiled wickedly. Even if Alyssa had no intention of using them as a weapon, it was the cringing and look of fear she had induced that she enjoyed.

Beth never told her parents that Alyssa had broken all of her exquisite cut-crystal perfume bottles. One by one she had tossed the lovely collection in the air, letting them land on the sandstone-tiled bathroom floor. The spiteful prank left a dangerous scattering of sharp shards. Beth knew that in Alyssa's mind, she had successfully punished her sister—for being a loving daughter, for her perfect report cards from school, for being too pretty, but most of all for the years of never showing any anger. Her actions communicated her thoughts clearly: *Let's see if this can raise some rage.*

Beth had quietly held the dustpan while the housekeeper swept the fragments into it, and decided she would wait until she had her own apartment to have fragile collectibles. The housekeeper reported the incident to Elizabeth, who put her arms around Beth, knowing she endured pain caused by her sister's uncontrollable malice. "My darling, after you graduate from college and have your own place, I will start a collection for you of the most beautiful antique perfume bottles." They felt helpless, not knowing how to handle the problem called Alyssa. Elizabeth and Christopher wordlessly seemed to agree that the only solution, with determined patience, was to bide the time until Alyssa left for college. Afterward, they would buy her a condominium and give her an allowance. They were ashamed to admit, even to each other, they wanted her out of their house and perhaps out of their lives.

Beth began a countdown—the days until she would leave for college. However, a conflicting feeling kept coming to her, the disturbing fear of leaving her mother alone with Alyssa. She discussed her worry with her father, who confided that he also didn't trust Alyssa and promised he would no longer play golf with the guys unless Elizabeth had plans with her friends. "When Alyssa and your mother are at home, I will be at home. I will take good care of your mother, my college girl."

* * * *

On the terrace, Alyssa moved to a chair closer to her brother-in-law. He wore a bored expression, and she was familiar with the feeling. She had always been bored at this house. She thought, *It's the perfect time to offer him some excitement. He hasn't shown any interest in me before today, but now he doesn't have Mother looking over his shoulder. He'll get my message.*

* * * *

Raymond and Beth, both thirty-five years old, had been married for ten years but not yet had children. During those ten years of monthly disappointments, Beth would go to her mother for comfort, and Elizabeth, with her usual positive attitude, assured her that pregnancy would happen. She reminded Beth it had taken five years for her to arrive and another five years for Alyssa. "We are just slow to conceive, don't stress yourself about it. Soon I will be Nana to a sweet little girl. I will buy her too many pink dresses, and you will tell me to stop spoiling her. I wish your father was here to overindulge her with me." They both laughed, realizing that Elizabeth was talking about a nonexistent grandchild.

* * * *

Alone with her brother-in-law on her mother's terrace, Alyssa was sitting in the pink and orange multi-flowered fabric, cushioned wrought-iron chair next to Raymond, thinking, *He's too handsome and sexy for my dull sister. I'm sure she doesn't appreciate his attributes.* Humidity had engulfed the area and Raymond had removed his jacket, rolled up his shirt sleeves, and unbuttoned several buttons on the top of his shirt, revealing a provocative chest with just enough hair. Alyssa leaned toward him, got his attention, and pointedly let her eyes wander over his muscular arms, bared chest, and down to his lap. He smiled, knowing the look. She had always flirted with him at holiday family gatherings, but he had never encouraged her. He used to think, *I'll stay with the older daughter, who has the best chance of inheriting the bulk of the estate and will probably be named executor, in control of the trust. This younger daughter will be under her sister's thumb, and I'm not going to jeopardize my gold mine for a fling inside the family when I can get sex outside the family anytime.*

Raymond looked at Alyssa, thinking she wasn't the same wild kid rebelling against her parents, seeking adventure in forbidden seas. Now she sailed calm waters, with a well-thought-out destination of her own choosing. He'd always felt she wanted to have sex with him, probably so she could throw it in her sister's face, but that would cause a divorce and certainly make their parents angry with him. But the parents weren't there anymore, so he no longer had to make a show of being the dedicated husband. He was sure the rebel daughter had experience, which could be fun. He suddenly felt tired of the pretense and knew his wife would be depressed, sullen, crying as she had been all week. He no longer had the patience for it, especially as he looked at Alyssa and saw the expression he had seen many times on women who wanted him: *I'm finished here, let's have some excitement!*

"Alyssa, let's go to the club," he said. "They haven't closed the pool yet, and we can swim a few laps to cool off. Isn't the heat and humidity stifling this afternoon? Go get your bikini, I'll meet you in the car." It was generic talk per chance it was overheard, could have been said to anyone, purposely made like it was a hot, boring afternoon and any company would suffice.

Alyssa went into the house without hesitation, giving him no chance to change his mind. She and Beth kept some clothes in their old bedrooms at their parents' home, just to be prepared for a change of plans. Raymond sat for a moment, casually retrieved his jacket by the collar, flung it over his shoulder, and walked on the hand-laid flagstone path around the side of the house to the circular driveway in front of the garage. As Alyssa passed through the foyer, she saw Beth's purse on a chair. She opened the flap, reached inside and took Beth's wallet. There was no plan, only the thought of how much trouble it would cause her; replacing credit cards, driver's license, cash. She came out the front door with a small tote bag hanging from her shoulder, got in the car at the same time as Raymond. He smiled. "That was fast."

"I'm ready." She displayed the same wicked smile as when she'd shattered Beth's collection of perfume bottles. She had been unconcerned about that mess and now was unconcerned about any consequences from driving off with her sister's husband. She hoped Beth saw them from an upstairs window, wished she had seen Beth as she hurried down the stairs, so she could have said, "Ray and I are going to the club," because it would have contained mean, implicit intention to hurt.

Beth heard the footsteps scrambling down the stairs and hoped Alyssa was leaving. She didn't want to confront her again. She walked slowly down to the main floor, into her mother's bedroom, and sat at Elizabeth's ornate French-style desk that stood in the center of a huge bay window where she would look at her gazebo, surrounded by New Dawn climbing roses, and jot down notes for poems she wanted to write later. There were still a few fully bloomed flowers with ready-to-drop petals hanging on to their last days, but the leaves were turning yellow and Beth knew a cold wind would be the end of them for this year. She thought, *My mother wouldn't like to know I am moping around here. I'll take some of the food from the caterer to Charles, talk to him for a while, make sure he's okay. I know losing his good friend is going to be difficult for him.*

Beth walked out of the spacious bedroom, holding herself erect as she knew her mother would expect, into the kitchen. The caterers had left labeled containers of leftover food on the granite countertop. She glanced outside at the unoccupied terrace, felt the lonely quietness, the empty calm of loss. She decided that Alyssa and Raymond had probably gone to play tennis. She certainly didn't have the energy or the desire to see people at the club or to play tennis, so she was glad they had left without her. She did, however, feel like talking to a friend about her mother, someone who would listen to her reminiscences about their long lunches with laughing gossip, the shopping excursions when they'd bought unnecessary, silly items, like the time they came home with little glass birds for their desks. They had unwrapped the treasures to show Beth's father, who rolled his eyes, then listened to snickering as they told him they had bought something for him and offered a half-eaten box of chocolate creams. Laughing, he always said, "You two girls can't be trusted out together." He was, of course, happy his wife and daughter enjoyed their frivolous outings and a close relationship that somewhat relieved the tension Elizabeth endured, caused by Alyssa. For her parents, Beth was the sugar on the bitter-lemon tart.

Beth picked up two containers marked "Curry chicken salad" and "Melon balls and sliced strawberries," walked out the front door over to Charles's house, and rang his doorbell. Leaning on his cane, he reached for her with his free arm, drew her to his wide, comforting chest. "Come sit with me, my dear girl, and we shall awaken memories of our beloved Elizabeth." Even his voice was like a bear hug.

* * * *

Raymond drove his white BMW convertible, Alyssa in the front passenger seat, past the Green Hills of Clarington Country Club. "Where are we going?" she asked as they passed the entrance gates to her parents' club. She didn't care where they were going; she had finally caught the attention of her sister's husband, and she planned to make the most of it. She would show him what he had been missing. Raymond sensed her desire, her craving for adventure, excitement, felt her looking at him, and knew that she would follow his lead as easily as a trained dog wanting to please. He thought, *This is going to be fun. I deserve it. The atmosphere around Beth is morbid; it's bad for my health. I need laughter, merriment. I bring my own amusement to the party, and today my amusement is sitting in my car.*

Raymond drove into the parking lot of the Sunset Acres Country Club. "This is where I'm most comfortable, Alyssa. I have lots of friends here, they'll like you." He saw the flashy red BMW that belonged to Joel Wolfe and knew he would be at the pool following an afternoon of tennis. "Bring your bag, Alyssa—you can change in the ladies' locker room. I want you to meet my best friend." He put his arm around her shoulders, pointed to the locker room door, and met her at the other side that led out to the pool area.

They joined a collection of young men and women, so fit, so blatantly tanned, laughing loudly showing straight, sparkling teeth as if they were being filmed for a toothpaste commercial. It was a reckless, carefree group, spoiled, bored, looking for new thrills to produce even more stimulation in their indulged lives. Each one was without noticeable flaws, as if they had been culled from a group and only the perfect selected.

The women had long, radiant, straight hair that draped down their backs, and they swung it around as they talked like heavy fringe on a shawl being flung over their shoulders. They wore skimpy bikinis that revealed flat stomachs and bodies toned to perfection. Smooth, loofahed feet pedicured with shiny red polish rested on a male thigh. They were animated dolls just lifted from tissued boxes. Basically they looked alike, without any individualism making one stand out. It caused them to diligently vie with one another for attention, compete for the crown of being chosen.

The men were arrogant, cocky, overbearing, and confident; after all, they were the ones being vied for. They drove impressive, fast cars and had affluent parents, which gave them the confidence to misbehave. Some of the men were married. But these young women liked being chosen for sex by a married man. It was an exciting challenge to play the game, contend, strive to be the superior one, possibly persuade him to leave his wife for her, which would be proof she had won. Also, these sex partners enjoyed seeing him at club parties, where he would be accompanied by his wife. They would smile at him, perhaps with a slight nod, with eyes that quickly surveyed the body, acknowledging their sexual feats, their secrets.

Alyssa, however, stood out from this group of women like the new kid on the block, totally self-absorbed. She was content in her own style and wouldn't think of conforming, becoming one of the group. She reveled in her diversity, looked down on the look-alike girls as if a queen among commoners. Alyssa had inherited her father's thick, wavy hair and she kept it cut short, so it fell into natural dips, swept back in place with gel, layered close in a brush cut to the nape of her neck. It was a style that stayed the same from the moment she ran a brush through it after stepping out of the shower, outlasting wind, rain, hats, and exploits in her bedroom. It was naturally dark brown, but she dyed it black. She liked to wear eyeliner at the base of her thickly mascaraed eyelashes, upper and lower, and the whole effect was exotic-looking. Alyssa was a jogger, which kept her legs muscular and her body shapely with zero fat. She had full, round, firm breasts and large, sensitive nipples that became hard when she wanted sex, which was as soon as she spied the object of her desire. She often had a full-body wax and liked standing naked to flaunt her smooth curves for protuberant, raspy-breathing, impatient men—whom she caught off-guard with a leather-belted wallop across their bare chests, followed by a canyon-echoing laugh.

Raymond had yet to discover Alyssa's enjoyment of giving and receiving pain. He saw himself as the suave, smooth-talking, urbanely sophisticated, ultimate sexually desirable, perfect specimen of man, always the leader, in charge and all wrapped up in a handsome package. There was a big surprise for him bundled up in Alyssa's flirting. She was craftily alluring the insect into her web of dark, secretive intrigue. Once the bedroom door was closed, he would be astonished to realize he was not the leader, nor would he be in charge.

Alyssa and Raymond stopped at thick-cushioned lounges near the pool, and Joel came over when he saw them. Raymond made introductions and told Alyssa to relax on the lounge while he and Joel ordered margaritas at the pool bar. Joel leaned close to Raymond's ear. "Wow, can I have her tonight?"

Raymond laughed. "She's been giving me the look for years. Tonight, I'm going to indulge myself."

* * * *

Beth Alexander and Raymond James had met at the Chicago Life Fitness and Physical Therapy Center where Beth was an ardent physical therapist. She researched up-to-date therapy for each injury that was assigned to her and kept her craft current by attending workshops. She had told her parents, "I don't want to be the society girl with an allowance, I want to earn money and support myself." Her father adored her, was impressed by her independent spirit, and told her they wanted to help her, would always be there for her. "Please keep your credit card that you had during college. We are happy to pay for your clothes and other charges." Beth was frugal in her spending, as she had been in college, so her mother regularly took her shopping.

Raymond had injured his rotator cuff, the muscles that encircle and support the shoulder, when he had overreached for his tennis opponent's blistering backhand and fallen on his shoulder. After surgery, his doctor sent him for therapy to get the shoulder moving again. Raymond had been assigned to a young male therapist with a bodybuilder's physique who led him in a series of exercises, combined with massage and electrical stimulation. Raymond dreaded the painful exercises three days each week, but he contented himself by intently watching a tall and very pretty therapist lead her patients through rehab exercises. One long wall of the room, packed with machines, was mirrored for patients to watch themselves do the exercises correctly. The time passed faster for Raymond when he watched Beth in her shorts or tights that revealed long, shapely, athletic legs. Her long, dark-blond hair was neatly banded at the nape of her neck, with lighter streaks that glistened under the bright lights. After three weeks of therapy, Raymond requested he get transferred to a different therapist, preferably the female. The receptionist smiled and put him on Beth's schedule.

As Beth demonstrated exercises she advised him to do at home on the off days he wasn't at the Therapy Center, he thought, *If I must do this boring therapy, I can at least enjoy the view.*

Beth was serious about helping her patients with their rehabilitation, pushing with encouragement—the conscientious teacher wanting her students to advance.

With the new therapist as his romance-challenge, Raymond looked forward to each session. "Will you play tennis with me and be gentle, so I can build up my game?" he asked, flirtatiously, flashing his perfect-teeth smile and flaunting his golden tan. Beth, a serious competitor, had played first court on her college tennis team, and opponents had become well aware of her powerful two-handed backhand that could go down the line or crosscourt without any warning. At her parents' club, she played first court, singles, in the ladies' league. Raymond stirred her competitiveness and she thought, *He's offensively cocky, I would love to beat him.* But she said only, "I don't play tennis gently, so if you want to play with me, you'd better concentrate on your therapeutic exercises." Her feistiness aroused him.

Raymond had asked around about Beth Alexander. He didn't want to waste too much time on a working girl; a few sexual encounters were all that interested him, but when he researched her father, his interest jumped to a new level. He decided she was worth putting some energy into the pursuit—and he was fueled for the race.

At six feet tall, not as tall as the handsome movie star, Cary Grant, Raymond had comparable good looks. He liked to let his thick, dark-brown hair grow long enough to fall over his ears and hang windblown-messy across his forehead. It made him look vulnerable, like an innocent schoolboy, and it tempted women to get close enough to push the disorderly hair back into place. They were seduced by his handsomeness and well-proportioned athletic body, and then he would turn on his charm, which he had practiced and perfected. The charm led to sex, and sex without a commitment was Raymond's goal, unless there was money involved. He was scouting for an heiress, a trust fund—after he tired of the current woman, that is. When the sex turned cold and boring, he was ready to move on to the next female challenge. Pursuit and conquer was his modus vivendi, his way of life. Raymond was like the spoiled child with overly indulgent parents who doled out too much candy, except he was the one permitting the excess, allowing himself too much candy.

Raymond graduated from Illinois State University, where he was popular on campus but academically at the bottom of his class. For male friends, he singled out fellow students who came from wealthy families and who probably would fall into the family business after graduation. He thought, *A good friend in the family business will be a good place to get a job without the hassle of job hunting.* Also, they would belong to country clubs and he could get himself on their guest lists and have no obligation for membership charges, simply sign tabs with the friend's name. Of course—and very important to him—country clubs were where the daughters, who would come into trust funds, could be found.

Exactly as Raymond had plotted, after graduation he got a job with the Lobo Insurance Agency, owned by the father of his classmate, Joel Wolfe. Both young men worked at the agency writing policies during the week, partied at their favorite singles bars every night, and played tennis at Sunset Acres Country Club on weekends, where Joel's father maintained a family membership. For Raymond, the country club was his dream come true. He signed Joel's name to his bar tabs and impressed the girls with his build in a Speedo swimsuit. Joel considered Raymond his best friend, and when Mr. Wolfe presented Joel with a new BMW, a gift for his promotion to Partner at the Lobo Insurance Agency, Joel gave his three-year-old BMW to his best friend, Raymond James. Luxuries came easy in Chicago's sumptuous suburbs.

Chapter 2

Charles led Beth through his two-story black slate foyer, arduously, due to the accumulated extra weight after retirement bearing down on fatigued knees. In the kitchen, he put the leftover food in the refrigerator and pulled out a chair at his breakfast-room table for the lovely young woman, the daughter of his best friend. He had always enjoyed the company of beautiful women, and they brought out his most charming manners—leaning toward them, looking into their eyes, being attentive. These were traits he'd had all his life and even now, at eighty-five, he still made a woman feel she was important, that she had something worthwhile to say.

* * * *

Charles Sullivan was born in Wales and had come to the United States with a troupe of Shakespearean actors who had been engaged to perform on the New York stage. He had been singled out and embraced by the reviewers. The audiences had returned many times to enjoy his clear, brisk, stage voice and handsome face. Shakespeare companies sought him for their productions, and he traveled to Montreal, Seattle, Sydney, and back to New York. Three times before he was fifty he had married and divorced glamorous, deep-voiced, velvet-dressed actresses, but none of them wanted to give up stage time to have children. One of his uncles, the youngest of his father's siblings, who had followed a young college student to the United States then married her, had bought a house in Clarington Hills, died, preceded by his childless wife, and left the house to Charles, his Americanized nephew. At that time Charles had been retired for ten years and was living in his co-op apartment in New York City. He came to Clarington Hills intending only to meet with a realtor and sell the property. He drove from O'Hare Airport through the grassy suburb with white wooden fences and bushes of gigantic purplish-blue hydrangeas, each bloom a hundred-flower bouquet. The tranquility filled him with a peacefulness he felt was missing from his life. That had been five years ago when he was eighty years old. He had walked through the carved, shellacked front door of the red brick two-story Colonial-style house, out the back French doors to the huge semicircular bricked terrace that reminded him of a stage. He stood in the center, and as dozens of rose bushes looked up at him, he knew he had found his last audience.

His neighbor, Elizabeth Alexander, a sixty-five-year-old widow, brought him a loaf of her lemon banana-nut bread as a welcome-to-the-neighborhood gift. They had sat on his terrace-stage and told each other their life stories.

* * * *

Thoughts of Elizabeth had filled Charles's mind all morning, but he tried to push them back now and let Beth talk, hopefully release some of her tense, emotional strain. He sighed, sat heavily into his chair, and said, "When it's humid like today, I spend the hours holed up like a fat woodchuck in my air-conditioned house." He saw the signs of tears on her face, took her slender, strong hands, engulfed them in his large, dramatic hands, and kissed her fingers. "Beth, my darling, tell me your plans. I couldn't bear to think I won't be seeing you. Will you and Raymond move into your parents' beautiful home? If you sell it, you must promise to come visit me."

"I have much to tell you. First, I'll make us some tea." She took two Earl Grey tea bags from the tin on the counter, put them in two Portmeirion mugs, and filled them with boiling water from the instant-hot faucet. She started talking as she placed the mugs on coasters on the inlaid oak table, feeling the warm comfort of sharing with a friend, letting go, untangling the knots that restrained her heart, her consciousness. "In the desert, nomads drink hot tea because they believe if the inside of the body is warm, they won't feel the intensity of the sun as much."

He laughed. She reminded him of Elizabeth with her bits of wisdom that she had probably read in some magazine. "I'm not sure that applies to the ninety-nine-percent humidity of Chicago, but hot tea is good for the soul."

Charles had been a father-figure for Beth since he'd moved into the big house next to her mother, not wanting to interfere but giving his opinion, advice, sympathy. She talked candidly to him as he rested a stubbly chin on intertwined fingers and listened.

Beth reminded Charles that she and Raymond had been married for ten years. She had undergone fertility tests without finding any problems, not once a late period to hope for a pregnancy, a discouragement that was a heavy weight. She confided that she knew Raymond had been seeing other women for their entire marriage. She'd never believed the excuses he made for nights he wasn't at home; her friends had told her they'd seen him in downtown Chicago restaurants with beautiful women, and when they'd confronted him, he had introduced the women as clients. Many times his shirts smelled of perfume, but what really bothered her was that she didn't see a way out, feeling she was locked in a cage and couldn't find the door. There was no love between them, and she thought perhaps that was why she wanted a child, to have someone to love. It was confusing, she told Charles, because sometimes at home Ray was thoughtful, brought bouquets of orange tiger lilies or pale shrimp-colored roses or little gifts of scented candles or bath salts, which made her doubt herself, thinking that maybe it was all somehow her fault or maybe just her imagination. She kept thinking, she said, if only she could get pregnant, a child would bring them together, make them into a family. However, this last year, she felt his behavior had changed—he couldn't hide the fact that he was restless, impatient, bored when they were together, spent more time with his friends at Joel's club, never invited her, criticized her clothes and her hair. She asked her mother to help her pick out more sophisticated clothes, thinking she had gotten too lax with her casual choices and started to pay more attention to their finances to see how much she could spend using both of their salaries and not be dependent on her mother. She knew her husband was handsome, but he also dressed beautifully, expensively—cashmere or silk knit sweaters and fine-wool slacks.

Charles knew all this, but his gaze never left her face. He let her talk without interruption, thinking it was good for her to voice it. Her parents had given her an American Express credit card years before she was married and the bill went directly to their accountant for payment. After she married they told her to keep the credit card for her personal charges. Raymond had found the credit card in her wallet and somehow gotten a spouse-card for himself on the same account. Elizabeth had told Charles her accountant had called, told her Raymond maxed out the card every month with charges for designer clothes, custom-made shirts and suits, and expensive restaurants. Elizabeth had not complained to Beth; it wasn't a financial strain for her. But she didn't want to buy him anything, she didn't like him. She also didn't want to catalyze more emotional distress in Beth's marriage. However, Beth started using her credit card to buy nicer clothes for herself and go to the beauty shop. She checked her credit card account online, curious about her own monthly charges, and saw the personal purchases Raymond had made. She was distressed and intended to talk to her mother about what to say to Raymond, but she kept putting off that conversation.

Raymond liked to take his current sex interest to fancy restaurants that had sophisticated atmosphere—he was adept at setting the stage, giving flourish to the drama, adjusting the mood to his advantage. His own paycheck was used for two purposes: to stash money away, and to have cash for flaunting, giving the impression of his importance and wealth. He lived free of expenses at home because bills were paid by Elizabeth's accountant. Beth told Charles she knew Raymond was taking advantage of her parents' generosity, but she didn't know how to handle it. After her father died, Raymond, thinking his bills wouldn't be monitored, wanted more and more—a newer, fancier car, top-of-the-line skis, racing bicycle though he didn't race, state-of-the-art tennis equipment. It was a problem for him when Beth started using her credit card for her own purchases. The card had a cap and left less for him to spend.

Beth told Charles she had never related to her mother that Raymond wanted to sell the townhouse her parents had bought for them when they got married and buy a condominium in downtown Chicago. "That's where the action is," he told her excitedly. She frowned. "But living in the city would mean sending children to private schools. The public schools in Clarington Hills, supported by high taxes, are advanced in teaching techniques and have art, music, sports, extracurricular activities."

"Beth, we don't have children." He smirked condescendingly and turned away, annoyed that she couldn't understand the boredom of suburbia as opposed to the excitement of the city. "It's living instead of just existing," he impatiently scolded.

They had few mutual friends and rarely entertained. She had met his best friend, Joel Wolfe, but they were only together as couples at special parties held at either country club when the two men made the arrangements. Though they only saw each other at these parties, she liked Joel's wife, an attractive, petite woman who was involved in her children's activities as Brownie leader, homeroom mother, and driver to gymnastics, tennis, ice skating, ballet, and whatever else she felt they needed to experience. Beth felt a pang of envy.

Charles could see from Beth's pained expression that she was exasperated. "Charles, I feel like I have wasted ten years of my life. He doesn't love me, and I don't love him. His feelings for me are worse than no love; he is indifferent, totally indifferent to me as his wife, indifferent to my feelings and what I want in our life. My father would be so disappointed in the way my marriage has evolved." She stopped talking and took a few sips of tea, looking out the double French doors at drooping, fading, last roses, thinking, *I refuse to join those sad-looking flowers in their decline, I will stand with the evergreens.*

He put his hand on the side of her face and kissed her forehead. "You keep coming back to the children issue, and you said you have gone to fertility doctors. Raymond has told you he had his sperm tested, but do you know for sure that is true?"

Beth felt his concern for her, the lingering doubt and mistrust of Raymond. She put her mug down and her eyes filled with tears. "Charles, he used to be so patient with me when I brought up my disappointment at not being pregnant, always said it will happen anytime, but the months passed and then the years and now I'm thirty-five, on the road to forty. This last year he made no pretense of sympathy toward my distress, even seemed aggravated when I wanted to talk about it. I don't know if he really went to a doctor, I always just believed him."

Of course, Raymond didn't want children. They were a nuisance, an obstruction to good times. He was too selfish to give of himself; there was sacrifice and steadfast diligence connected to raising children. Since it took his determined patience to be pleasant to people he didn't like in order to get what he wanted from them, he certainly didn't have patience for children who couldn't do anything for him.

Beth continued, "I mentioned to Raymond I wanted to separate, but he said we could work it out. It really just delayed the inevitable; our relationship didn't improve. Then last month I told him we should start thinking about a divorce. I think I have finally given up on having a family. I'm sorry now that I didn't confide all this to my mother. It was so difficult to admit my failure at marriage to her, or maybe to admit it to myself. She never asked about Raymond or our relationship. I think she didn't want to be the interfering mother. I also knew she didn't like him."

"Elizabeth loved you so much, Beth, she wanted you to be happy, and if you had told her you were suffering in your marriage, she might have advised you to divorce. Your mother was aware of your difficult relationship; both of you kept putting off that discussion. Don't dwell on regret, dear girl. Start making plans for your future."

Beth looked at her mother's old friend, his unruly white hair hanging over his ears and shirt collar, his matching bushy eyebrows over expressive, kind eyes. He had moved next door shortly after Beth's father died, and she was happy her mother and Charles had each other's companionship. She felt fortunate to have him in her life, as she was sure her mother had felt. "You're right, I need to take control of my life. It's ridiculous to continue in this loveless marriage. Tomorrow I will make an appointment with our family law firm."

Elizabeth had explained the will and trust to Beth, set up by her father. In addition to her allowance, money for Alyssa was to be paid at milestone ages, as Christopher didn't feel she was responsible enough to get a lump sum when her mother died. The house, all Elizabeth's personal possessions, and a large amount of money would go to Beth, plus control of invested money. There was no provision for Raymond. Her father had told the attorneys that, when the time came, to advise Beth to make her own will, to continue giving money to her parents' charities and to outline a trust, to keep Raymond from taking over her assets. Her parents and their attorneys were suspicious of Raymond, and after calls from the accountant concerning Raymond's excessive charges, many at expensive restaurants without Beth, had hired a private investigator to check his past and to follow him when he left home alone. The file on Raymond was thick with deceit, but Elizabeth had recently thought about discontinuing the investigation, feeling it was an invasion of her daughter's privacy, unless she had permission, and intended to discuss the findings with Beth. They never got to have that discussion.

Beth stood to leave. "Please know I feel so guilty for hating Alyssa and Raymond. I grew up trying to repress feelings like that." She leaned down to kiss Charles's cheek. "I've exhausted you with my problems; let's talk again tomorrow, I'll bring lunch. I'm going to take a hot bath and sleep in my mother's bed tonight, feel her love and presence. Just telling you all my concerns has made me feel better, Charles. I will start making my to-do list, and tomorrow will be a make-the-phone-calls day. Don't worry about me, I'm going to be fine. Thank you for your love and your friendship."

As Beth walked into her mother's house, sadness took hold of her again. She told herself, *The only way I will be able to live here is to realize and accept that my mother wanted me to have all her possessions, including this house. She specified that in her will and voiced the desire to me in person before she died. I will embrace her lovely things as part of the remembrance of her, like saving the good memories.* Beth's thoughts went back to the story her mother liked to tell about when she had met Christopher....

* * * *

Elizabeth worked at the Saks Fifth Avenue store on Michigan Avenue in Chicago, where she was the buyer for the Women's Designer Boutique. She had been behind the accessory counter, choosing a scarf to complete the outfit on one of her mannequins, when a distinguished man who looked too young to have gray hair thought she was the salesgirl. He leaned toward her and in a sorry-to-bother-you voice said, "Excuse me, miss, could you please help me choose a scarf for my lady friend?"

Elizabeth looked up and met the smiling sky-blue eyes of the most beautiful man she had ever seen. Christopher, at thirty-nine years old, was prematurely gray, with hair combed back from his face in a series of natural but perfect waves, as if a hairdresser had formed them with gel and sprayed them in place. He wore a pale-gray sport coat that was the exact color of his hair and a shimmering silver tie, obviously dressed for dinner and buying a last-minute gift.

"Of course," Elizabeth whispered, as if he had taken her breath away. "What is her favorite color?"

"Well, I'm not sure." He smiled, seemed embarrassed that he didn't know such basics. "Would you choose something that you would wear? I'm sure she will like your taste." It was a playful, flirty comment, but Elizabeth liked it and wished to herself that she could meet a handsome man like him who would thoughtfully buy her gifts. She made a mental note to make sure she told her next boyfriend her favorite everything.

"I was just admiring this pink and gray Dior, it will go very well with black or charcoal or even beige like the background."

* * * *

He watched her talk and heard the sincere fondness for her job. He liked her dark-blond hair swept back into a French twist, revealing a high forehead and dark-blue eyes, the color of a deep ocean, thickly fringed with mascaraed lashes. She was tall and wore four-inch heels that brought her up to almost six feet. He unconsciously straightened himself to let her know he was taller, although, he thought, it probably was not important to her. Somehow he knew that a person's inner goodness and kindness would be important to Elizabeth. He saw those traits in her lovely face and heard them in her smooth, soothing, helpful words.

Christopher Alexander was successful in his investment business—buying faltering shopping malls, remodeling and enlivening them. Also, he bought old apartment buildings, gutted and reconstructed the units, and sold them as condominiums. He was socially active, enjoyed parties, dating, attending performances of opera, plays, symphony. Christopher was at the top of Chicago's list of Most Eligible Bachelors but confided to his friends that he wanted to settle down, just hadn't met the woman he could envision beside him for the rest of his life.

He wanted to linger his gaze on her lovely face, talk, listen to her voice, but he would be late. He was never late; that would be rude. He was never rude.

"I'll take that scarf." He handed his credit card to her, and she hoped it wasn't obvious she had glanced too long at his name before she processed the sale. As she gave him the Saks shopping bag, their eyes met again and he said, "You have been so helpful. What is your name?"

It was a casual question, often asked by customers satisfied with the service, as though they might ask for the same salesperson next time they came into the store.

"My name is Elizabeth."

His gaze hadn't left her face. Something stirred a brightness around them like the sun appearing from behind clouds on a rainy afternoon.

* * * *

She thought, *I probably won't be at this counter if he should come in again, but I will never be able to pick out a scarf without thinking of him.*

Monday morning, she was sitting at her desk looking at pages of new designs she had ordered from New York and were due to arrive the following week, thinking of displays to attract a buyer's attention. Her phone chimed and she picked up, her mind still in the world of fashion. "This is Elizabeth."

"Hello, Elizabeth, this is Chris Alexander." The surprise of hearing his voice made her hesitate to answer and he continued, disappointed that she may have forgotten him or perhaps not taken notice of him at all. "You chose a lovely silk scarf for me last week."

"Yes, I remember. What can I do for you?" She could feel her heart beating, vibrating in her chest. She thought, *Did my words come out in a rush, all at one time, jumbled together? Does he want me to choose something else for his girlfriend?*

And then came the friendly voice attached to a smile but with serious intent. "Elizabeth, I am hoping you will have lunch with me tomorrow. I can give you references. My mother thinks I am the perfect son, and she will tell you that her only son is quite trustworthy." He laughed, didn't let her answer yet, and continued talking. He asked her questions about her job, her favorite restaurant, and what food she preferred. He told her he had grown up in the city, worked for the family business, which had been started by his grandfather. He was single, never married, lived in his condo on Lake Shore Drive.

After making plans for the lunch date and before he hung up, he asked, "Oh, and what's your favorite color?" They laughed together at the memory. He thought, *I have this strange feeling my life has just changed, like I've turned a corner and found the pot of gold beneath the tip of the rainbow.*

Elizabeth sat at her desk, unable to concentrate on work. She hoped she hadn't responded too quickly, too eagerly, given the impression she didn't have many dates. Elizabeth had lots of offers, but men friends only lasted for a couple of dates. Her friends told her she was too picky.

She knew that thoughts of meeting Chris would fill her mind. It would take hours to decide what to wear. She would be nervous until she looked once again into his striking blue eyes.

She wore her new Armani navy-blue suit and tied a long, narrow, aqua scarf around her neck into a double bow that looked like a huge flower flopped on its side, four-inch strappy heels, turquoise earrings.

When she entered the Waldorf Astoria Chicago's hotel restaurant, Elizabeth saw Christopher standing, smiling, waiting for her, and she knew in the grand scheme of life there was an element of destiny. She believed theirs had been a predestined meeting—she had decided to get a colorful silk scarf to embellish the outfit on her mannequin and had been at the accessory counter at just the time he came in the store. Now, as she stood beside him in the restaurant and looked at his handsome face, she was drawn by a strong magnetic charm and realized she could not look away. He pulled out her chair and as she sat down, she felt she had blown out all the candles on her birthday cake and raised her head to find that her wish had come to life.

Chapter 3

Raymond and Alyssa joined the stragglers who had paired up and were still at Joel's country club, inside the casual Grill-Café for hamburgers. The air had cooled and the men covered bare chests with long-sleeved T-shirts, the women with plunging V-neck cotton sweaters, still competitively displaying their assets. Raymond's cell phone vibrated. As he excused himself and walked outside, he saw on the caller ID it was Beth. She told him she would not be home, would stay at her mother's house tonight. He didn't ask how she was feeling but only thought, *Great, now I don't need an excuse to not go home and can stay the night with Alyssa at her condo.*

On Chicago's north side, in the trendy upscale area of Lincoln Park, Raymond and Alyssa entered her condo and walked straight to her bedroom, Raymond excitedly following close behind. She turned to face him and slapped him with an open-handed blow to the left side of his face. Before he could recover from the shock, she said in a guttural voice, "Get your belt out of those loops, you're going to use it and take off your clothes." There was no gentle, sweet kiss with slow, skilled, secret unbuttoning. Enjoying the stunned expression on his face and smiling mischievously, she removed her clothes and stood naked for a few seconds to let him look. She put her arms on the back of an overstuffed chair for support, bent over, stuck out her shapely buttocks, and turned her head sideways looking up at him. "Do you need instructions? Fold the belt," she said slowly, pronouncing each syllable as if she was a teacher coaching a child. "Stand behind me and strike my butt with the belt."

Raymond had heard friends talk about rough sex, but he had always been successful with honey-coated words and gentle coaxing, rubbing, exploring. He suddenly knew he wanted sex like this—raw, no pretense. He whipped the belt across her butt and she laughed low and throaty, shaming him. "Again, like you really mean it!" He drew his arm back and whacked her, the belt making a whipping sound. In an instant Alyssa turned and grabbed two fistfuls of his lush, wavy hair. His mouth opened in an expression of pain as she derided him. "I hope you fuck harder than you use that belt." She pulled him by his hair as she backed up to the wall and put one foot high on the arm of the cushioned chair. Her hands went around his neck in a strangling grip, and he thought she might choke him. He looked down at her heaving breasts as she labored at breathing, and his eyes glowed at the smooth mound between her separated legs inviting his hard erection. Raymond bent his knees slightly and rammed into her with the force of a jackhammer, grasping her butt with open hands, holding her to him. Alyssa threw her head back, growled a laugh from the depths of her belly as her orgasm trembled through her body, not even aware of Raymond's lusty surrender.

There was no interest in satisfying a partner in this sex match. Grossly indecent and obscene, it was all about self, an exploitative behavior to use each other for their own excitement and gratification. Feelings of deep affection, personal attachment, warm concern, and profound tenderness did not exist in their relationship. They would hang on to each other to sate their selfishness, she because it was maliciously destroying something—a marriage that belonged to her abhorred sister—and he simply because it was a new, extravagant, seductive, salacious adventure. There were no morals to abandon, no respect to forsake, no hidden intimacy. This was open recklessness with no concern of consequences. This was a joyride in the true meaning of the word.

Alyssa's condo was across the park from Lake Michigan. The next morning she and Raymond jogged on the path along the lake, sweatsuit collars zipped up against the cold wind. They stopped at an awninged café but opted for an indoor corner table. As Alyssa held her hot latte with both hands to feel the warmth, she tilted her head and mockingly asked, "Ten years of wedded bliss and no babies? My sister must be so distraught and probably angry that you haven't produced the proper sperm for offspring." She was ridiculing him, making him feel inadequate, which disturbed Raymond's core. He would have to prove himself to her, reveal he was chief.

Raymond put his elbows on the table and leaned toward Alyssa. He was preparing to tell her his secret. His eyes narrowed into slits, and his face expressed contempt for the subject she brought up. He wanted to show her he was in control of that situation. "When I was twenty-one, I knew there would never be children in my life. That's when I had a vasectomy."

* * * *

She laughed at the vicious joke on her sister. This was the confidence she wanted from him. She was sure he had never told anyone this secret. She had heard her sister distressing to their mother about "no sign of a pregnancy." Alyssa probed more. "And your facade has never come undone? The family rumor was that you told them your sperm tested alive and well, which they didn't believe, but Beth still expected to be pregnant each passing month. You have never told her you don't want children?" He nodded and she wallowed in the wonderful information. How she would love to fling this news in her sister's face!

He snarled, "Every month for ten years she thought she might be pregnant. I had to live with her disappointment, feign sorrow, pretend to care, give her sincere encouragement."

* * * *

Deludingly, to Beth, he had said, "Next month, for sure, sweetheart." To Alyssa, he confided, "Do you know how difficult it's been to keep my composure, put on an act? I'm finished. I'm off the stage."

Raymond sat back, satisfied with himself. He had outlasted her parents and now he would rid himself of the burden and get the cart full of money.

"If we kill her," plotted Alyssa gleefully, "I will inherit everything and we will never have to work, we'll travel around the world." She had news of her own for him. "All the money is in a trust, and your name is only mentioned to say you inherit nothing. You tried to put on a good show, but my parents didn't like you. I have seen the will, and Beth is the co-executor with the attorney."

But Raymond wasn't buying into Alyssa's plan. He wanted to be the one in control and have it all for himself. After all, he might tire of Alyssa next month. He knew he shouldn't tell her all his thoughts, but he was on a high, he had to brag. She wanted him, and he would play along, let her think she was part of his plan in case he needed to use her. Slyly, he looked at her. "If Beth is incapacitated, and I have power of attorney, I can sign her name and become owner of everything, keeper of the Inn."

* * * *

Alyssa sat up, interested in this new scheme. She loved that she and Raymond were conspiring together and she had an ally against her sister, at last. "How is she going to become incapacitated, and how are you going to get her notarized power of attorney?"

His smug smile delighted her. "Just watch me."

When his mother-in-law had been on her deathbed, Raymond began plotting. He had already called Beth's doctor and told him she was horribly depressed with no appetite, no energy, and she was talking about going to sleep and not waking up. That was not true, but Raymond was a skillful convincer, a trait applied with charm and earnestness which helped him achieve his goal of successful deceit. Her doctor said he knew Beth seldom took medications and a light dose of Zoloft would help her depression. He trustingly asked Raymond to carefully administer the dosage. Raymond grinned with superiority, amused at the easily successful beginning of his plan. Now all he had to do was pick up the Zoloft prescription and stop at Starbucks for Beth's favorite chai.

* * * *

He said to Alyssa, "I will mash a bottle of drugs and stir it up in her chai. She will tell me I am so thoughtful for bringing it to her. When she gets drowsy, I will remind her she promised to sign the title to my car—our cars are in both our names, so I can trade it in for a new one. She will actually be signing a power of attorney for me."

* * * *

Alyssa looked intently at Raymond, thinking about the holes in his plan. It wasn't waterproof. Quietly, doubtfully, she said, "I don't think a bottle of antidepressants will incapacitate her. It has to be mixed with another drug." Alyssa had never taken drugs. She felt they would interfere with her sex life. She had seen too many people under the effects of drugs and unable to function. An antidepressant, which her friend, Cheri, took regularly, sounded too tame.

"But there's a great possibility that a large dose might send her into a coma. Then I could get her institutionalized for being suicidal, where she would be kept drugged so she won't harm herself. If she dies too soon, Alyssa, I won't have a chance to get the money. First, I want her in a coma. I'll convince the doctors of her depressed state, and tell them she took the antidepressants to kill herself. It's a start, then I'll see how it goes and decide what to do next."

Alyssa shook her head. "It's too iffy! I'll just shoot her. I have several guns and I'm an excellent markswoman." Guns were permanent and dependable, not inconsistent like drugs.

Raymond leaned closer and hissed, "Alyssa, I need that power of attorney. I know several people who will notarize her signature for me as a favor. We can think about shooting her later. Maybe that will be Plan B."

* * * *

He thought, *She idolizes me, but I need to keep her restrained, tighten the reins, and not let her take over with irrational behavior.* She was sitting upright, clearly intent on every word he uttered, putty in his hands. *She is easily manipulated. If I decide to kill Beth and want her help, she'll do whatever I say.* He was sure he would be able to control her, just like the rest of them.

He relaxed, softened his voice, looked at her condescendingly, and pretended to confide in her. "I'm going to the office now to put in some time and make a good show. I have three appointments today to write some home insurance policies. I will play on my clients' sympathy—poor Raymond, such a nice guy and has big problems with a suicidal wife. I will chat with the other brokers and the office staff about how tormented I am over Beth's depression and let them know I am going to pick up a prescription of antidepressants for her. I will anxiously plant the words 'fear of suicide' in their heads. Alyssa, you can't rush something like this or you'll step into a hole and drown yourself. You have to test the water, keep your footing, and be sure there's a boat nearby. I've been thinking about this for a long time, waiting until the time was right." He smiled at her with confidence, smugness, thinking of his rewards—one reward would be tonight, with her.

He was used to sending out bait. "When I'm finished with Beth—she's staying at her mother's house—I'll come to your condo. Do you want me to stay with you again tonight?" Then the charm-smile, a spark to revive her memory.

* * * *

He still didn't realize Alyssa was holding the rod and reel. Her mind flashed back to last night—the shocked expression on his face when she'd slapped him, his muscular body, and the wide grin when she stood naked for him. Low and throatily she said, "Yes, there are things I want to show you."

He leaned close to her ear, thinking she was hooked. "I'm going to suck your nipples until they turn purple."

She looked at him with squinted eyes. "That'll be a good start."

* * * *

Alyssa had majored in art and art history. She was inventive in her artwork and probably, with her father's influence, could have gotten a job at an advertising agency. But she hated the idea of being in an office sitting at a computer all day. Instead, she worked at a small, exclusive men's store on Michigan Avenue. The clothes were expensive and the men who came in the store were intelligent, successful, and accustomed to gratifying their whims. If they suited Alyssa, measured up to her qualifications, she showed them a different kind of gratification.

* * * *

As Raymond drove north toward the Chicago suburb of Clarington Hills, he thought about his new life. He had used up ten years to get to this point and now he would have it all—money to spend on whatever he wanted without conniving or lying, and freedom to indulge in his sexual escapades without sneaking around his wife. With the power of attorney, able to legally sign Beth's name, he would sell the townhouse and also sell Beth's parents' house she had just inherited. He would buy a condominium on the north side of Chicago where there were parties every night, and he could have his choice of beautiful women without excuses, without explaining, without obligations.

It wasn't like he'd ever resisted any temptation put before him. Raymond placed himself in the middle of temptation like taking a dinner plate to the dessert buffet and loading up for his big appetite.

He decided that after everything was settled he would quit his job at Lobo Insurance Agency. Joel had been a good friend, and he would invite him to his new place, even have a room for him where he could bring women and stay as long as he wanted. Raymond thought about how difficult it had been to keep Beth content—all that whining about pregnancy. It had consumed his energy to placate her, but it would soon be worth it. As usual, Raymond justified his actions—he was a good husband, patient, loving, kind, brought her flowers and gifts. He was a good son-in-law, polite, respectful, always accompanied Beth to family celebrations. *How exhausted I am from being pulled in so many directions! But all my patience has paid off. I'm an independent, wealthy, free man. I have worked for this retirement. I deserve it all.*

* * * *

Raymond parked in the driveway of his in-laws' stately residence and opened one of the garage doors using the combination pad on the frame. In the kitchen, he poured the paper cup of chai into a mug and warmed it in the microwave. He removed a white oblong paper bag with several pages of warnings and directions, attached with a staple, from the pocket of his Ralph Lauren Blue Label blazer. He emptied the contents of the plastic container on the granite countertop and mashed them with a heavy, metal meat tenderizer. Then he scooped the pile of powder into the hot mug of liquid and stirred, making a little foam on top. As Raymond picked up the mug he made a superficial swipe at the counter to clean up after himself, pleased with his cleverness, and the prospects of his new life. He'd phoned Beth and told her he would drop by for a few minutes. She asked him to wait until tomorrow, told him she was fine, wanted to be alone, but he insisted. When he arrived, she was sitting up in her mother's bed in the master bedroom, propped on a plump, white linen backrest, intent with the *Chicago Tribune* crossword puzzle. He bent and kissed her forehead. "Sweetheart, I knew I'd find you in here. I stopped at Starbucks and bought your favorite chai latte to help you relax." He suspected she wanted to talk about divorce again. With a slight smile he thought, *Tomorrow will be too late, Sweetheart.*

* * * *

For a few seconds Beth thought she might not say what she had planned, but she knew she had to put her foot on the starting block in order to get going on organizing her life. It was the first item on her list. She countered his charm and turned the mood serious. "Ray, we need to have a long talk. Please come here to Mother's house after work tomorrow." Beth didn't want him to stay with her, she just wanted him to go home and come back tomorrow so they could have time for a long discussion.

Then, to let him know she mistrusted him, she reprimanded, "I tried to call you last night, but your phone was turned off."

"Sweetheart, I forgot to tell you—Joel and I had plans to take clients to dinner. We're writing the insurance on their house, cars, and boat." Raymond knew Joel would back up his excuse if needed. They had used each other as an alibi many times. "Sweetheart, shall we meet at Guido's Italian Bistro in town tomorrow evening?"

He held the mug up to her lips; she took several sips. "No, Ray, I would like you to come here, so we can talk with privacy." She was boosted by her own serious tone. Within reach was liberation from unhappiness: The process had been started.

"Whatever you say, sweetheart. I'll call you when I'm on the way. Let me sit here with you while you drink your chai. You look so tired."

Beth took the mug of milky, spiced, honeyed tea that disguised any drug bitterness from his hands and drank. It was warm and comforting. She was relieved they had plans to talk. Tomorrow she would make a list of everything she wanted to tell him; primarily, she was going to initiate a divorce. Also, she would tell him she would live in her mother's house and he could have the townhouse.

* * * *

Raymond was watching her, waiting for just the right moment, drowsy but still awake, so he could ask her to sign the document. She was talking about her mother—how she had handled the knowledge of inevitable death, bravely, gracefully, even taking care of the arrangements for the service herself and getting her monetary affairs in order with her attorney.

Raymond noticed her speech was slightly slurred. "Your mother was a wonderful person. I loved her. Sweetheart, you stay here and get some rest, and I'll see you tomorrow after work. Oh, I almost forgot—my car is in both our names. Will you sign the title so I can trade it in? It needs new tires, new brakes, some other things, and it's a good time to get rid of it instead of paying to fix it up. I have the title here." He took a folded paper from his breast pocket, placed it on top of the newspaper on her lap, and put a pen in her hand, pointing to the line with her name typed below it.

Beth felt listless, nauseous, she wanted him to leave so she could lie down. The writing on the paper was blurry, but she signed her name where he was pointing, thinking, *He doesn't have a mortgage to pay, thanks to my parents, so I guess he can afford a new car.*

He kissed her forehead, whispered, "Good night, sweetheart." He stopped in the master bathroom, placed the empty Zoloft container, lid, bag with warnings, and the empty mug on top of the white marble vanity. He smiled to himself. *How sad, this is where she took that whole bottle of Zoloft with the chai I thoughtfully brought her.* On his way out, passing through the bedroom, he glanced at Beth and saw her head back, eyes closed. As he drove out of the driveway, he felt the pleasure of accomplishment. He had finished the race in first place, broken the tape, the confetti was raining down on him. *It's all mine now, sweetheart.*

* * * *

Raymond called Alyssa to boast of his success and let her know he was on his way to her condo. He was riding on a high, laughing aloud in his car. He felt he was standing on top of the mountain, the world beneath him. *Nothing can stop me, I'm too clever for mere mortals.*

* * * *

That morning Alyssa had gone to work, using up time. Working served two purposes—it kept away boredom and provided endless prospects for sexual encounters. She spent the day mentally outlining her evening plans with Raymond, the image of his muscular, naked body imprinted on her mind. A news-known Chicago attorney came into the shop and went directly to her, but she brushed him off. She already knew him, had played with him, he was old hat.

* * * *

Alyssa opened the door at Raymond's tap and backed up for him to look at her—totally nude, wearing only black stiletto pumps and dangling two narrow, black silk cords from her long black-painted fingernails. He knew the games had begun. "That looks harmless," he teased as he started unbuttoning his shirt, stepping out of his slacks, shorts, and revealing a mounting erection.

"That depends on what gets tied up." The black cord had metal tips, and she whipped it across his bare chest. It stung like knife pricks and he reached for the cord, but she was on her way to the bedroom. She turned to face him, then quickly looped the slinky cord over his head, tied it once around his neck, and pulled the ends tight. He clasped his hands around her throat thinking, *One stranglehold deserves another.* He was getting the hang of pain threats—they meant more hurt on the way. She curled her tongue inside her mouth, hissed like a snake ready to strike, and slithered her body against him. "Can you feel my hard nipples?"

He gave a quick, breathless nod, waiting for instructions. She handed him the other silk cord. "Wind this around my nipples, tight, tighter, *tighter*." And the snake struck. In a flash she removed the cord from his throat and wound it around his genitals. He fell to his knees and she pushed him over with her foot, digging her high heels into his shoulder. He lay on his back, holding the throbbing bundle between his legs. She crawled slowly over him on all fours, starting at his head. She placed one nipple in his mouth, and he sucked eagerly. When he opened his mouth for air, she switched nipples, and he did his expected duty. She took a wide-mouth bite near his belly button and crept down farther, sucking his penis into her mouth. Her smooth mound was over his open panting mouth, and she pressed to receive a strong suck, the way he knew she liked. He felt a sensation like a vacuum device devouring his male organ. He loved her, he hated her, he loved her, he hated her. When her body spasmed, it was his permission to release, and he experienced an orgasm so intense his entire body vibrated. She had led him into darkness, down into a dungeon where pain intensified pleasure.

Chapter 4

Charles Sullivan had been reading in his den, dozing off in his too-comfortable overstuffed chair. He thought, *Before I get myself ready for bed, I will check to see if the lights are still on in Elizabeth's bedroom...her sweet daughter, Beth, is staying again tonight...going through a stressful time...should allow herself plenty of sleep. I must help her through this difficult period.* He walked heavily to his corner living room window and looked across the side yard to the glow coming from behind the large draped window. Before he turned to go to his bedroom, the lights of Raymond's car shone across the front of Elizabeth's house as he entered the circular driveway, like a searchlight making an arc, then stopped in front of the garage. As he often did when he was alone, Charles talked to himself. "I hope she isn't going to bring up divorce tonight…he's a fearful bastard, especially if he sees the hold on her fortune slipping away from him. I'll call tomorrow morning to make sure she's not overly stressed."

Charles got into bed, but he couldn't relax enough to fall asleep. He didn't like Raymond, who had been the subject of his and Elizabeth's many talks. Out loud, he worried, "She didn't like him, either, didn't trust him, had a mother's intuition that told her there was something phony in his actions." Anxious thoughts occupied his mind and he repeated them aloud as if he was talking to Elizabeth. "You revealed to me that Christopher perceived Raymond to be pretentious, narcissistic, and dangerous if someone got in his way. Oh, my dear Elizabeth, you never criticized him, never ruffled his feathers. How upset you were for your daughter! You tried to think of how to help, preferably to suggest a divorce, but you didn't want to plunge her into the emotional distress."

Charles got out of bed and went to his window again. Raymond's car was still there. "Is she going to let him stay with her tonight?" As he turned away from the window, car lights flooded his living room, and he watched Raymond's car go around the circular driveway, out to the street. He looked at the glow from the bedroom window, as if that would assure him she was safe. "Now I can get some sleep."

Charles headed for his bedroom again. He lay in bed thinking about Beth and the conversation they'd had yesterday after her mother's service. "She's taking on so much now, at this sad time in her life—the estate, dealing with the attorneys, the persistent problem of Alyssa, and now the plans to divorce Raymond." Again, Charles got out of bed not knowing exactly why. Her night table light still shone in the bedroom window. He picked up his phone and punched the house phone number, but it rang until the answering service responded. He found Beth's cell number, but the call was forwarded to the answering system. She had switched it off for the night. He punched the number for the house phone again, but the answering service came on. "Okay, I'll put on my robe, go to that front door, and ring the doorbell. She already knows I'm a doddering old fool, so I won't have to explain my senseless worry."

Charles rang the doorbell again and again until he started to shiver in the chilly, end-of-summer night. "Okay, I'm here, I might as well open the garage door and call her name when I get in the kitchen, so I won't frighten her. I just have to see for myself that she's all right." Charles and Elizabeth had given each other keys to their houses and written sticky notes to keep on the inside door of a kitchen cabinet with the outdoor combinations to their garage doors. "In case of emergency," they had agreed.

There was no answer when Charles called Beth's name, louder and louder as he apprehensively approached the master bedroom. He struggled to breathe as he saw her when he barely got through the open door. She was collapsed on the white, deep-pile carpet like a rag doll fallen to the floor. He took deep breaths, trying to stay calm enough to push three important numbers on the phone he grabbed from Elizabeth's desk.

Charles sat on the edge of the bed staring down at Beth's limp body and the splotches of milky-brown liquid around her. He saw the passing minutes pop up on the digital clock. "That bastard has poisoned her!" Impatiently, he was going to punch nine-one-one again when he heard voices. The emergency medical squad from the ambulance had entered through the open garage door and were calling from the kitchen.

He watched a swarm of people fill the bedroom. His sadness and regret were so heavy his body seemed to roll up and sink into the down comforter as if he were drowning. *Why did I wait so long to check on her?* Charles felt a gentle but firm hand on his shoulder. He looked up at young, sympathetic eyes and asked, "Is she alive?"

Quietly the answer: "The technicians believe there is a faint heartbeat. You may have saved her life. They'll do all that's possible. I want to take you back home now, sir."

Chapter 5

The staff at Northern Illinois Hospital left messages on Raymond's cell phone, but he didn't get them until he and Alyssa were out the door for a morning run. He stopped at a park bench on the side of the jogging path and listened to a call from a Detective Rice. "This is just a routine call about your wife in the hospital. Please call back." Raymond decided it was a call he would make later, but thoughts of the message crowded his mind. *How did she get to the hospital? She couldn't have been conscious enough to call nine-one-one. Maybe the housekeeper found her unresponsive this morning. I need some answers.* He stopped again and called the hospital, getting the nurses' station outside the Intensive Care Unit. The nurse gave him no information, only asking him to come to the hospital ASAP. He pressed her for knowledge of Beth's condition, but she would only tell him Beth was in ICU and her doctor would give him details when he got to the hospital. *If she's okay, they would tell me*, Raymond reasoned. *She must be in a coma, they can't say that on the phone.* "I'll be there right away," Raymond assured her. He gave Alyssa a complacent smile. "Everything is going as I planned. Let's finish our run."

Chapter 6

After the ambulance left with Beth, a young officer from one of the two accompanying squad cars walked Charles to his back door. He dressed, called a taxi, and anxiously arrived at the Northern Illinois Hospital. He informed the young woman at the emergency room desk that he would sit in the waiting area until he received some information, even if he had to sleep there for a week. A nurse finally came out, sat beside him, and patiently explained there was no news yet. "Mrs. James is receiving emergency procedures." She handed him a small paper from her notepad with the extension number of the ICU nurses' station and called a taxi for him.

Charles didn't get into bed when he got home. He sat at his breakfast-room table where he and Beth had had tea only yesterday. He went over their conversation—her plans to divorce Raymond, to live in her mother's house, to get on with her life. Aloud he analyzed, "She was sad, but I wouldn't say she was overly depressed. She was handling her mother's death with strong character." He relived the horror of last night, made a cup of strong tea, and decided his first call would be to the family attorney, Lawrence Simon, or Larry the Lawyer, as Elizabeth called him. Charles had met Larry when Elizabeth recommended him, and he had helped Charles with his will.

Larry the Lawyer answered the phone himself at eight o'clock, having arrived at the office early before the receptionist to get some paperwork done. Charles explained how Raymond had driven up to Beth's house, let himself in through the garage, and left after twenty minutes. Then Charles told of his worry and the manner in which he'd found Beth. He included his personal opinion of "that bastard Raymond," and his suspicion of attempted murder.

Larry listened attentively, assured Charles he would call him back with any news about Beth, and also that he planned to have his investigator check Raymond's involvement. "We will get to the bottom of this, Charles."

After talking to Charles and before planning his own private investigation, Larry called his friend, Detective Dan Rice, of the Chicago

Police Department. Larry and Dan had met twenty years earlier at a rowdy sports bar on the edge of the Loop in Chicago. Daniel Rice, a young policeman, went to the bar on his days off to watch the ballgames he couldn't afford to attend. Lawrence Simon went to the bar for the companionship of sports enthusiasts in a warm, friendly environment as opposed to the cold, windy weather coming off Lake Michigan at Soldier Field where the Chicago Bears played football. Daniel was fifteen years younger than Larry, but after seeing each other at several broadcasts, the two men began fan-type exchanges and telling each other bits of their life stories. Larry called Dan often and they would meet to watch Chicago sports games together. Through the years Larry treated Dan to Chicago Bulls basketball games at the stadium.

Larry repeated the conversation he'd had with Charles and asked Dan to meet so Larry could turn over the file from the previous investigation of Raymond that his office had done at the request of Beth's father.

* * * *

Daniel Rice grew up on the unforgiving streets of Chicago's south side. Early in his life he became well acquainted with drugs, dealers, gangs, guns, and being asked to leave the dilapidated house where he had been left by his mother, when Aunt Belinda had "company." Everything changed one day when a young policeman saw Daniel running down the street, and the neighborhood grocery store owner yelling and shaking both fists in the air. The new officer drove around the block, parked, and grabbed Daniel's ragged hoodie when he tried to duck into an alley. He dragged Daniel, kicking and punching, pushed him into the backseat of his patrol car, and got in beside him. The policeman showed sympathy on his face and in his voice when he said, "I'm not going to hurt you. Let's talk. You stole from the grocery store."

"I'm hungry."

"Where do you live?"

"Quincy and Locust."

"At those streets are three vacant lots and a playground."

"So?"

"Do you live on the street?"

"Most of the time."

"You remind me of myself. Would you like to live in a house and go to school?"

Daniel saw a light in the policeman's eyes and it transmitted a small ray of hope. Through the police department's recommendation, a saintly couple took in Daniel as their tenth child. The house was cramped and messy, but it was a family and they took care of each other. Daniel learned that he had a future, a life he could look forward to, and he worked toward becoming a policeman. His goal was to be like the policeman who came to visit him every month and take him to Chicago Cubs baseball games, eat hot dogs, and yell their disagreement to the umpire, who turned and smiled at them.

* * * *

Now, towering, strong, intimidating, intelligent, and street-smart, Detective Daniel Rice had an understanding of the criminal mind. Larry gave Daniel the phone numbers, address, and workplace of Raymond James and asked to meet at Northern Illinois Hospital. On his way, Larry called the doctor in charge of the ICU and filled him in about Raymond. Larry also called the accounting department to let them know he would be bringing copies of Beth's driver's license and insurance card, which he kept in his files. He had gone to the Clarington Hills home to get her wallet, which would have the originals, from her purse, but couldn't find it.

Dr. Stein met Larry and Detective Rice in the waiting area and took them to his office. "Beth's husband has not arrived yet, but we've been communicating with Charles Sullivan, who probably saved her life and claims that Mr. James tried to kill her. It was an overdose of antidepressants, the empty container found in the bathroom. Of course, there is the possibility that she took the pills herself. We will leave that investigation to you, Detective."

A gray-haired woman, ID hanging atop her ample bosom, serious faced, obviously the no-nonsense nurse in charge, appeared in Dr. Stein's doorway. "Mr. James is at the ICU desk, has not asked to see Mrs. James, smilingly wants to know 'her condition,' and could he 'please talk to the doctor?' He acts like he's posing for the *Tribune*'s social page." Raymond liked to show off the bulging muscles in his shirt and in his pants, but Nurse Martha was not impressed.

The detective raised his eyebrows, and all three smiled at Nurse Martha's assessment. Dr. Stein suggested that Detective Rice stay in his office, and he would bring Raymond there to get his side of the story. Larry gave his card to Dr. Stein, asked to be called with updates on Beth's condition, gave his friend their usual man hug, and returned to his law office on LaSalle Street in the Chicago Loop.

Detective Rice rose as Raymond, with Dr. Stein, entered the doctor's office. "Mr. James, this is just routine when there is a drug overdose." And then the routine question. "When is the last time you saw Mrs. James?"

Raymond put on his somber face, looked straight at the detective, and gave his dutiful-husband story. "Yesterday, I was so distressed about Beth's depression, I called her doctor for help. She was very close to her mother, and the funeral service seemed to send her over the edge. She had been depressed for weeks after learning that her mother wouldn't survive the spreading cancer. On the way to my mother-in-law's house from the office, I picked up the prescription and her favorite chai. She was in her mother's bed, which frightened me. It was spooky, like she wanted to join her. She asked me to leave. I left the prescription in the bathroom, thinking I would be able to talk to her about it today. She did drink some of the warm chai and was quiet, tranquil, when I left."

"Where did you go?" Raymond didn't squirm, but Daniel saw a flicker in his expression like it might be a question he didn't like. He had hesitated for one second, and Daniel knew it was a think-before-answering second.

"Home. I had to work today. Beth asked me not to stay, said she wanted to be alone. She was frighteningly down, quite depressed. I should have realized something like this could happen. I shouldn't have left her."

"Okay, Mr. James." Daniel thought, *That's overkill explanation.* "Thank you for your cooperation. Is it okay if I call you, just in case I forgot something for my report?"

"Of course, call me anytime. I'm happy to help."

Detective Rice drove to the luxurious suburb of Clarington Hills to keep an appointment with Charles Sullivan, whom he had called earlier. There was no unbiased opinion from Charles: He harshly accused Raymond of attempted murder. He gave the detective more information than he could hold in his little notebook, including the conversation he'd had with Beth the day of the funeral. Charles emphasized that she was sad but planning to call her lawyer, get the estate plan, then talk to Raymond about divorce.

It seemed to the detective that a motive for attempted murder was developing. He thought, *Thank God for a nosy but concerned, loving neighbor.*

* * * *

The next day Detective Rice walked into the Lobo Insurance Agency without an appointment, showed his badge in a friendly manner, and asked to talk to Mr. Wolfe. He was glad Raymond was not at work yet; he wanted to talk to him separately. Joel joined his father and the detective in Mr. Wolfe's ample, expensively decorated office. Mr. Wolfe shut the door with an annoyed slam, turned to the detective, and with an irritated tone said, "What's this about? I don't appreciate you flashing your badge to my staff. Is this some petty thing that could have been taken care of with a phone call?"

The detective smiled slowly, patiently. "Mr. Wolfe, this concerns the wife of your broker, Mr. Raymond James. She is in the Intensive Care Unit from an overdose of antidepressants."

Mr. Wolfe cut Detective Rice short. "What the fuck would I know about that?"

"It's our job to check household members when there is a drug overdose, and we thought, as his employer, you could give us some information about Mr. James."

Joel knew his father didn't like Raymond and had recently been upset when his accountant reported charges at the country club signed with Joel's name, dated when Joel was away on vacation with his wife and kids. Joel answered for his father. "Detective, Raymond is a friend of mine. Why don't you come in my office and I'll tell you everything I know."

Joel was a true friend. He and Raymond had each other's backs when both took risks in their game of cheating on their wives. He told Detective Rice about their friendship beginning at university, and that they still shared a close relationship, socialized together with wives, worked together with clients, played tennis every week—and yes, he knew Beth was quite depressed. Raymond had related his anxiety about her to everyone in the office, including telling them he had called her doctor for medication.

The detective had read the files from Larry the Lawyer, and knew Raymond was not an upstanding card player, in fact was adept at cheating. Detective Rice upped the ante. "Mr. Wolfe, just because someone is depressed doesn't mean they would try to kill themself."

"Oh, she was definitely suicidal. Raymond was worried sick about her."

Detective Rice put his cards face up on the table. "Concerned enough to give her a whole container of drugs?"

Joel didn't have a poker face to hide his surprise. The detective put his business card on the shiny, rich mahogany desk and left.

Mr. Wolfe bristled into Joel's office. "You tell your friend to clean up his act or I want him out of here. He doesn't write enough business to pay for my aggravation or his margaritas."

* * * *

This was Chicago. Interesting news swirled around the Windy City and as fast as air-speed traveled to the *Chicago Tribune*. A reporter found Raymond at the Lobo Insurance Agency and tried to antagonize him. "You're being investigated for your wife's drug overdose."

Raymond was somber, smooth, smug. "No, no, just routine questioning. She has been extremely depressed, suicidal. Her behavior was so frightful I called her doctor for help."

The reporter located Charles Sullivan and got a different story, especially the biased opinion he was happy to tell and getting angrier with each telling. Charles thought, *I will let the world know about that indecent bastard. He will not get away with his attempt to kill her.*

The article came out on the second page—no accusations, just news about socialite Beth James in the hospital for an overdose of antidepressants. Accomplished tennis player and working girl, oldest daughter of the prominent Alexander family of Clarington Hills. Father, the late Christopher Alexander who established the Alexander Foundation, which funded many charities. Mother, the late Elizabeth Alexander, who sat on social and charity boards. And at the end of the article—currently married to Raymond James, a broker at the Lobo Insurance Agency.

Mr. Wolfe called Joel into his office. "That article is the beginning of a serious problem, and I don't want our company associated with a problem that will cause us to lose business. Two things, Joel: He cannot work for us, and he cannot avail himself of our club. It's one thing to be your guest, it's another thing to sign your name and pretend he's you. I know you've been friends since college, but he is causing trouble for both of us and taking advantage of your friendship. Blame it on me—tell him you will give him a good recommendation when he applies at another company."

Joel took Raymond to lunch and told him Mr. Wolfe's ultimatum. "We've been through a lot together, Ray, but it's bothersome you didn't level with me about Beth and the overdose. You didn't come to work for two days or even call me. It was a shock when that detective came in saying you were being investigated, followed by a *Tribune* reporter. Dad is furious. I'll help you any way I can. We've been through some turbulence, but we were always there for each other, we always stick together." Joel had also been called on his marital cheating and used work with Ray for his excuse.

Raymond got in his car. His mind was racing. Now he could give all his attention to his new life. He had unloaded the job that was a roadblock. He shifted his scheme into overdrive. *I have power of attorney, I will turn everything into cash and stash it away.* He called a realtor, informed her he wanted to put the townhouse and his mother-in-law's house on the market. He called an estate-sale expert about selling the contents of both houses. He was heady, intoxicated with his legal control. *I'm going to the big house to find the key to Elizabeth's safe deposit box. What good stuff I'll find in there!—jewelry, more even bigger diamond rings she always flaunted, cash, title to her Mercedes, deeds to properties.* He was calculating his plunder, the predator circling his prey, salivating, tasting the blood.

His thoughts slipped back to his loyal friend, Joel. He knew Mr. Wolfe had put the screws to him. He could still count on Joel's help if he got bored and needed a reference for a job. He was also aware he had taken advantage of their friendship, gotten careless about the country club charges. It had been so easy. He smiled to himself. Joel was such a pushover, and he liked following Raymond into trouble.

Raymond turned onto the hand-cut-stone driveway in front of the Alexanders' stately home. After trying the combination several times, he could not get the garage door to open. Irritated, he got back in his car and found the leather Gucci key case in the glove compartment. Beth had given him one of her house keys ten years ago. He had never used it, never been to his in-laws' house without her, but had instinctively stored it away, knowing it would someday be useful to him. However, the key did not open the massive, carved entry door. As he stepped off the porch to walk on the path around back to try the kitchen door, two patrol cars pulled in the driveway. One parked behind the white BMW convertible, the other stopped alongside.

Raymond thought, *That damn lawyer probably has a watch on the house!* With his friendliest demeanor, he greeted the policemen. "Good afternoon, officers, I'm Raymond James, Mrs. Alexander's son-in-law. My key isn't working." He held up the fancy designer key case, proving his legitimate entry. He was family, this was his and his wife's house now.

Politely, meeting Raymond's eyes, the uniformed senior officer with holstered gun on his hip spoke with calm authority. "Mr. James, the locks have been changed. There was an attempted murder of the owner last week." The police had Raymond's car description, license number, and the instruction: Do not allow Raymond James, suspect, to enter the premises.

"Oh, no, officer, the owner is my wife, Beth. She has been suffering from depression, tried to—you know—it's difficult to talk about." His square-jawed face was serious with frown, wretched with worry, begged for pity.

There was no sign of sympathy from the officer who had read the report from Chicago Detective Rice: *Suspect under investigation, handsome and charming.* It included quotes from neighbor Charles Sullivan, who had called nine-one-one after seeing Mr. James leave the house on the night he found Beth collapsed on the bedroom floor. The officer's mouth was set in a straight line, an unwavering hands-on-hips attitude, a blank-stare posture. The charms were falling off Raymond's bracelet, but he continued to smilingly grasp an amulet of persuasion. "Officer, I'm taking care of my wife's business while she's hospitalized, and this is the home of her deceased mother. Beth is not able to tend to it, a house this size; we have a small townhouse. We're going to sell this property, and I'm here to initiate that process. As you can imagine, I have a big load on my plate—a demanding, sick wife, a time-claiming responsibility."

The senior officer lifted his chin and looked eye to eye at Raymond. "I have known the Alexander family all my life. I don't remember that Beth was demanding or overindulged."

Raymond started to interject something, perhaps that he had been misunderstood, but the officer kept talking. "This property is closed until the investigation is finished. You can call the attorney, Lawrence Simon, for more information."

Raymond soldiered himself upright. He told himself he was not playing games with this guy, he was legally in charge. He bravely countered, stepped toward the officer. "This is my wife's estate and she has given her power of attorney to me. Please open the door so I may attend to my business."

"Mr. James, do you happen to have that power of attorney with you?"

From the breast pocket of his custom-made black alpaca blazer, Raymond withdrew the folded, notary-public-witnessed signature page of the twenty-page document he had written himself, finding a sample on the computer. The senior officer handed it to his partner who folded it again and put the paper in his pocket without looking at it. Raymond grinned, amused, and thought with a smirk, *It's only a copy, officer—keep it.*

"Thank you for understanding my position, Mr. James—orders, regulations, all that. I'll get back to you. We'll move the squad car now and you can back out."

Chapter 7

Larry the Lawyer was sitting in his orderly LaSalle Street office. Files to be put in the cabinet were organized in squared columns, short stacks of legal-size papers on his desk were arranged in neat piles. The phone, copier, pencil box, pads of paper, each had its own space. One wall was papered with world maps from the pages of *National Geographic*. Cities around the world were marked with ball-head pins, not where he had been but where he wanted to go someday. He did take time every day to swim, his only exercise, but he ate sensibly and his weight had stayed the same for thirty years since law school. Larry had been engaged to be married once, to Alice. She was taller than Larry, with frizzy red hair and freckles. She was gentle-voiced but had a worried facial expression, and suffered from depression. "A manic-depressive," the doctor had said, "or bipolar disorder as it's known now." One day she'd just packed her bags and gone home to Indiana to live with her mother—no explanation, no note, no good-bye.

Larry had a quiet voice with an even tempo, and he always seemed to think before he talked unless he was talking to himself. His hair was gray and thin on top but trimmed short, practical. He wore comfortable wing-tip brogues he ordered from London, tailored light-wool pants, and a button-down shirt with a V-neck sweater. His sport coat waited on a hanger on the back of his office door.

Larry was examining Beth's signature on the last page of the power of attorney the officer had given him over coffee when they'd met at Starbucks in Evanston last night. He grumbled out loud to himself, "Not the perfect penmanship as when she has signed papers in this office, the name isn't on the line, slants up, rushed, messy, and where is the rest of the document? And why wouldn't she come to me if she wanted to do this?" He frowned as he listened to his messages—a real estate broker contacted by Raymond James to sell the Alexanders' Clarington Hills house, a luxury estate-sales representative contacted by Raymond James to sell the contents of the Alexanders' Clarington Hills house, both wanting keys to get in. Two messages from Raymond James, needing to get into his Clarington Hills house.

It was seven-forty-five in the morning. The receptionist wasn't in yet, so calls to the office number got left on the answering system. Larry's cell phone rang and he looked at the caller ID—Charles Sullivan. Larry smiled out loud, "I love this guy." It was Charles's second call that morning, the first when Larry was in the taxi on the way to his office. He didn't answer, deciding to call him back later, remembering Charles always had a lot to say. He had left a message asking Larry to return the call right away because he had important news.

"Good morning, Charles. Tell me about Mr. James being intercepted by the Clarington Hills Police Department, and the two real estate ladies that came to your house."

"Can you believe they wanted to know if I had a key to Elizabeth's house? I do, and they would have to step over my dead body to get it. What I want you to know is that Beth is not safe. He will cleverly find a way to either harm or kill her. He is egotistical enough to believe he can talk his way out of a box, even if that box happens to be jail. They'll never hold him on suspicion of attempted murder, and next time he'll be successful. She needs a bodyguard."

"Charles, you have acted in too many Shakespeare plays about those numbered Henrys who killed off their unwanted wives. And if you keep aggravating Raymond, you are going to need a bodyguard, too—making two people I'll have to keep watch over. Will you please let me handle the Raymond problem?"

Larry knew Charles was right about Raymond; he could be a dangerous man. The hospital was planning to release Beth from ICU to a regular room in a few days. They wanted to slowly start her eating and exercising. "Yes, how to protect her, that's my major problem, especially since she's going to want to go home. Even though 'home' will be her mother's home, she'll still be vulnerable."

The nagging headache-thoughts that had kept Larry awake and pushed him early to the office revolved around the troubling meeting he'd had with Alyssa late yesterday. "That crazy girl might be more dangerous than Raymond," he confided to the empty office. He had called Alyssa to meet with him and discuss her mother's will. She had been left plenty to live on and didn't seem upset that Beth had been left the bulk of the estate including the family home. But her answers kept echoing in his head, the words bouncing around, ringing bells of warning. "Beth will leave all her money to me." She had an air of superiority and confidence, Larry recalled. Her attitude had been one of unconcern. *And why is she thinking of inheritance from Beth, who is alive and doing well?*

Larry asked her, "Have you visited your sister in the hospital?"

Annoyed, she had replied, "No, Raymond checks on her, and gives me a report."

Ring! An alarm went off in Larry's head. "Raymond gives her a report? Something is going on here. Are they having sex?" *Ring!* "If they're sexually involved she may think Beth is an obstruction." *Ring!*

Larry called Dan Rice, whose insight and intuition he respected. "I would like to ask for your advice—and I may need a big, mean, smart shield—an overly protective bodyguard."

* * * *

Larry's private investigator confirmed his suspicions about Raymond and Alyssa. A dangerous, selfish combination—nothing would stop either one from pursuing their goal. Raymond wanted money, Alyssa wanted Raymond all to herself, and now they were sexually involved, paired up, on the road to their destiny.

Larry gave a copy of the investigator's report to Detective Rice. "Dan, to me, Raymond's intentions are obvious—if Beth survives intact to continue her life, he is out of the picture with no big bucks and he knows she's thinking divorce. If he attaches himself to Alyssa, and they get rid of Beth, he is back in the family portrait. I could let her go home with a nurse and a bodyguard, but I don't think she'll agree to it. She won't want to give up her privacy. When I saw her today she said she doesn't believe Raymond drugged her, she thinks she had stomach poisoning. It seems to be difficult for her to believe he would want to kill her. I just dropped the discussion. Maybe his intention was to put her in a coma, use the power of attorney to take over her assets. Think about this, Dan—if he finds out she's going to survive the overdose and continue her life without him, she is in imminent danger. Dan, what can we do to protect her from two people who may be thinking of killing her? Is a bodyguard the answer?"

Dan Rice came from the streets. He was a survivor, a thinker, a planner. "I have an idea. I'll get back to you."

The next day Dan called Larry to present his suggestion. Larry asked Dan to meet him at Gene & Georgetti Steak House on the near north side of Chicago and treated him to a sizzling, perfect steak dinner. They skipped the trendy front room where the bar was five deep with laughter and propositions and sat in a quiet corner in the back room of the restaurant.

Dan cut a large rare chunk, gave his friend an appreciative smile, and picked up a crispy slice of pan-fried potato with his fingers while chewing. "I have a friend, Douglas Green, who is a detective with the County Sheriff's department in Wisconsin. Outside of Madison is a beautiful little town called Green Valley. Everything grows there. They have vegetables I've never heard of. I've been to food stands off the county roads selling ripe, good-tasting fruit, not the stuff picked green and ripened in a warehouse. Doug and I have worked together on a couple Illinois/Wisconsin cases that were intertwined in both states. We were assigned to interview a patient at a private hospital in Green Valley, owned by two doctors, father and son, both MDs and psychiatrists. They care for and rehabilitate drug addicts and mental health problems but no pro bono; it's expensive. They are strict about visitors—security cameras, fences, guard at the gate. They'll help her get back on her feet, she'll be safe and won't need that bodyguard until she gets home. By then you could get an order of protection, since Raymond is under investigation. The hospital is called The Plum Tree Haven Clinic and it has a good reputation. I have the phone number for you here in my contacts. Tell the doctor you want her to recuperate from an overdose. That's right up their alley—or, rather, their valley." They smiled at each other.

Larry was ecstatic. "I owe you one."

"Another steak dinner?"

"With Key lime pie."

* * * *

Larry called Dr. Mitchell Matthews of The Plum Tree Haven Clinic and explained his dilemma—the responsibility of a daughter of old clients who needed help to recover mentally and physically from an overdose of antidepressants. "My friend Dan Rice, a trustworthy, good man, will accompany the ambulance in his private car, as a personal favor and will represent me. Please fax the documents for my signature and Detective Rice will return them to you with the check."

* * * *

Dr. Stein had suggested that Beth allow them to give her a tranquilizer to make her comfortable for the long ambulance ride to Wisconsin. She reluctantly agreed. Larry had convinced her that the Clinic would be a good place to recuperate from the drug overdose. "Or whatever it was. Just give us your cooperation so we can get this ordeal sorted out. Then, we'll talk about going home."

Beth was somewhere between clouds, feeling weightless, frivolous, giddy like she may start giggling. She was swaying gently as if in a hammock on a breezy summer day. With unopened eyes she saw fluff, pink, cotton candy angels with stretched-out wings, conscious yet gloriously half asleep. Her state of exaltation was interrupted by voices and being lifted. When she felt a warm blanket, she turned on her side and returned to the lightness, the dream, the calm of a cocoon.

The morning sun glowed into the private patient's room at The Plum Tree Haven Clinic, filling every corner as if it was searching to waken a vine of morning glories. Beth's eyes gradually opened, slowly adjusting to the unfamiliar, concentrating to find answers. Scenes were coming back to her in flashes like flipping through pictures in an album. A man said he was Dr. Stein, she was in the hospital. He asked, "Did you take lots of pills?" She had wanted to ask what kind of pills, but she just shook her head. She wanted to tell him she wasn't a pill person, rarely took aspirin for a headache, always thought, *It will go away.* Then through a fog she saw a woman in a white blur. "We're weaning you off the antidepressants, just rest, you're going to be fine." When she opened her eyes again, there was a plastic bag that dripped fluid into a tube connected to her arm. She remembered sitting up in the hospital bed, slowly sipping bland chicken broth, then chicken soup with overcooked carrots and the nurse helping her walk in the hall. Then another scene—she was suspended in air, looking down at herself in a small, moving enclosure, happy, carefree. Then the interruption, wanting to go back to the warmth and the postponement of time.

This morning Beth's attention gathered in this room. It smelled of freshly laundered sheets, the walls were pale green like creamy celery soup, hung with pictures of pale roses and lilacs. At the large window were open-slatted wood blinds, also beige drapes on each side gathered back into a brass holder. She was lying in a high-tech hospital bed with side railings and found the remote control—Blinds, TV, Radio, Call Nurse, Bed

Positions. She pushed the Up Head button and slowly sat up with a down pillow behind her. She was wearing a soft yellow-flowered-print hospital gown tied with silky ribbon at the back of her neck. She felt strange, like she was coming through a haze, her head and limbs moving in slow motion. *I need a cup of hot tea.*

Beth's nurse was watching her on the monitor at her desk, taking notes, reading the new file. In the small kitchen she poured a mug of hot tea, placed a fresh croissant on a plate, and took the breakfast tray to Beth's room.

"Oh, tea—how did you know?" Beth clumped some strawberry preserves on the warm croissant and took a big bite. "Wonderful!"

"We know a few things about you, but maybe you'll tell us more." The nurse was paving the way for the psychiatric interview.

At that moment a white medical coat, over a starched shirt and purple silk tie, embroidered with a name over the right pocket, casually entered the room and stood at the side of Beth's bed. "Good morning, Beth, I'm Dr. Matthews. Dr. Stein from Northern Illinois Hospital transferred you to The Plum Tree Haven Clinic yesterday. You are in Green Valley, Wisconsin."

His voice was low, masculine, authoritative yet friendly, with a slight welcoming smile. She focused on his face—a perfect hairline framing a wide square forehead, a matching square jaw, dark hair sprinkled with gray cut so short it barely was long enough on top to bend left. The soft gray eyes enveloped his subject, offering help, renewal, doctoring. *A doctor?* She thought, *he could have been a retired quarterback, handsome enough to be a TV commentator.*

She had intended to call Charles from the hospital before she left, but Dr. Stein and Larry had told her that she could call him when she got to the Clinic. "Dr. Matthews, I need to make some phone calls."

"I'll help you with that. Yesterday, I talked to Larry Simon, your attorney, who has taken care of all the arrangements for your care."

"First, I would like to talk to my friend, Charles Sullivan."

Dr. Matthews switched his cell phone off mute, brought up the touch pad. "I'll dial the number for you. Do you mind if I put it on speaker?" Cameras were recording the scene, a video with audio for the record and to be analyzed.

The early-morning hoarse voice answered. "Who's calling?" Charles hadn't recognized the caller ID.

"Charles, it's Beth."

Then came the caring Charles, softer, calmer. "My darling girl! Now I'm happy. I know where you are, Larry called me—to hear your voice is a blessing."

Beth smiled at the drama. "Charles, tell me what you know. I remember the evening after I was at your house, Raymond came over."

"Let me ask if he brought a prescription to you?"

"No, he brought me a cup of chai from Starbucks."

"And he gave you antidepressants with the chai?"

"Charles, you know I don't take drugs. I wouldn't take an antidepressant, I was fine. You and I had talked all afternoon. I told Raymond we needed to have a discussion, and he said he would come back the next day. He left, now I'm in a hospital. Fill in the blanks for me."

"Beth, my dear girl, it was terrible. I thought I had lost you. I saw his car leave, I was worried about you, and when you didn't answer the phone I went in the house and found you unconscious on the floor. I called nine-one-one. They said, at the hospital, it was an overdose of antidepressants."

"I don't understand—they must be mistaken. I didn't take any pills, I just drank the chai."

"Just get well and come home, my dear girl."

"Charles, I brought leftovers from the caterer to you. I thought they might have sat outside too long. Did you get sick?"

"I just nibbled on the fruit."

Dr. Matthews thought, *From this conversation it seems the damn guy put the drug, a large amount according to the hospital report, in the chai and may have intended to kill her.* "Beth, I would like you to relax, we have lots of magazines and books. Your nurse is going to help you continue to exercise, and when you feel up to it I would like to see you in my office."

After two days of stretching, walking, basic yoga with the physical therapist, Beth's nurse let her sit at her desk, talk on the phone to Charles and Larry, who asked her not to call Raymond yet because they had not told him she had been moved from the Illinois hospital. "Beth, I told him I wanted you to recuperate, and Dr. Stein felt you shouldn't have visitors until later. Raymond didn't argue, seemed content to have the update. I don't want you to worry, but he is under investigation, though it is your word against his about how you ingested the pills."

"Larry, I don't believe Raymond gave drugs to me. I probably ate something spoiled and got food poisoning. The leftovers from the caterers very likely sat outside too long."

* * * *

Beth was sitting on a small sofa in Dr. Matthew's office. He stood from his black-leather desk chair and sat across from her in one of two cushioned club chairs. She was wearing the lightweight sweat-suit provided in her room, hanging in the closet next to the fluffy white terry-cloth robe and foam-rubber-padded slippers on the floor beneath them. A fresh gown was brought in every night, placed folded on the foot of her bed. On top of a small dresser was a comb and hair brush. In the top drawer there was a net bag of toiletries—shampoo, conditioner, body lotion, face moisturizer, hand cream, huge bar of soap, all scented with lavender. There were only six rooms like Beth's in the front part of the Clinic. The other rooms were through a combination-locked door and did not contain the posh robe and amenities. The patients there were unstable, questionably dangerous to themselves and other people. The male nurses and aides were strong bodied and keen eyed.

"Shall we talk about your family, Beth? I know your father passed away a few years ago, and your mother recently. Tell me about her."

She looked at his unshaven, handsome, stubbled face and wondered if he was just starting to grow a beard. She had never liked facial hair on men; it didn't look clean, like they had been camping or perhaps the hair was concealing something or the men were hiding behind it. To her, a beard was like a woman wearing excessive makeup: What was being covered up or disguised? Also, she felt facial hair was prickly when kissing, whereas a freshly shaved face was cuddly.

Beth frowned at his conflicting look—dressed so perfectly yet an unkempt face. Then she looked away, thought of her mother, and gave that thought her attention. "My mother was a collector of friends, a giver of herself with an infectiously positive attitude. She was the volunteer who never said no, would always find the time to help and did it willingly, pleasantly. When it was cloudy and gloomy, she told us the rain was great for the flowers. If insects or birds ravaged the fruit in her orchard, she would sigh and say, 'All living creatures need to eat.' She never criticized, only said, 'Who am I to judge?' I always told my friends she had a sun-will-come-out-tomorrow disposition. She was beautiful, fun to be with, and my father adored her." Beth looked away, remembering her mother's words the day she died. "You have always been immeasurable joy in my life."

Dr. Matthews listened to the loving way Beth talked about her mother and wondered if she had the same attitude towards her sibling. He asked, "Can you tell me something about your sister?"

His question brought her attention back to the room, but it contained sadness. *I will entrust this private opinion to the psychiatrist. I need to say it aloud to someone.* Her voice was quiet, as if she was relating in confidence. "Alyssa blocked the sun and cast a wide, long shadow where the family huddled. When she was at home, I stayed in my room, away from her glaring threat. Even our little dog and cat avoided her, actually hid when she was at home." Beth recounted the memory she had never been able to bury—her mother, shaken, crying, had called Beth at university to tell of an incident. Alyssa had tried to kill Elizabeth's poodle and cat. That day after school, Alyssa came around to the back door of the house, saw her mother by the small orchard talking to her gardener, and went in the kitchen. From the refrigerator she got a brick of cheddar and a paring knife to cut a thick slice. She noticed Elizabeth's cat and dog curled together on the dog's oval bed, sleeping in the cool air-conditioned house. The cat, eerily, felt the predator-like eyes, lifted his head, and jumped up as the narrow pointed knife barely missed his head. The poodle got the warning but wasn't as fast—the sharp knife caught his shoulder. He yelped as blood soaked into his curly white coat. Both animals ran to the safety of Beth's room, under her bed. Elizabeth opened the kitchen door, saw Alyssa holding the knife over the dog bed, blood on the cushion. She stared at Alyssa "What have you done? Where is Sugarfoot?"

Alyssa looked at her with scorn, as though her mother was too loathsome to understand. "Mother, those two are totally useless creatures." She tossed the knife in the sink, took the chunk of cheese from the counter, and went calmly to her room. Elizabeth frantically searched her bedroom, calling her pets' names. As she got to the living room, she noticed drops of blood on the carpeted stairs, found the cat peeking from behind Beth's down comforter, the dog whimpering under her bed. She gathered both in her arms, ran to her car, and drove to the vet. The dog's scrawny shoulder required twelve stitches. "It seemed to me she hated all of us," Beth continued to Dr. Matthews. "She never let up on her rude, insensitive, disrespectful, inconsiderate behavior. Talking about her brings such sorrow, not for myself but because of the heavy grief she imposed on my parents. My mother, the eternal optimist, never stopped believing that tomorrow, next week, next month, Alyssa was going to change, be the darling girl she knew was inside just waiting for the right moment to come out. When she wasn't at home, my father and mother and I laughed at every little comment or facial expression or noise, just so we wouldn't forget the wonderful way laughter sounded."

* * * *

Outside The Plum Tree Haven Clinic, the wind angrily threw tree limbs back and forth, thunder growled, and lightening zigzagged in the darkening sky, all turning into a torrential rainstorm. The usually sunbathed atrium, a wide oblong room that jutted out the side of the Clinic, felt cold and deserted. It had been a long afternoon, a struggle to concentrate enough to read, not hungry but waiting for dinner. Beth was sitting in a double-sized woven seagrass chair, her feet tucked under her, covered by a soft velour lap robe, absently turning pages of a *Vogue* magazine. Two young girls entered the atrium wearing Plum Tree Haven sweats, laughing as they talked animatedly with busy hands and arms, too loudly, using those youthful facial expressions that said more than words. They spotted Beth and invited themselves to sit in the two chairs next to her. She thought, *Their fresh faces remind me of my college days, so much has happened since that carefree time.* She felt protective of them. *Why are they here?*

Lindsey was a brunette with streaks of ash blond in her long, straight hair that hung down her back and swayed like tall grass when she talked. Long-legged, slim, a jaunty manner like the popular girls on campus, she was confident, pretty, distrustful, which caused her to come across as haughty. Meghan had unmanageable shoulder-length, over-bleached platinum hair, growing out two inches from dark-brown roots with a slight natural curl that gave her a messy, unkept look. She was several inches shorter than Lindsey, with a full bosom; a rebellious college dropout, gum cracker, pot smoker. Both girls suffered the highs and lows of bipolar disorder. Meghan had been to the Haven three times, one drug overdose and two suicide attempts. She looked at Beth's neat hair, pulled back in a scrunchy to the nape of her neck, and decided she could probably style hair—an older woman with years of experience fixing her own hair.

"Can you do braids?" she asked Beth. "I just saw an old movie, *Ten*. I want to look like Bo Derek."

Beth thought, *Ten is considered an old movie? I thought Casablanca was an old movie.* She smiled. "I can make a French braid starting below one ear, up and across the top of your head, ending below your other ear. It will look like a crown. My mother taught me, and while she braided my hair, I practiced on my doll, then I used to braid my friend's hair in high school. I haven't done it for years, but I think I remember." When Beth saw little girls with pigtails, she dreamed of her own little girl and braiding her hair.

"Oh, please, do that to my hair tomorrow."

The girls were so childishly uninhibited, Beth thought. They had no secrets, talked about their pain, the distress of being bipolar, the side effects of their medication, difficulties fitting in at home, the frustrations of dealing with siblings and parents.

"Why are you here?" Lindsey asked Beth in the unreserved way of youth.

"They think I had an overdose of antidepressants, but I really just had food poisoning."

Both girls rolled their eyes at each other, then together said, "De-*ni*-al!"

* * * *

After breakfast the next morning, Beth and the girls met in the atrium, Meghan bringing her brush, a rattail comb, some yarn-covered rubber bands. "Look, they let me have my cell phone. I'm out of detention—they moved me into the sane section!" She explained to Beth, "Yesterday I was only out of lockup for the day—a test, to observe my behavior. If I had a jacket, I could take a long walk on the path around the property, maybe they would send that cute intern with the dimples and blue eyes to watch over me." She looked at Beth to clue her in on the procedures. "They only let you take a walk outside if you've graduated from confinement, but they always send a nurse, who's really a guard, to make sure you don't try to climb over the fence."

Beth thought, *She's right: a walk outside would help me feel better. I want to breathe some fresh air. It looks cold, I need a jacket. Would it really hurt to ask Raymond to do a favor for me? He should do something for me after all the misery he's caused me these last ten years. Larry doesn't want me to call him, but I'm sure he's been to the hospital and found out that I've been moved.* "Could I use your cell phone to call my husband?"

Raymond answered the phone with a question mark, not recognizing the area code or name on the caller ID.

"Ray, it's Beth."

"Sweetheart! How are you? I'm happy you called, I've been so worried about you."

"I'm in Green Valley, Wisconsin, outside of Madison, at a hospital called The Plum Tree Haven Clinic. Could you bring me a jacket, some jeans, sweaters, a couple bras, panties, and my Reeboks? Thank you." As Beth disconnected the call and handed the phone to Meghan, she felt a hollowness in her chest. She was empty of any feeling for him and wondered if she had just made a terrible mistake. Then, to herself, she justified the call. *Larry is too suspicious and overly protective.*

Meghan looked at Beth with a frown. "You have a husband? I was going to set you up with Dr. Matthews."

Lindsey wrinkled up her young face in displeasure. "I was thinking about making a play for him, myself."

Meghan shook her head and pointed her finger. "No, no, no! He's too old for you. Take it from me, you don't want an old man. They just want to lie there, let you do all the work. Half the time they can't get it up, more excuses than a juvenile delinquent."

Lindsey insisted, "But, I haven't had sex for two months, I'm so horny. The male interns laugh in my face! I think they're afraid of losing their job."

"Lindsey, just get yourself a vibrator. You can have three, four, five orgasms without a groping, sweating, heavy-breathing male. It's so peaceful and satisfying." Meghan turned her attention to Beth. "You could handle an older type, you would probably have the patience it takes. What do you think about Dr. Matthews? You could have some fun while you're here. Have any yearning for him? Don't you think he's a pretty sexy-looking old guy?"

Beth laughed at her new young friends. *Twenty-one years old, too early in their lives to endure a complicated illness.* She told Meghan to sit at the desk chair, stood behind her, started parting her hair to make a continuous braid around her head. "I'm sure Dr. Matthews wouldn't have sex with a patient, and anyway I don't like that stubble on his face. He wears a nice shirt and tie, and doesn't shave. I don't get that."

Beth's comment frustrated Meghan. She sighed. "That's something my mother would say. Hair on a man's face is sexy, hair other places, too."

Lindsey had been at the Clinic for over two weeks and observed Dr. Matthews daily. "He's not growing a beard, just doesn't shave often. Sometimes he comes in shaved on Monday morning, late. I think he shaves when he has a date over the weekend, probably with an older woman who doesn't like 'facial hair,' trying to get lucky."

A nurse came in the atrium. "Meghan, your hair looks great! The physical therapist is ready for both of you."

As the girls left, Beth stood alone at the window watching the squirrels scampering, searching for something to store away. Worried thoughts went through her mind. *Raymond will be here this afternoon. Larry is going to be angry with me. I should have thought more carefully about that call. Now Raymond definitely knows where I am. Did he really try to kill me?*

Chapter 8

Alyssa got home from work, opened the door of her condo, saw a large black duffel on the floor in the entry hall with a shiny, red, quilted parka thrown over the top. A memory of her sister wearing the jacket flashed through her mind—white fox fur around the hood, hip length, zipped up the front. She saw their mother gushing, "How pretty you look!" Annoyed, she gave it a little kick, saw Raymond watching from the sofa.

"Why the fuck is this here?" she demanded.

Raymond had had a busy day of his own, working. After receiving Beth's phone call, he drove home, put her requested clothing in a bag, retrieved a jacket from a hook by the back door, and threw it on top of the bag. He was curious about her move to Wisconsin, angry that Larry the Lawyer hadn't consulted with him, worried that she might fully recover—*she sounded stable.*

He hadn't been able to get into his mother-in-law's house yet, but he checked out Beth's drawers. In her vanity he found a small mirror-covered jewelry box that contained several items her mother had given her. He put two in his pocket—the five-carat Marquise diamond ring that Christopher had given Elizabeth on their engagement, plus a lovely three-carat heart-shaped diamond pendant. *She seldom wears these, she won't miss them, but I could say I forgot to lock the back door and they were probably stolen.*

Among the chic, picturesque shops of downtown Clarington Hills was an antique store. They sold old family jewelry which had passed through generations until it fell in the hands of young women who had no feelings for the possessions of the great-great-grandmothers who had cherished them. The antique store also sold beautiful ornate, vintage, sterling tea sets, crystal wineglasses with garlands of flowers etched around the rims, and assorted pieces of Lalique crystal, among other treasures. As Raymond looked in the window before entering, he thought, *If I'm successful in here today, I'll have much more to sell later.* Raymond walked into the shop like the privileged few who kept or discarded on a whim, his chin high, a pleasant smile, but not too big. He was wearing a deep-taupe vicuña blazer and matching Egyptian-cotton shirt, casually open at the neck. Nonchalantly, he addressed the gray-haired owner. "We're cleaning out.

If you're interested in these, I'll bring more later." *Soon as I get in the big house.*

Raymond's demeanor was impressive, projecting the image of a prosperous husband with an excessive wife desiring new, getting rid of the old. It was an excellent performance. He thought about the ease of looking wealthy, walking into the right store with the right merchandise, a few convincing words and walking out with a big check, no questions asked.

Raymond's next stop was the BMW dealership, on the edge of Clarington Hills, in a row with glass-fronted showrooms displaying Mercedes, Lexus, Porsche. The manager recognized him. "Hi, Ray, you're looking good. How's Joel?"

The manager opened the showroom double doors. The salesman drove the metallic-gray BMW 650i that had been on display out to the driveway. Raymond got in his bigger, more luxurious, leather interior, never-driven, sparkling-new car and headed for Chicago's north side.

This suits a man of my stature. All it took was the generous check from the jewelry store, plus the trade-in of my outdated BMW, the balance put on my credit card which is paid on time every month by my mother-in-law's accountant. I love CPAs, they're so efficient.

Raymond was grinning at his easy achievement and planning his next step.

Tomorrow I'll drive to Wisconsin, tell the doctor at that Haven, a mental asylum, I think, they must keep her, she's dangerous to herself. They will be responsible if they let her go and she ends up killing herself. Maybe I can get her committed indefinitely. I'll sign the papers, she'll never get out of there.

He was pumped, excited about his life's path; it aroused him sexually. *Tonight I am going to do some heavy drilling.* He shifted his butt; the thought of sex with Alyssa had started an erection.

* * * *

After the busy day, Raymond was sitting in Alyssa's apartment. He'd been impatiently waiting for her to get home from work and looked up from the sofa, naked, ready, as Alyssa came through the door. "Come here, I have something for you."

Seeing Beth's jacket in her entry changed Alyssa's mood to sullen. "Hold on to it. I'm going to shower."

He smiled to himself, went to the bedroom, sat on the edge of the bed, anticipating, his heart beating like the runner at the finish line.

She can get belligerent because she's strong, aggressive, resentful that I'm dominant. I know she got upset when she saw Beth's jacket, but I'll change her mood.

Alyssa slinked out of the bathroom, barefoot, nude, no makeup, her hair wet, eyes clouded with half-closed lids, a wolf stalking. She held up her hand, revealing a six-inch sheath, clicked a button, and a slim steel blade ejected like a lightning flash.

"No knives, Alyssa, no cutting." He held up both hands, palms facing her. "Put the knife down." He was scared. *What am I doing here with this nutcase?*

Her mouth was open, taking in more oxygen. She tilted her head with phony pleading. "Ray, I want us to exchange blood. A small cut under our forearms, then we'll put the cuts together while we fuck, our blood will mix, flow into each other."

He was looking at her heaving body, inviting him. Her other hand was sliding over her breasts, down past her smooth, waxed mound, two fingers entering the opening. He watched. Then, in an instant she made a half-inch cut, without flinching, between her wrist and elbow, the blood trickling down her arm. "Give me your arm and lie on the bed, I want to be on top."

His body was pulsing. *What's a little cut?* He held out his arm. The cut was as rapid as his blink; in shock, he fell back on the bed, stretched out, his penis a post for her mounting. She lowered her body onto him, intertwining their fingers, cuts oozing together adhering their arms with sticky blood. Her movement felt like a motor vibrating his body. The room and his head spun around him. She was out of control. His orgasm was bursting him apart, sending him flying in different directions. He slowly gathered himself, his mind, opened his eyes. She was looking at him with no emotion, just a quiet demand: "I want more."

He was trying to comprehend what she was saying. Hesitantly, he answered, "Give me a few minutes."

She laughed in scorn. "So naive, you have a fist with a glorious thumb." She rolled on her back, spread her legs. "Get up, fuck me with your thumb like you're in a boxing ring."

Raymond didn't hold back the short, fast, punishing punches. Her arms were above her head holding on to the headboard, back arched, and she was screaming joyously like she was on a roller coaster. With his other hand he grabbed his now swollen penis and matched the rhythm. She came, shouting his name, he, sweating, panting like a dog, then plopped on his back. She followed on top of him. They sank into an exhausted deep sleep.

.

Chapter 9

The Plum Tree Haven Clinic began as the private office plus a twenty-four-hour care facility founded by Dr. Miles Matthews, medical doctor and psychiatrist. It offered six patient rooms, two doctors, three nurses, and three aides. In the early days, in a small room next to Dr. Matthews's office, a two-year-old boy played alone and waited patiently for his daddy or the cook or an aide to join him in coloring, drawing, putting wooden puzzles together, building Lego towers or, best of all, reading to him. At least five times every day, his daddy came into his playroom, picked him up with strong arms, took him outside to listen to the birds, tickle his nose smelling roses, and play on his swing set. "You, my son, are the most wonderful boy in the whole world. I love you more than all the stars we see in the night sky. Today, we must go home early to check our strawberries. Lie on your mat, take a nap, and I will be back for you." Miles kissed his child's face, placed the fuzzy teddy bear to the lean chest, covered both with a light blanket, and closed the door. Mitch fell asleep, dreamed of walking the strawberry field in back of their big house with his daddy.

* * * *

Beth was in the workout room, next to the physical therapy space, sitting on a mat, cross-legged in a yoga position, eyes closed, thinking of life without being married, without Raymond, without her parents. She came out of her trance upon hearing her name, gently insistent. The therapist was saying, "Dr. Matthews would like to see you." When she walked into his office, Dr. Mitchell Matthews was already sitting in the chair across from the small sofa. He started talking in a serious tone as she sat down. "Beth, we just received a phone call from Raymond. He is on his way to the Clinic, bringing the items you asked him to get for you from your house. It was my understanding that you were not to contact him. Larry is quite upset."

Even though she had doubts, she decided to justify her actions. "Larry is overprotective. I'm not sure Raymond gave me drugs. I need some clothes, shoes, a jacket so I can go outside and walk, breathe, get better. I want to go home."

Dr. Mitch Matthews took a deep breath. *She needs to know more about her situation.* Calmly, gently, he explained, "Beth, we have a problem. There is an investigation proceeding at this moment, evidence is being collected. Larry has told me that Raymond called your doctor and got a prescription of Zoloft for you. He would never have been able to get that prescription without the doctor seeing you, if he wasn't an old friend of your parents and has known you all your life. If someone wanted to pursue it, I believe he could be in trouble for doing that. Signs of that prescription were found on the kitchen counter where it is believed it was ground up and added to the chai. The empty container was found in your bathroom, looking as though you took the drug after Raymond left. The Zoloft was in your system, but, thankfully, you vomited some of it with the chai. Charles Sullivan was concerned enough after seeing Raymond leave, and, not able to reach you on the phone, he entered the house, found you unconscious, and called nine-one-one. I'm being straightforward with you because it's time for you to understand you're in a dangerous position, and you are hindering efforts being made to protect you. Larry meant this Clinic to be a safe place for you until the investigation is finished, and then, hopefully, Raymond will be arrested. These are facts from the crime lab and the detectives, not speculation or probabilities." Dr. Matthews leaned toward her, watching her expression of exasperation, then sadness. Both were the effects of the confirmation of a failed marriage and the realization that her husband had tried to kill her. His voice became softer. "Of course, I know it's difficult to believe someone you have lived with for ten years would try to harm you." He couldn't find the courage to tell her Larry also said Raymond was staying at her sister's apartment.

Beth started to cry, silently, tears streaming down her face. "I've suspected he married me for my money. My parents were very generous to us, and he took advantage of them, and he also knew I would have a large inheritance. I've felt for a long time he didn't love me. I mentioned divorce to him several times."

"I'm sorry to give you this burden just when you are regaining your health. You will need great physical and mental strength to get through this time, but I will help you. I talked to Larry after Raymond called. We would like to tell him he cannot see you because you are still bedridden, in and out of coherency, and that you called him yesterday during a short, assisted walk and haven't been up since. An armed guard will be in our front office as a safety measure because we don't trust him and, of course, everyone who enters our facility is recorded on video with audio. If he asks for me, I will talk with him. We don't know his intentions; it's possible he only wants to drop off your clothes. How do you feel about this, Beth? Do you want to talk to him?"

The straight-forward words of Dr. Matthews had rocked her world. She sat up, gathering her strength. "No, I won't interfere again. I'll let you, Larry, and the police handle this problem."

Beth left Dr. Matthews's office and sat alone in the small library, near a window that looked out on a rose garden. The bushes were bare, trimmed, neat piles of mulch mounded at the base of the stalks, ready for early frost. A flagstone walkway wound in and out of the garden with scrolled-iron benches scattered throughout. Her thoughts went home.

Looking through this window reminds me of my mother's yard and how she loved spending time there, both working and having tea in her gazebo. Time passes and life is never the same again. I will keep the good memories. I can let myself sink into depression or I can get on with my life, which is what Mother would expect of me. Mom, you gave me fortitude, backbone, confidence, and overflowed my soul with your love. There are wonderful people to help me get through this burdensome time so I can take control of my life. I am going to call Larry, tell him it's time to get the divorce attorney and start the procedure.

Two walls of the library were lined with bookshelves, interspersed with decorative baskets, brass bowls, wooden sculptures. At one end a circular staircase led to a cozy reading loft. She walked up the double circles and found an inviting open space with two comfortable chairs to relax into and get lost with a book. Soft lap robes had been placed over the arms and the end tables held piles of magazines. The window in the loft looked out over the main entry of the Clinic. On the left, near the end of the building, another door with a covered vestibule, used by patients, nurses, and aides, led to acres of landscaped space across from the main entry. The fruit trees and blackberry bushes along the stream and walking path were all perfectly groomed and in the process of changing seasons, except for the thick hedge of evergreens that hid a chain-link fence surrounding the property, only visible in a few places from the upper level of the library.

Beth saw two couples—one woman being pushed in a wheelchair, another pair sauntering along the stream that ran lazily down the middle of the property. To her right, the driveway led to a heavy iron gate with a gatehouse and guard, light posts that included cameras. Beth sat in the suede-like upholstered chair, tucked her feet under her, still looking outside, thinking the grounds must be beautiful in spring, pale-green new growth on the evergreens, the many plum trees in bloom, bushes and bulbs flowering. *I look forward to being at my mother's house in spring, seeing her garden come to life. I need to get a pad of paper, make a list—calls and errands when I get home. Tomorrow I must call Mom's housekeeper, Ada, about Sugarfoot and Sam. She became their guardian.*

A shiny, elegant, pewter BMW rolled slowly up to the front door. Raymond got out, stretched, opened the trunk, took out a duffel and her red parka, and went into the building. She shivered, thinking of her conversation with Dr. Matthews, and that Raymond was so close, just downstairs from her right now. From the corner of her eye she saw the passenger door open. Alyssa got out of the car, walked through an opening and into the huge landscaped area. The sight of her made Beth recoil into the chair.

Why did she come here with Raymond? She certainly isn't interested in visiting me. She always flirted with him, could he be going after her, knowing our divorce is imminent, and she could support him in his accustomed style? What a pair they make! He'll try to use her, sure that he'll be in control, but he's no match for her viciousness. I'm too numb to feel any sympathy for him, as if my senses have been novocained.

Beth watched Alyssa approach the couple, who were now standing on a picturesque bridge over the stream, leaning on the railing, talking, watching the water find its way around the stones. Alyssa talked to the male attendant who nodded, then she continued past the stream, surveying the area. *Why is she interested in the walking area? What information could she want from the attendant?* Beth wanted to look away, go downstairs, sit at another window, another view, but she couldn't move. Her gaze followed Alyssa back to the car, staring as if she was in a trance, moving backward, away from the window, trying to put more distance between them. She continued watching as the car turned around in the circle and left through the gate. She felt a relief—they were gone.

Beth heard someone calling her name. Dr. Matthews was at the bottom of the stairs.

"How did you know I was here?"

"Your nurse always knows where you are, it's part of her job. Come with me to my office, I'll relate the conversation with Raymond."

She walked beside him, slowly, dejected, thinking, *Ten years of my life wasted, thrown away. Why did I keep thinking he would change? A rotten apple just keeps getting more rotten.*

* * * *

Dr. Mitch Matthews knew that Beth could see the main entry from the window in the library loft. She would have seen Raymond and Alyssa drive up to the Clinic entry. He wanted to put his arm around this lovely woman, say he would not let harm come to her. He wanted to loosen her hair and feel it against his cheek. *How unprofessional of me,* he scolded himself.

Raymond had asked to see the doctor in charge. Dr. Matthews led him to an office in back of the reception desk, used when interviewing new patients and guardians. Sweetness oozed out of Raymond like spilled syrup—the lowered chin, the soft voice, the sad eyes, so concerned about his wife. "Beth has a lawyer who is her executor, but I have her power of attorney. I'm surprised you didn't ask for my signature when you admitted her, but I'm happy she's here. I want her to have the best care. I can sign papers now for her continued commitment. I'm afraid for her to be alone—she tried to kill herself once, so depressed, unable to handle life after losing her parents. This is a great facility, I know she'll be safe here. Do I sign regularly for her commitment? Annually? Shall I bring some winter clothes for her?"

Dr. Matthews was a good listener. He sat forward, elbows on the desk, hands clasped together, attentive, serious faced. "Mr. James, we will let you know when we need more papers signed for Beth's continued stay. We would like to keep a copy of your power of attorney in our files, with your contact number and your signed Health Care Directive. I assume you don't want us to take any emergency procedures to revive if she should withdraw into unconsciousness, if brain damage is imminent?" *Would he agree, show any sorrow that such a terrible thing might happen to his beautiful wife, insist on reviving with hope of recovery?*

"No, no emergency procedures." Raymond handed him the twenty-page document. They stood, shook hands, Dr. Matthews watched him walk to his impressive car, then drive out the gate with his sister-in-law.

* * * *

Beth was sitting on the sofa in Dr. Matthews's office while he sat in the chair across from her. An older gentleman walked in who looked so much like Dr. Matthews, she knew they had to be related. Older brother? Father? "Beth James, this is my dad, Dr. Miles Matthews, founder of The Plum Tree Haven Clinic. He is supposed to be retired but likes to come in, give his opinion and advice." Beth would learn they liked to play a teasing game, but it was a rare relationship of dependency, trust, support, affection. When they glanced at each other, the love between them flashed like a lighthouse beacon.

The younger Dr. Matthews, Mitchell, had asked his father to observe his sessions with Beth on the monitor beginning the day he'd walked into her room and heard the call to Charles Sullivan, who had related the night he'd found her and called nine-one-one. Dr. Miles Matthews sat on the sofa next to Beth, looked into her eyes, and smiled. His was the face of a father, a protector, a healer. "Beth, we are going to help you get past this bumpy road; the smooth surface is just ahead for you. I want you to lean on us, depend on us, we are here for you."

"Thank you." She turned to the younger Dr. Matthews, searching his face, waiting to hear about Raymond's visit.

He was wondering how much to tell her, then decided she needed to know everything. Slowly, gently, he related the conversation. "He did not ask to see you, so I didn't have to tell him you were not available. He wanted to commit you indefinitely, gave me a copy of the power of attorney you had signed, which Larry is quite anxious to see."

"I never signed a power of attorney for Raymond."

"Larry suspects you signed it the night he brought the chai to you."

"I remember he said something about the title to his car. It's in both our names and he wanted me to sign the title, so he could trade it in. I noticed today he was driving a new BMW."

"Did you also notice someone was with him?"

"Yes." Beth's eyes teared up. "It's not that I care, I just feel so stupid allowing all this to happen to me. The warnings, the signals were evident, but I hid behind the smoke screen. I guess I didn't really want to see."

Chapter 10

Alyssa was quiet, brooding on the drive back to Chicago, thinking, *If Beth wants clothes to wear outside, even in a wheelchair, it means she's not in a coma. She's conscious, recovering from a drug overdose like many people I know, and they are going to learn she did not take those pills herself.* She was irritated at Raymond, jealous that he'd visited Beth. "Ray, I don't want you running up there every time she calls and wants you to bring something. Let Larry deliver her clothes, he's getting paid for catering to her whims."

In an irritated tone, Raymond stated, "I went to that mental asylum to commit Beth forever, so I won't have to see or talk to her again."

"Did you see her, Ray, talk to her?"

"No, she's bedridden. I told the doctor I don't want any emergency procedures if she sinks into a coma."

Alyssa was doubtful, suspicious. "I don't think so. Someone was watching me from a high window. I'm sure it was Beth. She backed away when I looked up."

"Alyssa, that could have been anyone. They have many patients, cameras all over the place. They watch everyone who comes through that gate, it could have been an aide keeping an eye on you. I'm sure there was a camera on me, but I don't care, I just want her to stay there."

"I wouldn't be surprised if she was walking around those grounds right now, wearing her cute red parka."

* * * *

It was a snide remark, said with scorn, and caused Raymond to worry. He thought, *I need to back off—this relationship may be winding down. With Beth committed indefinitely, I have control of the money. I won't end it yet, in case I need her. She's starting to get on my nerves, too possessive. I can't breathe with her stifling jealously.* He stopped in front of Alyssa's building. He was dropping her off.

"Where are you going, Ray?"

Then came the lies mixed with truth, at which he was an expert. "I'm meeting a realtor at my townhouse, putting it on the market, going to move downtown closer to you. I'll call you tomorrow."

* * * *

He flashed his familiar, sexy, winning smile, but this time it didn't win anything. Alyssa was upset, upset he was not staying, talking about tomorrow instead of tonight, upset he had chosen to deliver items to Beth, upset he had left without promising to come back, upset he was smiling and leaving. She had lost her hold on him. Upset, Alyssa hesitantly got out of the car. Something about Ray was different. She felt it and thought: *If he's successful at keeping Beth locked up, with her power of attorney he'll be in control of her money and won't need me. He managed to get himself an expensive car, then he'll sell the townhouse and buy a condo. But if she's dead, he won't get anything, he'll come crawling to me.*

* * * *

Raymond's appointment with the realtor was not that afternoon, it was the next day at noon. He was a glib liar, had so much practice. *I have to take a break from Alyssa, she's getting too possessive, too domineering. I need some breathing room and a little variety. The sex with her is fun, but it was scary when she held up that switchblade. Still, I got lost in the passion, but who knows what she'll come up with next. I don't understand that hurt-thing. She's more than a sadist; she likes inflicting and receiving pain, what's that called, sadomasochism, all under the guise of sex. It's new to me, I'm not sure I like the pain part. On second thought, I wonder if she'd let me fuck her butt. I'm sure she knows about that. I'll mention it tonight when I call her.*

As he pulled into his garage, closing the door behind him with the remote, Raymond was planning his next moneymaking schemes. He wanted to spend this evening looking through Beth's desk, hoping to find bank statements, perhaps a savings account not controlled by her parents' accountant, or perhaps money in her personal checking account he could close out. He kept thinking if he could get into her parents' house, he could get more jewelry to take to the antiques store, it was so easy. Alyssa would know the new combination to open the garage door, she might have the new key to the front door. He and Alyssa could drive there in her car, she would open the garage door for him. If the police came, she could talk to them, stall them while he rummaged through Elizabeth's desk, jewelry box, and he needed Beth's purse to get her car keys, he could sell it, easy cash. He felt sure there would be money stashed in the master bedroom, he'd find it.

Chapter 11

The sky was the usual fall, dismal gray in Wisconsin, a cold, crisp air, the beginning of winter's scolding. Meghan and Beth were standing in the atrium. Meghan was wearing her Plum Tree Haven yoga pants and a sweatshirt. Beth, in jeans and a heavy sweater, was holding her red sateen, quilted parka, waiting for two aides to accompany them on a walk of the Clinic grounds.

Beth looked at her young friend with motherly caring. Kindly she said, "Meghan, you're not dressed warmly enough."

"You sound just like my mother, only not as bossy."

A male aide walked into the atrium. Beth could tell he spent most of his spare time in the gym—thick neck, muscular shoulders and arms. He informed them, "Lindsey doesn't want to go outside, says it's too cold, she'd rather walk on the treadmill. Mrs. James, you have a phone call from Mr. Lawrence Simon."

"I've been waiting for Larry to call me back. Meghan, put on this jacket, I'll walk later." She held the parka open. Meghan put her arms through, Beth pulled the hood over her head, zipped it up like a mother helping her preschooler. The strip of white fox fur framed the young face.

"Wow! My parents would never buy me anything this fancy." Meghan ran her palms down the front of the shiny red fabric, smiled at the aide as if she was dressed for their date.

"Tell them I gave it to you because it looks better on you than it does on me." Beth walked out of the atrium to get her call from Larry the Lawyer. Meghan and the brawny escort headed outside.

Larry had distressing news for Beth. The private investigator had followed Raymond to the antiques shop. After Raymond left, the investigator convinced the owner to reveal what he had bought from Raymond, telling him it was stolen merchandise, adding the information that Raymond James was being watched by police. Larry called the owner and made arrangements to buy back the diamond ring and pendant. "Beth," Larry said gently, "Detective Rice, working with a private investigator, is stacking up evidence against Raymond. Unfortunately, the signing of the power of attorney is your word against his. The only person who is in trouble concerning that is the notary public; the document claims she witnessed your signature. She could say she came to the house with Raymond, and we would have to dispute her and prove she wasn't there. We're working on it. The good news is our divorce attorney is going forward with those documents. He says the law is on our side concerning the trust. Christopher and Elizabeth wanted to make sure Raymond didn't get anything from them."

It wasn't the money that concerned her. "How long until I can go home, Larry?"

"Stay at the Clinic where I know you are safe until we can get enough evidence to get him arrested. We're canceling your credit card, which will cancel his spousal card; a new one is being sent to you. Go shopping on the computer."

After hanging up the phone, Beth stayed in the desk chair within her nurses' alcove, a little slumped, trying to absorb Larry's torrent of news, mostly disturbed that Raymond had sold the lovely ring and pendant her father had given to her mother and sentimentally passed to her. *When will I get my life on track? He keeps setting up roadblocks.*

Beth's thoughts were interrupted by the sound of sirens, loud as if they were just outside the Clinic.

Dr. Matthews rapidly walked past, gave quick instructions to the nurse without stopping. "Keep her in that chair, don't let anyone near a window."

He punched the phone number for his dad who was at home, lounging with the newspaper in his favorite armchair, thinking about lighting the logs in the huge stone-faced fireplace. "I need your help," Mitch said. "A patient has been shot!"

The answer: "I'm on my way."

There were three additional doctors and two interns at the Haven, but when he needed serious advice or there was an emergency, Mitch didn't hesitate to call his dad, the rock foundation upon which the Haven was built, the uncrackable Dr. Miles Matthews.

The ambulance was pulling into the driveway near the main entry where there was a gate opening to the walking grounds. Four emergency medical technicians pulling a gurney ran across the scenic bridge, past the fruitless trees to a crumpled heap of a young man enfolding a red jacket, a red jacket that was spilling its color onto the holder, onto the ground, escaping, lending color to the colorless day. Meghan would have liked being held in his muscular arms, feeling him pressing tight around her as if he thought the pressure would stop the flow. She would have liked to have felt her head against his solid chest, under his stubbled chin, heard him calling her name: *Meghan, Meghan, Meghan.* She would have liked seeing his face awash with tears, but she was no longer walking happily as a child by his side, no longer teasing him about his muscular arms, no longer there.

The aide had managed to push nine-one-one on his cell, didn't remember saying, "In the meadow of Plum Tree Haven—shot—bleeding—hurry!"

The receptionist had heard two loud cracks, looked out, saw the red jacket being gathered up, called Dr. Matthews. "Emergency!"

* * * *

Lawrence Simon joined both doctors Matthews and Beth. She sat on the sofa with Larry, the senior Matthews in the armchair, the junior Matthews in his heavy black-leather desk chair he had rolled between them. Dr. Miles Matthews sat forward, looking at Beth's red, swollen eyes, her sad, tormented face. Her head was too heavy with sorrow to hold upright, her body slouched. Miles's voice was barely above a whisper. "Beth, please listen to me. Larry, Mitch, and I have a suggestion. You are no longer safe here." He avoided saying, *Our other patients are not safe with you here.* "There is a place we would like you to live, just for a short time, until the investigation is finished and you will be able to go home. Please try to understand this could have been a random shooting, an upset ex-patient or even someone angry with Meghan, she had many unstable friends. You are not to blame."

Larry put his arm around her. Beth felt dizzy, so many thoughts swirling in her head.

She was wearing my jacket—the shot was meant for me. Larry saved my life, calling at the exact time I would be out the door. Sweet Meghan was so happy to wear the red jacket. Could Raymond have tried to kill me? Again? But he wouldn't even profit from my death, maybe he doesn't know that.

She acknowledged to herself that these people in the doctor's office were trying to help her. She would agree to whatever they offered. Faintly she mumbled, "Okay."

* * * *

At Larry's request, Detective Dan Rice and his friend, Wisconsin Detective Doug Green, led the investigation into Meghan's death. They worked tirelessly, digging deep to get a shovelful of evidence that could get Raymond arrested. They examined tire tracks, finding that the bullets had come from a car down a narrow dirt side road along the hedged boundary of the Clinic, off the main highway. One bullet missed its target and lodged high in the trunk of an old Bartlett pear tree. They sifted the area for a witness who may have seen a car turning onto the dirt road, checked with the gate guard, who sometimes looked at that road with his binoculars, but not at that time that day. A search warrant gave them access to Raymond's townhouse and car. "I don't own a gun, I don't like guns, I don't know how to shoot a gun. Where is Beth?"

"That's interesting...he didn't ask how Beth was doing, just where is she." The detectives lied, as planned by Larry and the doctors Matthews. "She has been transferred to another hospital, in Michigan. We are not allowed to divulge anything further."

They re-examined the records from the private investigator, which led them from Raymond to Alyssa. Dan and Doug looked at each other like the sun had just come over the mountain and shown on their faces. At the same time they said, "Alyssa." Before obtaining a search warrant, they checked her activities, talked to professors at Southern Illinois University—poor attendance, excellent grades if she liked the class or professor, barely passing grades if she was bored, a runner, competitive, rough, soccer player, liked weightlifting, known for her association with a wild motorcycle group, an excellent shot at skeet shooting, took private lessons at a rifle range and often went there for target practice.

The doorman at Alyssa's building rang her unit. "Some detectives and Chicago policemen want a word with you."

She met them outside her open door as three experienced, callous, seen-it-all policemen, guns on hips, heavily badged, preceded the detectives out of the elevator. "Come in, I love men in uniform," she purred.

They had a search warrant but found no guns. The parking attendant said her car had been in the building's garage all week. The doorman said she always took cabs to work.

After leaving Alyssa's building, in a secluded corner of a coffeehouse,

Detective Green took a small pad of paper from his breast pocket then drew a diagram of The Plum Tree Haven Clinic acreage and nearby area. "Dan, if you drove a car down this side road to kill somebody, would you drive your own car?"

"No, I'd rent one, use an alias, someone's ID I had access to, like my sister's or mother's."

"What would you do with the gun?"

Dan looked at the diagram. "Is this a river running under the highway near the Clinic?"

"That little river is about a mile away with an access road down the side leading to a great apple orchard, where you pick a bushel yourself, go to the farmhouse, and pay on the way out. I've been there, it's a dirt road right next to the water—muddy, murky water. If you were looking for something in that water, it would be difficult to find."

"Doug, do you remember the owner of the private shooting range said she brought her own guns for practice? Guns, that's plural. Somewhere in that apartment is a key to a storage locker. If you use one gun and then get rid of it, there's more where that came from. Or, if you want to keep it, you need a safe, private place to store it."

"But we need that gun for fingerprints."

They sipped the rest of their sweetened, whipped-creamed coffee, smiled at each other. "Buddy, we have more work to do."

Chapter 12

Three generations of the Johnson family had grown up in the two-story farmhouse, a covered porch wrapping around two sides, solid oak-plank floors and stairs, with a curved banister to the second floor and then an attic that some years was used for storage, sometimes extra bedrooms. Carl Johnson, the patriarch, had been the county judge. Whether he had gone to law school was a debated issue, but people felt he had moral, just principles, made fair decisions. Carl had built the big house for his pretty, blonde Norwegian wife and filled it with ten children. After Carl and Inge died, the remaining children married, left the area. The old house passed to the only grandchild, who loved the deteriorating white elephant and promised the family she would someday fix it up and live there if they wouldn't tear it down to sell the fertile farmland.

Inge, named after her grandmother, whom she also favored in looks, had become pregnant at sixteen; and, after a botched abortion, which resulted in a hysterectomy, she left for the big city, Chicago, where her pretty face got her a job as a receptionist for a construction company that did remodeling. She dated one of the young carpenters, Luke, in an off/on romance. He kept breaking up to find someone to start a family with, coming back, breaking up, until after fourteen years and witnessing the problems his siblings were having with their kids, he decided a life with Inge would be fulfilling enough for him. They married at the Chicago courthouse with six other couples they didn't know, Luke's favorite brother and sister-in-law as witnesses. Inge took him to Wisconsin, showed him the old Johnson family home—the apple orchard begging to be pruned, the overgrown blackberry bushes promising abundant fruit in exchange for water, dozens of different-colored rose bushes, struggling but defiantly blooming. Luke recognized the quality of the building materials in the house, put his arm around Inge, and said, "This house has been waiting for us. Let's move here, spend the next year fixing it up, and we'll have a bed-and-breakfast and so many Viking apples and blackberries, people will lock their doors when they see us coming."

The house was in serious need of repair. Luke's brothers came out from Chicago on weekends to help. Inge drove Luke's truck through the suburbs of Chicago touring garage sales, replacing furniture taken by her sisters, cousins, aunts. Her mother helped sew curtains for the new kitchen, drapes with matching bedspreads for the bedrooms, taught her to make apple fritters and blackberry cobblers, and formed a new relationship with her reclaimed daughter.

* * * *

Mosel Porter drove Beth's new four-door Mercedes off the highway onto a two-lane paved county road, with Beth riding beside him. The road was interspersed with long, random driveways leading to spacious two-story farmhouses, surrounded by many-acred farms. A double-size silver metal mailbox, welded on top of two old scrollwork garden gates, had "Inge's B and B" scripted in forest green, with three white daisies painted on the side.

Mosel turned into the driveway, the heavy car crunching the gravel, and parked in the wide empty area off to the side of the front porch.

Inge, watching through the living room window, opened the door to greet them. "Mrs. James, Mosel, I have both of your rooms ready, let me show you around."

The four rickety steps to the porch had been replaced with thick, sturdy boards. A new railing, painted white, swooped around the side of the house. The original heavy, hand-carved wooden benches had been sanded, varnished to show the beautiful grain, padded with yellow cushions so bright it looked like the sun picked that porch to reflect its rays and left the surrounding area dismal.

Beth stepped through one of the weighty double doors with etched-glass windows. "What a charming house! My mother would have loved it."

Mosel filled the doorway, seeming to dwarf Inge, who hoped the bed was strong enough to hold him and made a mental note to cook large breakfasts and have sandwiches available for him during the day. She was happy with her first paying guests. Others had been nonpaying family members, and Dr. Matthews said these two might be staying for several weeks.

* * * *

Mosel Porter had been on the Chicago police force with Daniel Rice, both men aiming to become detectives. Mosel never made the promotions, maybe because he got noticed for being big, quiet, too nice, and not noticed for being smart, inquisitive, a thinker, a problem solver. When Dan

Rice made Detective, he looked at his friend's disappointed face. "Mosel, you should be a private detective or bodyguard. My friend, Larry Simon, will get jobs for you."

Larry recognized all the assets the Chicago Police Department had overlooked and hired Mosel as Beth's bodyguard/driver/protector, a responsibility Mosel took on with heavy seriousness.

* * * *

Larry and Mosel had gone to the Alexander home in Clarington Hills, gotten Elizabeth's sporty white Mercedes from the garage, traded it for a four-door, comfortable, dark-taupe sedan. Larry told Beth, "Later, when you get home, I want you to start cleaning out your mother's house, make it your home. This is a good place to start."

Beth agreed. "I'm not going to argue with you, Larry, but don't get a black car that looks like a limousine—it will look too pretentious."

* * * *

Beth had left The Plum Tree Haven Clinic and begun another step in her new life. She was sustained by the memory of her parents' abundant love, and no longer felt the victim of a deceptive, humiliating marriage. She was independent now, planning her own way, feeling happy to be free, like a pacing, caged animal released.

Mosel had driven Beth to Michigan Avenue in Chicago, waited for her at the door of each store, collected her shopping bags, hovered around her as they walked the few steps to the safety of the car. Larry thought it could be dangerous for Beth to go to her townhouse or her mother's home to get clothes and personal items. "Someone could be lurking, waiting for another chance, so just use your new credit card, buy everything new. You're starting a new life."

On the way back to Green Valley, Beth surveyed her pile of packages. "Mosel, today I spent a big chunk of my inheritance." Mosel smiled at her in the rearview mirror. Larry and Dan had told him her story, showed him the investigation reports, introduced him to Charles Sullivan and both doctors Matthews. He liked his charge and was settling in to his obligation, his new occupation.

* * * *

Beth followed Inge up the curved staircase, to the carpeted hall, into the only suite. The bedroom was spacious with an iron four-poster bed.

Rods across the top may have supported a canopy at one time; it now had cream-colored drapes hanging high at the four corners to the floor. An open arched doorway led to the sitting room with a two-cushion sofa and an armchair, two dining chairs at a small round table with a fringed tablecloth down to the floor, and an ornate refinished maple desk facing a draped window looking out on the surrounding farm. Mosel was making his second trip up the stairs loaded with shopping bags. Beth acknowledged the tedious work that had gone into remodeling the beautiful old house. Inge said, "Mosel, come with me, I'll show you to your room on the main floor by the stairs, and both of you please feel welcome to use the living room. I will see you tomorrow morning in the dining room. Start on the basket of fresh blackberry muffins while I make breakfast. Tea and coffee will be on the buffet."

Inge arranged for the *Chicago Tribune* to be delivered and Beth took it to her sitting room after breakfast every morning, settling into the crossword puzzle. Her new iPhone chimed. Larry or Charles called daily, but then an unfamiliar number appeared on the caller ID. Beth reluctantly answered.

She heard a cheerful masculine voice. "Hi, Beth, this is Mitch." She asked herself, *Is that Dr. Matthews's first name?* He was obviously amused at her hesitation and explained, "The guy in the white coat." Beth felt elated, like the most popular boy in school was calling her, then scolded herself. *I'm not in college! This is a doctor checking on me, but he's so handsome and I have thought of him.* He continued, "I met Inge and Luke, inspected their B and B before I recommended it to Larry. I thought you would like it." He repeated Larry's warning: "Remember, no one knows where you're staying. We put out the information that you were transferred to a hospital in Michigan. Still, all of us are happy Mosel is with you."

She admitted to herself, *I guess they don't trust me since I called Raymond while at the Clinic and revealed where I was staying.* She didn't want to dwell on the killing, though it was, often, sadly on her mind, so she just accepted the reminder and went on to another subject. "Inge and Luke did an incredible job on this beautiful old house. Inge is indulging us with her breakfasts, but Mosel picks up dinner at the Deli. I'm becoming quite spoiled."

"That's good news—you deserve to be spoiled." He paused, as if thinking about what he wanted to say next. "Beth, there is one good restaurant in town, a little French café—André's. Could I take you there for dinner tonight?"

She hesitated.

Am I allowed to go out with a handsome man? Isn't that why I bought a lovely new dress? Who better to wear it for than the "sexy-looking old guy," as Meghan had called him?

She had paused long enough, he wouldn't think she was too anxious. Still she answered shyly, quietly, "Yes, I'd like that."

Mitch quickly replied, "I'll pick you up at seven."

She was excited about the call. At the Clinic, she'd never allowed herself to think of the handsome doctor except as her doctor, but now she wasn't his patient and her mind wandered to male companionship, the flirting, the laughing, the touching, the compliments. She chided herself.

This is not a date, he is doing a routine follow-up to see how I'm progressing...no, this is a date! Tonight I am going to look good.

She called Mosel on his cell phone. He was in the driveway watching the passing cars, surveying the area. He answered at a half ring.

"Mosel, we need to go to downtown Green Valley."

He drove her to the beauty salon, situated in the front bedroom of the hairdresser's cottage down a tree-lined road off the one main street.

"Cut this hair off, make me look like a glamorous woman. No more ponytail for me."

Her heavy blond hair, parted on the side, swept up from her forehead, swooped down and back in a loose, wide wave at her cheek, then slightly turned under at the nape of her neck. She looked at herself in the mirror, approved. The now-short, thick hair moved like swaying ripe wheat. She wore her new black Armani dress, a sheath with long, tight sleeves, fine zippers going up a few inches at the wrists. She had treated herself to in-out diamond hoop earrings that gave a glimpse of a sparkle when she moved her head.

Beth heard the car crunch on the gravel driveway at seven o'clock sharp and was walking down the stairs as Mitch opened the front door. He watched her until she got to the final step. "Excuse me, miss, I'm here for Beth James."

She giggled and explained her new look like a schoolgirl. "I had a haircut today." She stood next to him in her very high-heeled shoes, almost eye to eye with the tall Mitch Matthews. "I can't offer you a glass of wine, I forgot to buy a bottle." She felt a little nervous.

"You look fabulous, Beth. We'll have wine at André's."

She put a huge square wool shawl of black, charcoal, and beige plaid folded into a triangle over her shoulders as Mitch ushered her to his car and opened the door.

"The doctor drives a yellow Corvette?" she exclaimed, amused, stepping down into the seat.

"Dad calls this my midlife-crisis car."

"How do I put the window down on this yellow machine?"

Mitch pressed a button. She saw Mosel walking toward her new Mercedes and leaned out the window. "Mosel, you have the night off."

"No, Beth, you enjoy yourself. I work every day, this is my job. I will just be around, don't think about it." He followed them to the restaurant, kept lookout in the parking lot.

Sitting across from Mitch Matthews in the restaurant, Beth saw a man different from the professional doctor. He laughed, told silly jokes, teased her about having a chauffeur because he knew she was self-conscious about it, then held up his wineglass. They had finished one bottle and started on another. "Here's to the woman who buys her own diamonds." She blushed. She had told him about her shopping spree and he sensed she was embarrassed, as though she had to justify it by saying her mother had been encouraging her to buy some nice clothes and get her hair styled.

He reached for her hand and put her fingertips to his lips, looking intently at her eyes. "Are you aware your eyes have tiny yellow specks that are hypnotic?" And he thought, *My feet haven't touched the ground since I walked in the room and saw her. I'm falling in love.*

She felt dizzy, giddy. *Is he this romantic with all women? I want to know if there are lots of women in his life. Do I need to be careful with my feelings?* With the aid of too much wine, she bluntly asked, "Where do I stand in the competition for the handsome Mitch Matthews's heart?"

"You're in the running by yourself. My dad says bananas last longer than my lady friends, says I'm too particular or too difficult, he's not sure which. I don't like sitting across the dinner table from a date young enough to be my daughter, makes me feel like a dirty old man. Also, I'm allergic to bubble gum." She laughed. He thought, *I may not be able to continue my life without hearing that laugh.* He wanted her to know more about him. "Beth, I'm a country boy. It's not easy to find a woman who thinks it's a fun date to walk down a dirt road and share an apple with the neighbor's horse. But I believe watching a running stream, walking among fruit trees, flowers, fields of anything growing is good for the soul. That's why I elaborated the landscaping around the Clinic and our house. This is me; you decide if I'm too much of a hick for you. I'm forty-two years old, divorced, my father lives with me because I insist. He gave me our family house when I got married, I remodeled it and included a suite for him. I'm not moving to Chicago, though I like going to plays, fancy restaurants, museums, the opera." He changed the talk to them. "Remember"—he smiled—"it was Meghan's idea that we get together."

It made her sad again to think of Meghan getting killed. Beth thought about their conversation in the atrium and told him, "She said you were a 'pretty sexy-looking old guy' and wanted to know how I felt about you."

"Yes, she told me and also let me know you don't like facial hair and advised me to shave."

"Did you shave for me tonight?"

It was an intimate question. He picked up on it, smiled. "Yes. Will it get me a kiss?"

"Ummm, depends on the dessert."

"Bring on the chocolate mousse."

* * * *

In the living room of the B and B, Mitch removed her shawl. Beth found it unnerving, sexual, and it made her feel warm, heady. *I've definitely had too much wine.* She sat at one end of the curved sofa, he sat close and put his arm around her, their faces only a few inches apart. He put his hand on the side of her face, his fingers extending over her ear, into her silky hair. His mouth covered her lips, easily. She kissed back with parted, sensual lips, leaning against him as their arms slipped around each other. She put her cheek against his. "Thank you for shaving for me." They relaxed, breathed into the embrace, letting the time pass, each thinking about the ease of being together. The extended kiss was too good, sending longing to their bodies. She broke the trance, whispered, "You should go home."

"Yes, I'll call you tomorrow."

* * * *

When he called, she was on the tollway heading to Chicago for an appointment with Larry the Lawyer and told him she would call him on her way back after dinner. The next call was from Larry, who was inside her mother's house. "Okay, now tell me again what you want me to bring from here. How about this beautiful mink coat with a hood?"

"No, I don't have anyplace to wear it."

"That's not what I hear."

"Private news travels far and fast! I would like some of those boots in the mudroom and a warm down parka from the back hall closet. It's starting to get cold here. On the shelf is a new tennis racket, I've only used it once, please bring it. There's a pro at the health club and two indoor courts. I'll take advantage of that."

Larry was in the master bedroom. "I'll bring this white leather jewelry box for you, mostly plain gold stuff in it, and you'll have a place to keep the heart pendant and diamond ring from your parents that I bought back."

"Larry, I'm so anxious to go home. I want to get my stuff from the townhouse and move into my mother's house, talk to Charles, get his advice. He always helps me clear out the cobwebs."

"Beth, try to be patient about that. Go to the gym, exercise, swim, have some fun with Mitch. Today we will get some preliminary forms filled out, but when you come back to Chicago next week for four, five days, I'll ask Mosel to bring Charles downtown to have dinner with you several evenings."

* * * *

On the drive back to Wisconsin she returned Mitch's call; he was still at the Clinic. "If you work every day, you won't know what day it is. How are we going to have a big Saturday night?"

"Tomorrow is only Friday, but I'll take the day off if you'll have breakfast with me." He didn't want to wait until dinner to see her. *I think about her too much. I need to take a deep breath and concentrate on my patients.*

She liked the sound of his voice. "The best breakfast is at Inge's. Would you like to join me and Mosel tomorrow morning?"

"Yes, and afterward I'd like to show you my house and, most important, the strawberry field—an important part of my life when I was growing up."

* * * *

After breakfast, Mosel followed Beth and Mitch two miles past the B
and B on the county road. They turned right onto a dead-end graded dirt
road with only two farms. On the left was the enormous, totally remodeled
Matthews house, sitting back from the dusty road, with a long hand-laid
brick driveway leading to the four-car garage on the side or circling wide in
the front to double doors with wild birds carved in bas-relief. Inside, the
entry was an art gallery that led to an open two-story-high living room, a
stone fireplace that looked like it belonged in a ski lodge, several sitting
areas, and a baby grand piano placed at a bay window. Behind the state-of-
the-art kitchen was an apartment for the housekeeper/cook, Hilde, and her
husband, Lech, who was in charge of the grounds with seasonal help.
There were two master-bedroom suites on the main floor, one was guest
quarters, the other was Mitch's, plus Miles's extensive suite, which was like
an apartment; also a paneled library, two more bedrooms, and four
bedrooms upstairs, each with its own bathroom. The back of the house
opened to a double-story covered, screened-in porch, complete with
stainless steel barbecue, tables, chairs, and lounges. From the porch, the
strawberry field stretched out seemingly with no boundaries.

As Beth and Mitch stepped out of the enclosed porch to the back of
the house, Mitch opened his arms as if to encompass the field. "Beth, in the
spring, these acres fill with the most beautiful, lush green plants that
produce giant, cardinal-red, sugar-sweet strawberries. This field contains
intimate memories of my childhood with my father, so profound, the sight
of it makes me want to put my arms around him, thank him again and
again. He taught me the unconditional, continuous, deep love of a father.
When I went off to college, he said, 'If you call me every day, I won't
embarrass you by moving in your dorm room with you.'"

* * * *

Mitch's father, Miles Matthews, was the only child of two doctors: a
gynecologist and a psychiatrist. He had a lonely childhood and all his life
looked forward to marriage and many children. He was thirty-two, an
established psychiatrist, when he married Marina, a nurse in his clinic. He
inherited the farmhouse his parents used as a summer getaway, only a few
miles from the clinic he built. Miles was overjoyed when Marina said she

was pregnant, but she informed him that she was not ready for a child and wanted an abortion. In disbelief, he stared at her. "You said you wanted a family!"

She ranted, pouted, gave him the silent treatment, inquired about an abortion on her own, unsuccessfully. She was "too far along." As the months passed, she became angry and abusive, screamed at him daily, "I'm not prepared for this!"

After a beautiful, healthy baby boy was handed to Miles in the delivery room, Marina left Wisconsin and they never heard from her again. Miles wouldn't hire a caregiver, saying, "This is my boy, I'll take care of him." They were together, at home and at the Clinic, every day until the half days of nursery school, when Miles parked the car, walked his boy inside, went to work, then picked him up. "Mommy doesn't live with us, she is in another place, but I'll love you and be with you for all my life."

Beth understood the father/son closeness and why Mitch insisted his father live with him. Perhaps he wanted to care for his father as his father had cared for him. She looked at the strawberry field, empty of fruit now on this warm autumn day, still in perfect rows. The small once-lush plants turning brown seemed to send a message of giving and receiving, abundant fruit for loving care. "What did you do here with your father that has remained as such positive and fond memories?"

"I learned about life—the plants growing, producing little white flowers, turning into tiny green buds that grew, changed colors, and became wonderful fruit. 'A cycle of life,' Dad called it, and somehow I knew the theory translated to everything living, we all had a cycle of life. Dad had back problems, and he would take a long stick out to the field—we called it the 'strawberry stick'—and every day, all summer, we checked the plants, me on hands and knees, he probing with the strawberry stick, watching, waiting for the surprise. There's one area of plants right in the middle that is always the first to ripen and produces giant deep-red strawberries. Dad would carry a three-legged stool; we sat in the field, selected and ate strawberries, and discussed our dreams, our plans, our future. We've done that every summer, all my life." Mitch stopped, looked at the field as if he was thinking something he couldn't share, but when he looked at her, he knew she would understand. "He always told me he loved me more than all the stars in the sky. I remember as a little kid, getting out of my bed at night, going to the window and looking at the sky to see how many stars I could find, so I would know how much my dad loved me."

They went quiet, each thinking of the father/son love that lasted through the years, continuing the cycle.

Beth broke the trance, wanting to hear him talk more about his life. "This is a big field. What can be done with so many strawberries?"

"Hilde freezes some, makes muffins, pies...we leave baskets in the back room at the Clinic for the staff, Lech takes the large ones to Ellie's Fudge Shop, and in exchange she gives some back to us dipped in chocolate, which we share with the staff. Everyone we know gets a basket of strawberries. Sometimes we come home and there's a big bushel of apples or pears on the front porch. The people around here would drop whatever they're doing if you called them for help."

Now I understand the sensitive side of this beautiful man, Beth thought. She wanted to know more, but didn't want to sound so serious. "I want to visit Ellie's Fudge Shop."

He laughed. "I knew that would get your attention. Ellie has been making copper vats of fudge for over forty years. It's even creamier than my old great-aunt Flora's."

He stopped to take his cell phone out of his khaki pants pocket. "Sorry, Beth, this is my new psychiatrist at the Clinic, please don't be offended if I take the call."

Beth walked toward one side of the magnificent house and saw a large vegetable garden, brown vines lying on the ground and hanging from a wide trellis.

I wonder what memories this garden holds?

She walked the length of the backyard to the other side of the house and was surprised to find a tennis court that looked newly resurfaced. Next to the four-car garage was a backboard, with a white line painted across marking the height of a net. Mitch came up behind her.

"Dad had this tennis court put here ten years ago when I insisted he live in the house and included a suite for him in the remodeling. That was at the time of my short marriage. He wanted to get a condo near downtown Green Valley, said a married couple needed privacy. Privacy wouldn't have changed the marriage. Our health club, one of a big chain, has courts, but Dad wanted the convenience of coming out here to hit balls against the backboard or have his buddies over, spur of the moment. Also, he thought we would play together, but I spend most of my time at the Clinic."

Tennis had always been a big part of Beth's life, an escape from her sister when they both lived at home, offering camaraderie with girlfriends and the competition of tournaments in high school and college. Now, standing on the court, she yearned for the feel of the racket, the strong grip, the body movement, the quick thinking to vary shots. She turned to Mitch. "Will you play tennis with me?"

He put his arm around her shoulders; she slipped her arm across his firm back. "Beth, there's an emergency at the Clinic. One of the patients tried to hang herself from a door hinge with strips of torn sheets. We have three doctors and two interns, but I need to help. I'm sorry to say I won't be back until late tonight. I would love to stay here and play tennis with you, but it has to be another time. Could we have dinner tomorrow night?"

She nodded, he put both arms around her, she held her face up for a kiss. They embraced for a while, the emergency call on their minds. "I had hoped to spend the day with you," he said. "It was a short day off."

Mosel and Miles were standing near the dirt road discussing the upcoming football game between the Green Bay Packers and Chicago Bears. Miles saw Mitch and Beth walking toward the garage and called out to Mitch, "Can you sub in our old-men's tennis game today? Beth could cheer us on." Walking closer, Miles continued, "I just got a call from Dale Clarke, his knee has gotten much worse, he's decided to finally go ahead with knee replacement, which is probably a year past due, anyway, we only have three for our game. We can take turns playing two against one but none of us like it."

Mitch told his dad about the phone call, the suicide attempt at the Clinic, that he was leaving now to make sure all was taken care of and to process the paperwork.

Miles asked if he wanted his help, but Mitch said he would call if he needed advice. Mitch knew the attempted suicide would wear on him. It would be a stressful day dealing with the parents, dictating the reams of paperwork, getting the staff back on their routines. Beth would be on his mind, but it would not be a good evening to be with her, to give her his undivided attention. He would need some time to let this incident settle.

Beth put her hand on Miles's arm, shyly. "I could be your tennis sub, if you don't have anyone else to call."

Miles didn't hesitate. He knew the guys would be upset with him, but he would not hurt Beth's feelings by refusing her offer. He smiled at the lovely, fragile-looking young woman. "Beth, I would love to have you play in our game and be my partner."

She was excited by the opportunity—it had been over a month since she had played, before her mother passed away. Beth had spent every spare moment with Elizabeth, giving up her tennis. To Miles, she enthusiastically said, "I'll go to the B and B, change into a sweatsuit, and be right back to practice against your backboard."

"Do you have a racket?" he asked.

"Yes, Larry went to Mother's house and got some stuff for me. I kept a racket and clothes there to play at their club."

"When you get back, I'll hit balls with you until the guys get here."

Mitch pulled his yellow Corvette out of the garage, and it seemed to blend with the yellow leaves as Beth watched him drive onto the dirt road. Mosel opened the door of her taupe Mercedes. "Looking at that canary-yellow car makes me think I'm too conservative, Mosel, but I'm branching out, don't you think?"

"You're doing great, Beth." He had become fond of his charge and quite protective.

By the time Miles had changed into sweats, gotten his racket and a new can of balls, Mosel and Beth had parked at the far side of the house near the tennis court. Miles watched as she stretched her limbs, bending, twisting. She pumped thirty balls with the racket, like dribbling a basketball, put two balls in her pocket, and walked to the opposite base line. Her balls came across the net low, fast, straight. Miles thought, *This is going to be interesting.*

Jackson Bradford, retired judge, and Ivan Van Camp, retired high school and private music teacher, both old friends of Miles, had been playing tennis together about forty-five years. Miles went to greet them as they arrived at the same time and parked in back of the garage, near the tennis court.

Miles gave them the update. "Dale has pooped out on us again, but I have a sub."

They looked at Beth, hitting backhands against the backboard, not noticing she wasn't missing any bounce-backs. Ivan gave a disgruntled look. "A girl?"

Jackson agreed. "We'll have to hold back on our serves, hit easily to her forehand. Come on, Miles, it would be better to play with just us three."

"Oh, like you're such hotshots. Be nice to this young woman, she's a friend of Mitch's." Both of them groaned. Miles said, "Beth will be my partner and we're going to clean your clock. Want to put a little money on it?"

Jackson and Ivan said, "Hello" to Beth, grouchily, announced that they were ready to play, whispering to each other, "We don't need to warm up to play with a girl."

Miles said, "Go ahead, Jackson, you serve first."

Beth stood ahead of the service line, in the backhand court, took three steps forward to the net after Miles returned the serve, then cut off the crosscourt return sharply down the center, four times.

"Love-forty, game, my serve." With an all-business tone, Miles loudly gave the score for Jackson, who was moodily quiet. Beth cut off their returns like they were feeding practice balls to her at the net. "Your serve, Ivan." Miles pitched him three balls.

They tried to lob over Miles's head, but she anticipated the lob from their stance, took several steps back, and returned the lobs as overhead smashes. Miles tried to hide his smile. Looking at the ground, he said, "Your serve, Beth."

Beth quietly announced, "I'll take two practice."

Grumpily, Jackson answered, "We just do first one in." She became intimidated, sensing that they were disgruntled, blooped her serve to Jackson, and he happily blasted it down the alley alongside Miles.

"Sorry, Miles, I won't do that again." Her next three serves were not returned; they either went into the net or off to the side. Jackson and Ivan finally admitted to each other they should try to hit everything they could manage to Miles, keep the ball away from "the girl" and won one game. Miles put his arm around her shoulders as Jackson and Ivan walked grouchily to their cars without asking Miles about their next game.

Miles couldn't help himself. In a bragging tone, he called, "Let us know when you want a rematch."

Beth asked, "Are they mad at me? They weren't very friendly."

"They are probably mad at both of us, but right now they're both thinking they will beat us next time. Don't worry, they'll be coming back for more. It's the best game we've had in years, and both of them liked the challenge. They'll get nicer; you bruised their male egos. I wouldn't be surprised if they try to talk me into changing partners. My dear Beth, you were fantastic—six-love, six-one. I haven't had a score like that for a long time. It was so much fun just watching the looks on their faces. Let's sit on the porch, have iced tea, and I'll tell you about Mitch selling strawberries out by the road every summer."

****

The next morning Mitch called while driving to the Clinic. "I just passed Inge's, are you having breakfast?"

"Lingering over tea and *Tribune*. How was the emergency?"

"Grim. Let's talk about us. Today is Saturday, could I pick you up at seven for André's again? I'm afraid we don't have much choice, André's or the Deli."

"I look forward to seeing you, Mitch. Could I pay for dinner this time?"

"No, thanks for offering, but I could use a tight hug and a wet kiss."

She smiled. "I'll bring that with me."

The waiter at André's poured the deep-red wine. Mitch held up a big balloon glass. "The thought of you makes me scribble hearts on pads of paper." She returned his gaze and smiled. The lovely compliment upped her heartbeat. She noticed he couldn't seem to look away.

She wanted to know more about him. "Mitch, will you tell me about your marriage?"

He took a deep breath. "I met Whitney at the health club here in Green Valley. Her parents had a townhouse at The Glen Vale Resort, came for summers and holidays. I had a private practice in town, felt the experience would be beneficial before joining Dad at the Clinic. The relationship and planning a new life was exciting in the beginning. I remodeled the house for her, but she thought it would be our summer house. I realized we didn't have good communication. She expected me to work in Chicago, lead the glamorous life, live in a glitzy Lake Shore Drive apartment. It was a superficial relationship, and when the deep feelings started to appear, our connection got lost. She didn't like country living year-round—her Jimmy Chou heels got stuck in the mud, metaphorically speaking." He smiled. "She didn't like the smell of the neighbor's horses, didn't like the dirt road, didn't like the one-main-street small town...and she didn't like me. Now she's happy, lives in Chicago, married to a LaSalle Street lawyer, wears Prada to the expensive restaurants, the maître d' knows her name. I've seen her in the lobby of the Lyric in Chicago, and she introduced me to her husband. He seems like a nice guy. I said, 'If you ever need my services, come up to Wisconsin.' I was just making small talk, but she thought I was referring to living with her and got all insulted and huffy, so now she gives me the big snub when I see her."

He wondered if it was too much information, then decided he wanted to tell her everything, open the book, let her know the whole story.

Beth thought, *Maybe he wouldn't approve of my parents' luxurious lifestyle.* "Do you go to the Lyric often? My parents had a subscription, and my mother wore Prada."

"Beth, please don't transfer anything I say about Whitney to you or your mother. I know you wore that beautiful Armani dress tonight for me, not to get the attention of everyone in this restaurant. It's a completely different story."

"How do you know it's an Armani?"

He gave a confident little grin. "Actually, I guessed. I have seen a few designer labels in my self-indulgent days." She knew what that meant. *Labels can only be seen when a garment is removed. I'm sure he has known many women, but he said there is no one in his life right now, and I like him.*

"Dad gets two seats with his subscription every year, and when he can't get one of his buddies or old girlfriends to go, I fill in, or use the tickets for dates. I enjoy the opera, the good restaurants—I just don't want to feel obligated to go, like it's an important part of my life. I want it to be an evening of choice, not to impress. We have a small two-bedroom condo with a maid's room by the kitchen where Lech sleeps when he drives Dad to Chicago. Sometimes Dad and I go together, stay for a couple days, shop, walk along the lake, go to a Cubs or Bulls game."

Beth surveyed the handsome man sitting across from her—intelligent, kind, courteous, sincere in his job, a clever sense of humor, truthful even if it didn't put him in a good light, a deep appreciation for his father. He was wearing a soft wool, dark-brown blazer, tan button-down shirt, open at the neck, no tie, and a freshly shaved face. *He's affectionate, romantic, and he looks at me with a tender yearning that stirs something inside me.* "Did you shave for me, tonight?"

"Of course."

She felt a warm flush. He continued, "There's an old-fashioned barbershop in town where I had my first haircut, four generations of barbers have owned it. They have one antique chair that sits in front of a row of up-to-date chairs, made of porcelain and steel, at least sixty years old, they're not sure. I've been sitting in that chair for forty years. It's sentimental, like comforting nostalgia. I reserve that chair for my haircut, then on special occasions I get a shave—hot towel, straight razor, and cologne."

"Did you go there before picking me up?"

He nodded.

"Let me smell." He leaned his face to her. She put her nose on his cheek, inhaled. "Very nice."

"Nice enough to snuggle with me by the fireplace? I'll give you the present I bought after my barber's appointment."

"What is it?"

"A box of Ellie's fudge."

"That's bribery!"

"A guy has to use all his resources."

She laughed that laugh again that made him want to hold her face with both hands.

Before leaving André's, Mitch called Lech, asked him to light the logs in the stone fireplace. Beth felt the warm glow as they came in a side door from the garage. They sat close together on a large, curved, sectional sofa in the high-ceilinged, spacious living room, with a bottle of champagne nestled in a wine bucket of ice cubes, two long-stemmed flutes, and a two-pound candy box on the oak-slab coffee table.

She smiled. *Some thought has gone into my visit.* "What if I had refused your offer?"

"I would come home, eat the entire box of fudge, and drink the whole bottle of champagne to drown my sorrow."

He handed the box to her; she slid the satiny white ribbon off the ends, took a whiff of the fresh chocolate, which enticed her to choose. "This is so much fudge."

"I got some of each kind. Let me guess your favorite—Rocky Road." He picked a square, broke it in half, and put a small piece in her mouth.

"Delicious! I'll share with you." She put her hand on the back of his neck, pulled him to her, his mouth covered hers, and with his tongue he tasted the sweet chocolate and felt the bits of pecans. She was thinking, *When did I become so forward? I'm certainly not hiding my desire for him!*

As he drew away he said, "I must remember to tell Ellie this is the best batch she's ever made." He poured two glasses of champagne, she picked a piece of maple walnut, he tasted it in her mouth, refilled their glasses. He took off her shoes, massaged her feet, slid his hand slowly, firmly up her leg, clasping her hip, her butt, his lips lingering as he kissed her neck.

She unbuttoned his shirt, slipped her hand inside, feeling his nipples, the hair, the firm pectoral muscles. *I have an incredible sexual urge for him.*

"Do you want me to shave my chest?"

"No, just your face. I like this."

He unzipped her dress, his hand warm, soothing, on her back. She thought, *So this is how he knows labels.* She put her lips to his ear and he barely heard her. "Take your shirt off, I want to feel your skin against mine." When he leaned back to remove his shirt, she stood up, stepped out of her dress, hose, and panties. He took off his pants, they embraced, holding on to the moment, both thinking it seemed right even if it had progressed in the fast lane.

"Beth, lie with me on the rug, in front of the fireplace, let me make love to you." She felt the deep pile under her and he pulled two small pillows from a pile of different sizes, put one under her head, another under her butt. He unhooked her bra, kissed her nipples gently. His tongue traced a line down her flat stomach, between her legs, lingering, sucking. With his fingers he felt her wet as his fingers massaged, listening to her moan. She spread her legs for him as he lay between them, supporting himself on his elbows, and began a rhythmic motion.

Somewhere in the back of his conscience a reminder flashed—*birth control, condom. I'm sure she has taken care of birth control. No, she probably hasn't used any device for ten years. This is so irresponsible of me—the condoms are in my bedroom night table. I will not interrupt her, I won't have an orgasm. I will just give the pleasure to her, I can restrain it...Beth, don't hold me so tight, don't lift your hips up to me, don't put your hands on my butt and press me closer!*

Her body trembled with involuntary spasms. Unable to hold back, his body joined with a releasing series of quivers. They breathed deeply, searching for air. She whispered his name and he thought it sounded like music.

The roaring fire had settled to burning ash. Mitch reached for an afghan to cover her. A strange sensation invaded his mind, a warm realization: *My life has changed.* "Beth, let's lie on my bed." She took his hands, he pulled her to standing, swooped her up in his arms, and carried her to his bedroom. They slept, entwined in each other's arms, then woke in a few hours, made love again, mindless of time or place or condoms, in a world of their own. The deep desire was still strong, but the urgency had faded, leaving the slowness of giving and receiving pleasure. Exploring with mouths, tongues, fingers, brought responses of gratification-sounds, all quenched their thirst for a tender relationship.

Beth heard him whisper, his lips against her forehead. "Are you awake?" She felt his naked body aligned with hers, his hand spread on the small of her back.

"Yes, but don't move. I want to stay like this forever with you. Promise you'll get rid of thoughts of all other women."

"No room in my head for anyone but you."

She smiled. "Wonderful answer. Today's Sunday, do you work today?"

"Beth, I work every day, and it will take all my willpower to get up from this bed. Until now, work has been my only reason for greeting the day. Let's have breakfast before I go to the Clinic." He raised up, pointed to a door. "Your bathroom is on the right."

There was an archway to a short hall. Left led to his bathroom and closet, right to a walk-in closet with padded satiny hangers, tilted shelves for shoes, twelve empty drawers, and a dressing area. Her bathroom contained a glassed-in shower, a Jacuzzi easily big enough for two, a marble vanity with a skirted stool and drawers containing the toiletries from the Clinic. *I'm jealous of every woman who has used this bathroom.* She stepped out of the shower and saw a sweatsuit from The Plum Tree Haven Clinic, folded, on the vanity stool. When she came out of the bathroom, Mitch was sitting at a round table, pouring tea from a thermal carafe. "I peeked at you in the shower when I put the sweats on the stool."

She thought, *As if he hasn't already seen everything.* On one of the chairs, neatly folded, were her clothes from the previous night. "Did you collect my stuff?"

"They were on the hall table outside the bedroom door."

"I left them strewn around the living room. I'm so embarrassed."

He smiled at her. She thought, *I'm sure it wasn't the first time Hilde has found a woman's clothes near the fireplace.* He had pulled two chairs together, side by side, placed a strawberry muffin from a ceramic basket on each plate. "I put a spoon of honey in your tea. Beth, I want to ask you a personal question. Do you take birth control pills or use a device?"

"No, but don't worry. I haven't used anything for ten years. I'm not able to get pregnant."

"During that ten years did you have a fertility test?"

He was sounding like a doctor. "Yes, Dr. Matthews. They didn't find any reason I couldn't conceive. This has been the dark cloud over my life."

Mitch continued in his serious doctor voice. "Was Raymond tested, also?"

Beth nodded and thought, *Perhaps he's interested in having children, and now that he knows I can't conceive, he may not want to continue this relationship.* This was the subject that always changed her mood, the bane of her being, the thorn, the burr. Her eyes saddened, her chin dropped, she fought tears.

"One more question, Beth. When was your last period?"

I guess when you've just had sex with someone, you can talk about these things. She sipped the tea, thinking, swallowed hard. "It was Saturday, two weeks ago."

Mitch put his arm around her. He kissed her wrinkled, puzzled brow, her turned-up nose, her soft lips. "Last night we made love at the time of your ovulation. I didn't use a condom, you could be pregnant right now. I want—"

"Mitch, please, stop. I have gone through the waiting, hoping, praying, every month for ten years. I can't think about it anymore, I can't bear it, it's too painful. There is no chance that I am pregnant."

"I want to tell you something—listen carefully. I know this is a supposition, but you must understand. If you are pregnant, I want to be in your and this child's life. If you are not pregnant, I want to be in your life. A week from Wednesday is eleven days after fertilization. I will buy a urine-test kit, we won't talk about it until then. I will be contemplating for both of us." He lifted her chin, smiled into her eyes, kissed her lightly on her lips. "Yum, tastes like strawberry muffin," he teased, trying to lighten her mood. "Okay, tomorrow you have meetings in Chicago, let's talk about tonight and when you get back to me."

"Mosel and I are driving to Chicago this afternoon. My meeting with the divorce attorney is at nine o'clock Monday morning, then appointments every day. We will be back late Friday."

"I can't wait five days—I'll drive to Chicago during the week."

Beth looked at his handsome face, his attentive eyes shining at her. She could feel his caring. "I'm anxious to proceed with my divorce. I will miss you, but let me get through this legal stuff. Larry has planned every day. Three evenings Mosel is picking up Charles, who calls me every day, then two old friends I grew up with are coming downtown to have girls' dinner with wine and gossip. I can't see you until next Saturday."

"How will I survive that long without holding you? No matter what time you get back on Friday night, will you come straight to my house? I'll have a hot bath drawn, and I give a good massage. I just want you to sleep in my arms. We'll make love the next night when you're de-stressed and rested. How's that for a schedule?"

"I like it."

When he looks at me I feel his warmth like the promise of new life at springtime. I know he's hoping I'm pregnant. Maybe he has wanted a child for many years, just like me. If there is anyone who can comprehend the longing for a child, it's me. He doesn't want to hear about the ten years I have not been able to conceive. Maybe it wasn't my fault, maybe it was Raymond's, maybe Mitch would consider in vitro or adoption. I'll talk to him about it when I get back from Chicago. How wonderful to love someone who loves you back.

* * * *

The meetings Larry the Lawyer had scheduled for Beth were stressful, yet she felt the blockades of progress to a new life were being torn down. Raymond had been served with divorce documents. He would be forced to get a lawyer, and that lawyer would go after Beth's assets for his client. The plan was to have everything in place, the timing had to be perfect—Raymond would be arrested for attempted murder, even though they were aware it would be his word against hers—he gave the drug versus she took the drug herself. The lawyers wanted him to appear in divorce court coming from jail after being arrested for attempted murder, knowing the probability of only holding him for three days—seventy-two hours. Beth's divorce lawyer wanted the judge to hear about his confirmed affairs with many women, including his sister-in-law, and the fraudulent power of attorney. They would produce the documents proving Raymond sold his wife's jewelry while she was in the hospital, for the sole purpose of buying himself a bigger, fancier car. Also, they would bring up his request to keep his wife permanently committed in an asylum. The senior psychiatrist, Dr. Miles Matthews, would testify on her behalf. It would be dangerous for Dr. Mitchell Matthews to testify since it might be discovered that they were sexually involved. Beth's lawyer would make a divorce settlement offer to Raymond of the couple's townhouse, which had been a gift from her parents. Of course, Raymond's lawyer would try for support from the trust, but Beth's team was prepared to show she had also worked for their entire marriage, and, importantly, that the trust specifically stated support for the daughters and nothing for the son-in-law. These were the plans being discussed in detail, carefully written like a term paper, edited and re-edited.

Larry wanted Beth to be informed about Raymond's past and his activities during their marriage, which hopefully would leave her with no room for sympathy toward him. Both doctors Matthews and Larry felt that by exposing Raymond's clandestine life, the proof included in the reports from the private investigators and Detective Rice, it would answer all her questions, crush her doubts, and enable her to leave the past behind her, bury it, go forward with her life.

Learning about the deception, the lies, the cheating, the selfish indulgence in whatever brought Raymond satisfaction, made Beth numb. *How will I ever be able to trust another man? The wasted years, ten wasted years.*

In the evening at dinner, she discussed the day's sessions with her mother's old friend. "Charles, you pull me up out of a dark hole and plant my feet on solid ground. Thank you for your sound advice and your love."

"My dear girl, Larry has debated these issues with those two psychiatrists. They are the ones helping you to get on the paved road to your future. You are strong, intelligent, resilient like your mother—you'll ride through this storm."

"Charles, you give me the boost I need to get over the hurdles. I'm so grateful for your support."

Two of Beth's friends met her at Castelli's Italian Bistro on Rush Street. During her ten years of marriage she estimated they had gotten together as couples with husbands less than twelve times. Raymond only wanted to socialize with her friends at the country club parties, when he could give them a few minutes and then be with Joel, so Beth only saw her friends at lunches and tennis games.

Daisy placed her hand sympathetically on her friend's arm. "I'm glad you can finally see the real Raymond. I understand how you would be blinded by his good looks and charm, but when I talked to him, I felt he was always watching the door, looking for someone else, not really interested in our conversation. He made me feel dull and boring, never tried to charm me, as if he knew it would be a meaningless endeavor. I can tell you now, all of us knew about his cheating, but we didn't want to hurt you by revealing it."

"I know you had good intentions, but I wish you had told me."

Beth had been friends with Daisy and Bobbie since high school, when they had sleepovers and stayed up most of the night discussing the merits and demerits of specific boys, gossiping about other girls in their classes, and any new information about sex—"Alice opened her parents' bedroom door, saw her mother on top of her father, but they were under the sheet."

These were the friends Beth could confide in. "I did suspect there were other women. He would sit in his car after pulling into the garage, laughing, talking on his cell. I challenged him about the rumors, the scent of perfume, the phone calls when he would leave the room to talk, but he'd make great, believable excuses for everything, or maybe I wanted to believe him. Also, he could become so thoughtful, kind, loving, it would make me think he had changed. Now I realize he has always been a con man. I was easy to take advantage of—a pigeon, so naive."

Bobbie related that her husband, Pratt, had run into Raymond at the tailor's several times where he was being fitted for custom suits, blazers.

"We knew he didn't make that kind of money, you supported him well." Bobbie wasn't the type to brag that her husband could afford the tailor and Raymond couldn't, it was just well known that Pratt and his father had inherited a fortune from his grandfather.

Larry had made her promise to not discuss details of the divorce, only to say she had retained a divorce attorney. "Don't give away our strategy, Beth—words travel fast."

Both friends were worried that Raymond could get dangerous if he thought he might lose financial support. They remembered her difficult, mean sister, and phone calls from Beth: "Can I sleep at your house? My parents are out, Alyssa is threatening me and I'm afraid to be alone with her. The housekeeper locks her door at night, I think she's afraid, also."

Daisy remarked, "It's disturbing that you had such protective, loving parents, yet you were surrounded by peril and perhaps you still are."

They talked past midnight, eating cannoli, sipping Chianti, then Daisy and Bobbie told her their children would be up early and it was an hour drive to Clarington Hills, they had to leave. "Please call and let us know how the divorce is proceeding. If you need us, we'll go to court on your behalf, tell everything we know about Raymond."

"Thank you. Your friendship means so much to me."

The old friends left her with mixed feelings—embarrassed that she couldn't see what everyone else had known, angry that he had taken advantage of her generous parents with his self-serving spending of their money, and sad she hadn't shown her mother she had the courage and strength to divorce him. *It's comforting to have friends I can trust and confide in.*

It had been an oppressive week, like an extended funeral service. She would get depressed, Larry would give her a boost, make her laugh. "We're going to get rid of this bum, then I want you to have sex with at least five men."

Beth laughed and thought, *One man is enough, especially when he says he can't wait for me to get back to him.*

Mitch called every day, leaving messages since her cell was turned off. "I miss you too much. I'm going to control myself, only call you once each day." Then there would be five messages twenty minutes apart. "What color roses would you like for our bedroom?" "I stopped by Ellie's, bought a box of Rocky Road." "My arms and my bed are so empty without you." "I've given up drinking tea, it reminds me of our breakfasts." "Bring jeans and boots and your tiara, so I can introduce you to Prince, the royalty among us farmers."

Beth returned his calls each night. "I'm mentally exhausted, just wanted you to know I got your messages." Then the little laugh he loved. "I miss you. Will you hold me, kiss my neck, and all those other places?"

"Yes, but if you talk to me like that I'm going to become a patient in my own Clinic."

Then the laugh. "Do you want me to bring something for you from Chicago?"

"Yes—you."

The five days of meetings drained her—discussions of strategy for the divorce, letting Beth be aware of Raymond's deceit by showing her the detectives' files, reports from the accountant on his ten years of spending, including bills from fancy restaurants and hotels where she had not been present, a copy of the power of attorney she unknowingly signed, receipts from the jeweler who'd bought her ring and pendant, the check endorsed by the BMW dealer and used for the trade-in. It all made her dizzy, gloomy, unable to think about a positive future until evenings when she talked to Charles and Mitch, who made her laugh, wouldn't let go of her hand, wouldn't let her fall backward into the hole.

"Now," Larry said, "we will wait for a court date for the hearing, then a precisely timed arrest of Raymond, so the judge will hear a request for divorce from the man accused of attempted murder, appearing in court straight from jail."

Beth called Mitch to let him know she and Mosel were on the tollway, driving to Wisconsin. She slept in the backseat of the smooth-riding Mercedes during the two-hour trip to the Matthews' home in Green Valley, dreaming of seeing Raymond enter the court in an orange jumpsuit, cuffs on his wrists and ankles, like she had seen on TV. The change from the paved to the dirt road woke her, and by the time Mosel had parked the car, Mitch was standing in the doorway. She saw his tall, slim outline, the foyer lights behind him. *I know that body, chest, nipples, hair. I wish it had been me in the gym ten years ago instead of Whitney. I met and married the wrong man. It's true what they say—I was in the wrong place at the wrong time.*

Her bathroom had a vase of one dozen roses, so pale pink, as though they had been dipped in pink lemonade. There were glass containers of lighted candles on the vanity, on a shelf above the oval tub, on the step to get into the tub. Mitch helped her undress, and the warm, scented water enveloped, relaxed her. He pulled the vanity stool close to the bathtub's edge. "Will you tell me about the week? Talking will get it out of your head, clear your mind, wash out the grime."

She thought, *I'm in love with my psychiatrist—me and every patient he has.* "It was all about ten disastrous years of my life. The facts don't show me in a very good light. I allowed a morally reprehensible man to contrive a means of control over my being." She admitted to the facts without crying.

There was only candlelight in the bathroom; she fixed her eyes on one dancing flame and thought, *I want him to know the truth.* She told him about the investigator's reports, Raymond's infidelity, the extravagant spending of her parent's money, the honesty of her girlfriends, the encouragement from Charles and Larry—sustenance from friends.

When she stopped talking, and he thought she might cry, he held up a soft terry bath sheet. She stood to be wrapped, he patted her dry. "Now, your massage with a soothing oil-based body cream before you sleep in my arms." Beth could feel the stressful effects of the harrowing week slipping away, her bruised soul being healed.

* * * *

When she awoke the heavy drapes were drawn open, looped to the sides in a large iron ring, the blinds slatted at half-open. He was sitting at the table where they'd had tea only a week before, reading, a vase of roses in front of him, white like the first snow. The last she remembered was feeling each toe being massaged.

She had been awake a few minutes, just looking at him, thinking of his hands rubbing her body. "You haven't played the piano for me. What are you reading?"

Mitch looked up. "You're awake." He sat on the side of the bed, pulled her to him, their arms around each other. "I'm highlighting some new ideas in the medical journals to talk over with my dad. And tonight after dinner I'll play love songs for you."

Beth saw her suitcase with the items Larry had gotten from her mother's house, two shopping bags and a zippered black garment bag in the corner. "My stuff from Chicago."

"Yes, you said you had bought jeans, so I asked Mosel to get your bags from the car. Will you unpack, hang things in your closet?" He was thinking if she had clothes in her closet he could feel she almost lived with him. "Put on some jeans, we're having ham-and-cheese omelets in the dining room, then walking up the road so you can meet Prince. I'll call Hilde, let her know we'll be there in a few minutes."

Beth didn't want to leave his bed, his arms, so tried to stall. "Thank you for the massage, I was awake until you got to my feet." She didn't want him to think the massage had been wasted on a sleeping body. "All the tension is gone from my muscles." She had been aware she was getting a professional therapeutic massage, gentle, yet working, probing, relaxing each muscle. "I could get you a job giving massages like that."

He smiled, "No, thanks, I only want to rub your body." He kissed her nose, her face, then stood, offered his hand to help her out of bed, watched her walk naked to the bathroom.

* * * *

The neighbor's house was across the dirt road, sitting back into trees and shrubs, summer blooming bushes now bare, surrounded by acres of farmland. Mitch and Beth crossed the road, walked on a path just wide enough for farm equipment, past the Andersens' house to a large area, fenced off to corral a lone horse munching faded alfalfa. The broad-shouldered yearling colt saw them walking toward him, tossed his mane, trotted in a wide circle then along the split-rail fence. He was the color of melted caramel with a pale-beige mane and tail that he swished side to side like teenagers flinging their long straight hair. His walk was a prance, knees lifted high like he was marching in a parade.

"Prince, this is Beth."

The horse whinnied, as if acknowledging the introduction, put his head across the top rail as Mitch scratched between his ears, then placed his head over Mitch's shoulder. "Yes, I brought apples." Mitch took an apple, already cut in half, from the pocket of his down parka, held his hand up with half an apple, and the horse lipped it into his mouth. Then he galloped around a few times, pranced back to the fence. "He's showing off for you, Beth." Prince took the rest of his treat, followed them along the fence to a bench, which in summer would be shaded by an old oak. Mitch and Beth sat and he scooted close to her, put his arm around her shoulders.

"Prince was foaled early last year. I had asked the Andersens if Dad and I could attend, and the call came at 3:00 in the morning. The veterinarian was there, making sure the birth went well for Queen B and her foal. It was an emotional experience, seeing a life coming out of an animal. Dad cried, perhaps remembering when he saw me being born. Prince wanted to stand up right away, on spindly, wobbly legs. I knelt down, put my hand under his belly to steady him, felt his breath on my face and I cried for the miracle of it all. Fritz Andersen said I could name him, and he has Arabian in his background, so I called him Prince. Also, his mother was known as Queen B. The Andersens have an eleven-year-old granddaughter, Kathryn, who comes up from a Chicago suburb with her mother. During the summer months, two summers now, she stays with her grandparents three or four days each week, but during school she comes on week-ends. The sad part is that Prince's mother died only a couple of months after he was born. The vet said she had West Nile. Apparently there's no treatment after being infected by mosquitoes with West Nile virus. The virus infects the central nervous system causing weakness, convulsions and fever. To Prince, Kathryn probably took the place of his mother. She used to play with Prince like he was a dog when he was a little colt. They would run around this corral, laughing, two kids at their own game. She held him by his mane when they walked, like it was a leash, always talking to him. Then, this past spring I saw them racing on this path. He seemed to never get too far ahead of her; he could certainly have outrun her, but he knew they were just playing. He would put his head down to her and I saw them cheek to cheek, she whispering to him, rubbing, scratching, then combing, grooming. One day late into this summer, she stood on this bench and straddled his bare back. He stood still for a few minutes, she laid forward, put her arms around his neck, said something, and he walked slowly down the path, she, holding on to his mane. It's quite beautiful to watch—the relationship, the communication."

Beth listened quietly, thinking he was a sensitive man, a psychiatrist who, perhaps, had a difficult time pulling himself back from the personal stories in his Clinic, so he could have space to analyze.

"Does anyone else, besides Kathryn, ride Prince?"

"No, he's Kathryn's horse and friend, my godhorse." Beth laughed. *A horse for a godchild?* "I check on him for her during the week."

"Did you bring Whitney down this path?" *Am I letting jealousy show its narrow-minded head, will it upset him if I ask questions about her?*

"Yes, once, the Andersens had two other horses before Queen B."

He thought, *I won't criticize or be negative about Whitney. My life with her was short and has been over for a long time. I don't think about her or even like to talk about her, but I'll answer Beth's questions. I understand she's naturally curious. I would be curious if I didn't already know a lot about Raymond.*

"Do you compare me to her?" Beth felt guilty about her question, putting him on the spot and then thought, *Okay, there it is, the other-woman question.*

"There's no comparison, Beth."

She smiled. *Wonderful answer.*

Walking back toward the house, Mitch and Beth passed Mosel, surveying the area, on lookout. "Want to walk with us, Mosel?" Beth asked.

"No, you two go ahead, don't pay any attention to me, I'll be around." He was wearing a bulky jacket, as if a gun might be hidden somewhere inside. His eyes scanned the area intently, watched a car turn in the Andersens' driveway, squinted at the occupant.

Beth and Mitch walked hand in hand as they crossed the road. Miles waved; he was in the front yard talking to Lech and a workman. Beth asked Mitch, "Would you like to invite your dad to join us for dinner tonight? I miss my parents, their opinions, sincere advice, unconditional love. When your dad met with us at the Clinic, he reminded me of my dad."

Mitch liked the idea of the three of them going out together and how thoughtful she was to want him on their date, probably realizing he would enjoy having his dad get to know her. "I don't know if he'll go with us, it would be like him to feel he's interfering, but maybe if you ask and call him Miles, he'll like that."

Miles was on his way to the side door as Beth called to him. "Miles, could I talk to you?" He turned, smiled at her, and she met him as he walked toward them. "I would like it very much if you would join Mitch and me for dinner tonight. I enjoyed my parents' company, I miss them."

"I would like it very much, also, Miles." Mitch bumped his dad's shoulder like two teenage boys with a secret.

Miles looked at his son. "I don't want to cramp your style."

Beth put her arm around Miles's waist. "Don't worry about Mitch, he can hold his own. Please join us. Mitch is going to the Clinic now, Mosel and I will pick up both of you at seven tonight. I am going back to the B and B and do some maintenance work on myself. I have a new burgundy dress to show off." She leaned her head on his shoulder; he felt like a father.

Miles put his arm around her, thinking, *I always wanted a daughter.*

When Beth was in Chicago, meeting every day with attorneys and accountants, instead of taking a coffee break between appointments, she'd asked Mosel to drive her to the exclusive shops. She had been in the Valentino boutique off Michigan Avenue with her mother, but never bought anything for herself. This time she chose a deep wine-colored V-neck dress with a double wide stole in matching fabric. *I guess I'm making up for all those years I thought it would be ostentatious to wear these expensive clothes, even though Mother encouraged me to buy them.*

* * * *

The Matthews men, father and son, looked admiringly at the lovely woman sitting with them in André's, the small French restaurant on Main Street in downtown Green Valley. In summer a black-and-white-striped awning shaded four round tables with chairs outside on the sidewalk for baguettes with sliced ham and Gruyère at noon, afternoon gelato and people watching, becoming a chic French bistro in the middle of Wisconsin. The red geraniums in the window boxes had given up at the last frost, the outdoor furniture was stacked, covered with a tarp in the back of the restaurant. Now, a perfect, deep-red rose in a bud vase flanked by two votive candles in small round cut-glass holders decorated each white-linened table.

Miles rested his forearms on the table, leaned toward Beth. "You should be featured on the cover of *Vogue*. The shine of your hair rivals these candles and your beautiful dress is the exact color of this rose. We are the envy of everyone in this restaurant."

"Thank you, Miles, now I understand where Mitch gets all that charm." She was wearing the three-carat heart-shaped diamond pendant her father had given to her mother on their first anniversary, then passed to Beth, sold by Raymond, retrieved by Larry the Lawyer.

Miles continued, "Mitch gave a heart-shaped pendant to a girlfriend, but her parents wouldn't let her keep it." Miles looked at his son. "Whatever happened to that necklace, Mitch?"

"Dad, I was eleven years old, in sixth grade."

Beth laughed. "I must hear this story."

Miles enjoyed reminiscing about Mitch's childhood. "Mitch loved Molly Larsen, it was her eleventh birthday, and he wanted to give her a present. In The Velvet Jewel Box, our local jewelry store, Mitch saw a tiny heart-shaped garnet pendant. It cost about twenty dollars. He took the money out of his savings account, combed his hair, put on a pale-blue button shirt, even tucked it in his jeans, and rode his bicycle to her house. The Larsens were farmers, hardworking people. They told him he shouldn't spend his money so foolishly, to return it to the store because she wouldn't be allowed to wear it. It was a good lesson for an eleven-year-old boy; we discussed it for days. I explained if the farmers have an unfortunate growing season—late frost, hail, drought with insects, horde of grasshoppers—that's a year's loss of money. When every dollar is accounted for, it's a lack of good judgment to spend twenty dollars on something so frivolous. Mitch argued that he had worked for that money just like Molly's parents—planting our vegetable garden, weeding, potting geraniums, the jobs for his allowance and selling baskets of strawberries instead of lemonade at a table out by the road. But the difference was that his money didn't need to be used to support a family."

Mitch added, "I still think I was right. They just wouldn't let Molly be part of my conviction."

Beth asked, "Where is Molly now? Do you ever see her?"

"She told me her father said I was a bad influence. We didn't know exactly what that meant, but she knew she was supposed to avoid me. I've seen her a few times in town and still when I look at her, I see that pretty, freckled-face girl with braids. She has a twenty-one-year-old boy who works at home and four other kids, teenagers. Her husband took over his family farm outside of Green Valley."

Beth knew he had wanted a family and wondered if he was thinking if all that had worked out, if Molly Larsen could have kept the heart pendant, he could have children of those ages now.

Miles smiled at his son, grateful for the privilege of being included and seeing his boy happy. He held up a balloon glass of Cabernet sauvignon. "Here's to ruby wine, red roses, and Beth in a burgundy dress, all quite pleasing."

After dinner, in the car, Miles sat in the front passenger seat talking to Mosel about the snowy, slippery roads he dreaded in the approaching winter. Beth and Mitch cuddled in the backseat, kissing, as if they were alone. Mosel parked at the front door. Miles asked, "Mosel, you want a decaf before you go to your room?"

Mosel had been assigned a room upstairs facing the front yard over Lech and Hilde's apartment for the nights Beth spent at the Matthews' home. Hilde had decided that, during the time he was there, he was her responsibility, so she left meals for him on a hot plate in the kitchen when he didn't go back to the B and B. Daily she left fruit and cookies in his room and turned on his night-table light if he was out driving Beth and Mitch at night.

"No, thanks, Dr. Matthews, I'm going to drive around, see if there are any stray cars parked off the roads."

"Don't scare any kids that think they've found a secluded place to park and neck, or whatever they call it these days."

Mosel laughed. "They might change the name, but it's still the same thing. I won't bother the cars that have steamed-up windows."

As they walked through the foyer, Mitch said, "Dad, I'm going to serenade Beth with some love songs on the piano, hope it doesn't keep you awake."

Miles teased, "Just let the piano music be the serenade. Beth, he plays the piano beautifully, but you don't want to hear him sing."

Mitch clutched his chest. "Shot down by my own father."

Beth hugged Miles, kissed him on the cheek, thanked him for dinner, then he went to his apartment. Mitch took her velvet-lined stole, which had been snugly double-wrapped around her shoulders, and they sat together on the leather-cushioned piano bench. She had told him her favorite songs. He played "The Music of the Night" from *The Phantom of the Opera*, expertly, with no sheet music, then "Love Changes Everything," choosing random lines to sing along, the singing more like a whisper. He continued into her most favorite, "All I Ask of You"—she knew the words, sang them in her mind to the music. She thought, *Is this really happening or am I inventing it like the girl who never gets asked to the prom? No, I'm at the prom with the captain of the football team.*

Mitch turned to her, put his hands on both sides of her face, kissed her lips. "I love you, Beth, I love you." He stood, offered his hands to help her stand, swooped her up in his arms, carried her to his bedroom. She kissed him before he set her down, then he unzipped her new dress, remembered it was expensive, and laid it carefully across the club chair. He sat on the edge of the bed, pulled her standing in front of him, cupping her breasts with his hands, sucking her nipples. He eased a hand between her legs, feeling her moisture, rubbing, massaging, exciting her with his fingers, listening to her moaning. He brought her onto the bed with him, they lay side by side, she felt his rigid erection and raised up to kiss his nipples, her tongue marking a damp trail down his stomach. She put his swollen penis in her mouth, wrapped her tongue around it, sucked as he whispered her name over and over, the love songs from the piano playing in her head. His chest was heaving; she straddled him, sliding onto his erection, moving for her own pleasure. "I'll come first, then I'll do it for you." She spasmed on top of him, the involuntary contractions sending sensual gratification through her body like electricity, then rested her head on his shoulder and whispered, "Your turn." She shifted her pelvis, causing a narrow, tight passage, and began a quick horizontal, continuous movement. He yelled her name, gasping for air, his heart throbbing, thinking, *I envy whoever taught her to do that!* She stayed on top of him, relaxed, feeling his hands moving up and down the back of her body. "My darling," she sighed on his neck.

"Beth, my love, I always want to be your darling."

Chapter 13

Wearing a zipped-up Italian sweatsuit on top of a matching tennis shirt and shorts, Raymond opened the front door of his townhouse to pick up the *Chicago Tribune* from the stoop. A FedEx van was parked in the driveway and a spry, uniformed young man was walking toward him.

"Mr. Raymond James?"

Raymond wrinkled his brow, nodded. The young man held out a clipboard with the signature form, then gave Raymond the large, white cardboard envelope. "This is for you, please sign next to your name."

Raymond looked at the return address—Lawrence Simon, Attorney at Law. The enclosed letter stated that Beth Alexander James was filing for divorce. His credit card was canceled as of today, the power of attorney he'd fraudulently acquired was being disputed. He was advised to obtain counsel unless he would prefer to sign and notarize the enclosed document, a twenty-page divorce agreement stating that Mrs. James was relinquishing ownership of their townhouse, asking for no alimony, each to keep their own car. However, if he preferred to contest the offer, he would be notified separately of a court date.

Raymond sat on a kitchen counter stool, staring at the letter.

Is she conscious? Could she say she didn't take the drug? I'll swear she was extremely depressed about her mother's death, I felt she was suicidal, I requested the antidepressants, gave her one, then left the container in the bathroom with the intention of giving her another the next day. She took the overdose on her own, but I obtained the best care for her at the hospital and at the Haven. That will be my story. Is she filing for divorce, or is this initiated by that crafty lawyer so he can stop paying my bills and keep me from getting my due money? What does he mean, "fraudulently acquired power of attorney"? It's her signature. He's pulling some lawyer bullshit, but I'll cover it up with petals of distress—my suffering with worry about my wife's depression, her attempted suicide. The judge will be overcome with sympathy and through compassion will award me support. I'll get the best Chicago divorce attorney, Beth will be required to pay his fees, he'll back me up, help get big bucks for me from that trust fund.

Raymond became pumped, enthused by the new plan to get maintenance from Beth. *Whoever has money has to pay support in a divorce, and her trust fund will support me for the rest of my life.* He called his friend Joel Wolfe. "Ask around—who's the sharpest, meanest, most expensive divorce attorney in Chicago?"

When Raymond became enthusiastic with scheming, it stirred his sexual glands. He then called Alyssa.

* * * *

"You have something interesting for me?" She was in a taxi, on her way to work at the Michigan Avenue exclusive men's store. "What's your desire?"

"My desire is to fuck your butt."

"Oh, Raymond, sweetheart, anal fuck will cost you."

"You can have anything you want." He felt safe saying that to Alyssa; she didn't need money. Then he remembered their last session. "But no knives. I don't want more cutting."

She laughed, low, down in her throat, like an animal growl. "No cutting, just branding and butt fucking. Come over at eight tonight." She thought, *No one drops me off. That stunt calls for a penalty to be inflicted. Branding will let him know what happens when I'm upset.*

* * * *

Raymond's mind went on a joyride. *I'll use her until I get tired of her, especially since she's willing to give me what I want. I don't like her, but she offers excitement and new adventures. That's what I need in my life right now. I'm not going to tell her about the letter from Beth's lawyer yet, I'll wait until I have more information. Besides, she gets jealous when I talk about Beth, who could be in a coma and this lawyer just acting on her behalf.*

* * * *

The doorman at Alyssa's Lincoln Park building recognized Raymond. "I'll call Miss Alexander, tell her you're on the way up, Mr. James."

At Alyssa's door Raymond tapped lightly; before he finished, Alyssa opened the door, stepped back. She was nude. He let his eyes wash slowly down her body. The games had started.

She turned her back to him, bent over, her head near her ankles. Raymond stared at the dividing line down the center of her buttocks, aware it was a preview, erotically suggestive. *She knows I want this. It's not a slam dunk; she's going to make me pay for it.* "Okay, get your whip, I'm ready."

Alyssa laughed, that throaty laugh he didn't really understand, whether it was derision or mischief or amusement. Something drew him to her, not only the sex games. They shared some personality traits—unconscionable acts of lechery to please themselves, conduct inconsiderate of others' feelings, selfishness so strong they would readily harm anyone who blocked their path to self-satisfaction.

Alyssa went to the sofa, extended her hand to someone who had been lounging, and assisted her upright. Raymond stared at the vision as she walked toward him—strappy five-inch heels brought her up to six feet tall, a nude body with skin so smooth she seemed to be sculpted of whipped cream. Her nipples were pink like her lips. Honey-colored hair was gathered to the top of her head like an upside-down ponytail, falling in curly-ribbon curls on her forehead and around her head that bounced as she moved. She slid her hands around the nape of his neck, kissed him with an open mouth. He jerked his head back, putting his hand to his bleeding lip.

"Alyssa, she bit me!" A child calling for his protector.

"Cheri, don't bite him. I told you to make him feel good, please him."

"But I like him, I could eat him up."

Alyssa stepped between them. "This is Cheri, she's carried away by your handsome face, but don't fret, I'll keep her in line. She's only here to help. She's going to guide your dick into my butt. That's what you want, isn't it?"

His voice got husky, the answer came like a low growl. "Yes." His breath quickened, his erection jumped forward.

Cheri started to slowly undress him, hung his cashmere sports jacket on a wide wooden hanger, unbuttoned his shirt, slipped it off, and ran her hand across his chest. She unhooked, unzipped his trousers, pulled them down, catching his brief boxers with her thumbs. He stepped out of them, proud of his masculine body, his long, thick penis, now at full attention.

In the fireplace, gas flames surrounded the real-looking logs, a long handle like a barbecue spit stuck out from the logs, the tip resting in the flames. Alyssa picked it up by the handle. The tip that had been in the fire was the size of a postage stamp—a script letter, the initial R. "Raymond, this is a very high-tech branding iron. This ring slips down around the letter to ensure the correct depth of branding, just the top layer of skin." She smiled. "Anyway, Cheri will spray on the deadener, then we also have a balm. I want you to brand me first, so you know there's nothing to it, sort of like a tattoo, but so small, not even noticeable," she lied.

Raymond got nervous. He wasn't concerned about branding Alyssa, he was worried about getting branded himself. "Where shall I brand you?" *If she screams, I'm walking out of here.* But in his gut he knew he wanted to participate in this extravagantly reckless behavior.

Alyssa pressed her breasts against his chest, and he could feel her hard nipples. "Put your initial just below my spine, so you can look at it when you fuck me. Cheri will help you."

She draped her body over the back of the cushioned armchair, the top of her head touching the seat, hands on the wide arms of the chair. Cheri sprayed the soft area above the opening in her buttocks, then spread a thick layer of white ointment from a tube. Raymond watched intently. "A double dose of deadener," Cheri explained. "I've done this several times, it's quite simple. I should start charging for my services."

She wiped off the white ointment with a tissue, took the branding iron from the fireplace. "You hold the handle, I'll guide it to the right place." She placed one hand on Alyssa's lower back, and with the other hand she steered the script letter toward Alyssa's butt, Raymond holding the handle above her hand. There was a sizzling sound, slight wisps of smoke, the smell of burning flesh. Quickly Cheri lifted the iron, placed it on the hearth. Alyssa never moved, not even a flinch, didn't utter a sound. She had absorbed the pain into her body like a sponge absorbs water, feeling the hot sensation swell inward, fevering her female organs, giving her a releasing, satisfying orgasm, a pleasant expression on her face.

Cheri had a lilt in her voice, like she was passing sweets around at a dinner party. *Care for another petit four?* "Finished, Alyssa."

Alyssa's voice came from the seat of the chair. She asked, "How does it look, Ray, your initial on my butt?"

He reached for her shoulders, pulled her off the back of the chair, put his arms around her. "Are you okay? Your skin is charred!" A pinched, concerned expression on his face, perhaps it was worry for himself.

"That will just fall off." The singing, musical, listen-to-the-birds-in-the-trees tone in her voice. Then quickly, before he could dwell on it, change his mind, Alyssa caressed his butt and purred, "Now bend over the chair."

Cheri sprayed, then applied the ointment while Alyssa was still giving him directions. "Put your hands on the arms for support." Her ecstasy came from the act of possessing, her euphoric desire to dominate him. Cheri moved soothing hands around his butt, up his back, then he felt a sharp, stabbing pain by his buttocks and smelled burning flesh. He howled like a wounded animal, but it was over, a script A burned into his skin. He hung limp over the chair, in shock, unable to move. The women rubbed his head, arms, shoulders, he felt a cooling spray below his spine. He scolded himself, *How could I have been so stupid? Just because she didn't move doesn't mean it wasn't torturously painful. She thrives on pain, both the giving and receiving. Now she is going to get her painful fuck, and I will enjoy inflicting the punishment.* "I'm going to kill you for this, Alyssa," he growled.

"No, sweetheart," she said in her breathiest voice. "You're going to have your dream fuck."

Cheri smiled, sprayed his branded butt again, then Alyssa helped him stand. "Come lie on my perfumed sheets, we're going to soothe your body with warm, wet sucking." He eased onto the bed, angry at himself for allowing her cunning deceit. *I believed their shit—nothing to it, not even noticeable. Who can think straight with two nude women caressing? I checked my mind at the door when I walked into this apartment!* He kept his hips raised off the bed, leery of putting weight on his butt. He felt a thick, soft layer of cotton with sticky ointment being placed under the branded place, then slowly, carefully, he relaxed his hips. His attention was diverted by four hands rubbing, ten fingers kneading his toes, inching slowly up his legs, and at the same time ten fingers massaging his head, ears, circling down his shoulders, chest, two mouths kissing, sucking. His body became a combination of pleasured relaxation and muscular tension as his sexual desire grew and the world shrank to this sensuous room. He forgot the branding, the pain, and escaped into a cloud of pleasure. The women pulled him to his feet, away from the bed. He watched as Alyssa turned her back to him, knelt on the bed, hooking her toes on the edge, knees apart, laying the side of her face on the cool sheet, her butt in the air. He stared at the smoothness, the charred R on her skin. *She's mine, I own her, she would do anything for me.* He was proud, his ego swelled with his accomplishment of dominance. Cheri put one hand on his back urging him forward. Her other hand, the palm slathered with lubricant, around his erection, slowly easing it toward its goal, guiding it to the opening below his initial. Raymond's anger and hatred for Alyssa returned, and he began the punishment, an evil smile on his face.

Chapter 14

It was Wednesday morning, eleven days after Beth and Mitch had made love in his living room, on the floor by the fireplace. Mitch was sitting on the edge of the bed watching her sleep, deep breathing, hair falling over her eye and cheek. In her sleep, after he had gotten up, she inched closer to his side of the bed, feeling for him, arm outstretched past his pillow. With his fingers, he hooked the drape of hair behind her ear like he had seen her do many times. She opened her eyes to his smiling face.

"Are you looking for me?" he asked.

"How did I get over here?" Her desire for him embarrassed her. *I am so forward, I show him my passion so easily.*

Last night, the lovemaking had left Mitch with a stirring in his soul. Their relationship was too loose, like two boxcars with an ill-fitting connection. They had talked late into the night—he telling her of his deep feeling of love, the emptiness without her, the meaningless days when she stayed in Chicago. "I love you so much it scares me," he confessed. "I want to hear you say you love me."

She had thought about it, wanted to respond with her own admission of love, but something held her back. "Mitch, I've wanted to tell you, but it seemed wrong to say it as a married woman, married to another man. I wanted to wait until I'm free and single and have the right to love whoever I want."

"I understand, but you're in the process of getting a divorce. To me we're a perfect match, two people fitted together, aligned, but I want more. I want to know if you feel the same, I want to hear it from you."

She sensed that Mitch wanted a commitment from her. *He doesn't realize I am committed. I would never have sex with two or more men simultaneously. I only want to be with him, but I also want to be divorced from the man who never loved me.*

She wrapped herself around him, pressing close, feeling his firm body. "I love you, Mitchell Matthews. I've loved you since that morning I had croissants with strawberry preserves and Earl Grey tea, and you walked in my room wearing a starched white coat, perfectly ironed shirt, and a purple tie. Many times at the Clinic, I would tell myself, 'All his patients are in love with him, just concentrate on clearing your mind.' You were quite professional, but too handsome." They relaxed into their embrace, feeling the comfort of one another, enveloped in the long awaited aura of love for each other.

After Beth had gotten back from Chicago, they had fallen into a routine. Nights were together, then he would go to the Clinic and she would spend days at the B and B or the health club in a yoga class, hitting tennis balls with the pro, or walking the treadmill. Larry had made her promise she wouldn't walk the country roads. Mosel would park in front of the beauty salon or a boutique and stand at the door watching, waiting for her. She became a regular in Miles's tennis game, and just as he predicted, Jackson and Ivan argued to be her partner, flipping a coin to determine the winner.

She and Mitch had dinner together every night, usually including Miles, sometimes a casual meal at the Deli, or Hilde would roast a chicken with lots of vegetables. Miles would initially refuse Beth's invitation to join them. She would put her arms around him and insist, telling him she needed more information about Mitch. She asked about both of their childhoods, loved to listen to his stories, and told him, "Miles, I don't miss my parents as much when you're with us, you fill a void in my heart."

The night she had declared her love to Mitch, they embraced each other as if the spell could be broken if they separated an inch. He had begged, "Beth, please move in with me. I want to come home to you every night, not just call to make a date. Let's live together like a family. You can even bring your driver," he teased. "When you must go back to Chicago, I want to go with you, we can't be apart again. I'll help you get through this trauma."

"Mitch, I want us to be together, but I can't move into your beautiful home. It just wouldn't be the right thing to do until I'm divorced. Let's wait and talk about it again when I'm a single woman." In the back of her mind she worried that he might no longer want a serious relationship with her when he finally accepted the fact that she could not get pregnant.

Beth had fallen asleep, enveloped in the warmth of his body, and in the morning after he had gotten up, she reached for him in her sleep, scooted over to find him. Now he sat on the edge of the bed, put his hands on her shoulders, and drew her up to his chest. "Beth, are you familiar with this?" He reached for a box on the night table, an e.p.t Pregnancy Test.

"Quite familiar. I've used it too many times, and I'm well acquainted with the red-negative window." She felt a tightening in her chest and told herself, *Don't cry, it's been a glorious ride, but the carousel has stopped, find your way home.*

He held up a fluffy white robe; she slipped her arms through the sleeves, looped the tie, walked downcast to her bathroom, holding the tester she had become accustomed to using. *He couldn't wait a couple weeks more to see if my period comes. Of course, it will come, it always comes. I might as well do this urine pregnancy test and get it over with.*

* * * *

For a moment he regretted buying the tester. *What if I'm wrong? She will be depressed and was just getting into a better place—having accepted the disappointment of a failed marriage, the realization of being married to a man who tried to kill her, and years of discouragement at not being pregnant. No, I'm right about this. She was tested and no negative results were found. I've had my sperm tested, a good count, which is why I've always been careful, until now. I would bet the problem was with Raymond and wouldn't be surprised if he had a vasectomy without telling her. This wonderful woman and I are going to have a family.*

Beth stood in the bathroom doorway, a smile, a frown, a smile. "I don't know if I did it right—it's blue-positive."

He lifted her off the floor, whirled her around, set her down gently. She was still holding the testing stick. He looked at the indicator, dropped it in his pocket, put his hands on the sides of her face, tears spilling down his cheeks, off his square jaw. She wiped them away with her fingers, but they kept streaming.

"Mitch, darling, this is not a blood test, it's not one hundred percent reliable. Don't allow your hopes to climb to the top of the ladder—the slide down is fast with a harsh landing. I've been there many times."

He sat with her on the foot of the bed and patiently explained, "Beth, this urine test indicates hCG, which is a hormone found only in pregnant women, and is ninety-seven-percent accurate. A blood test is ninety-nine-percent accurate. We can get that for confirmation in a few more days."

After too many disappointments, she was not easily convinced, even with Dr. Matthews's medical explanation. "I'm afraid to think about it until my period doesn't come and I have a blood test."

Mitch could not be deterred. "After years of disappointment, I understand that, but didn't all the previous urine tests show negative?"

"Yes."

"Is this the only test that indicated a positive result?"

"Yes, but I would like backup."

Gently, he held her close, their hearts together, beating with the same timing. "Beth, this is happening to us. Sometimes fate takes over your life and the inevitable happens that is totally out of your control, as if the strings to your destiny are being quietly maneuvered by something unseen, unheard."

"That doesn't sound like Psychology one-oh-one, too abstract."

"Today, my love, I choose to believe in fate. Let's share this incredible news with Miles. I may open the front door and yell it to the world!"

She watched as he sent a text message to his dad, who was on the other side of the house. *Are you awake?*

Mitch kissed her lightly on the lips. Then his cell beeped with the answer. *For hours, having coffee, reading the paper, what's up?*

Mitch punched in another message. *We're on our way to your room.*

Beth was standing next to him, still in her terry-cloth robe. "I wish you would wait a few more days for a blood test." Then she smiled at him. "Oh, let me get dressed."

"You look like you stepped out of the Saks catalog." He took her hand, towing her toward Miles's room, while she protested halfheartedly. Mitch knocked once and opened Miles's bedroom door, Beth behind him, embarrassed to intrude. He was sitting at a table tucked into a window bay looking out to the strawberry field, still in his soft-blue cotton pajamas, holding a mug of steaming coffee. "Dad, do you remember where you put your strawberry stick?"

"I'm sure it's in the toolshed, haven't used it for years." Miles looked at Beth and explained, "I used a long stick to search the plants, find the ripe strawberries, then Mitch picked them, loaded up his basket. He always called it 'the strawberry stick.'"

In his mind Miles pictured the years of picking strawberries with his boy. "Why are you asking about that?"

"You are going to need that stick to help this little kid find the strawberries. Beth and I are ninety-seven-percent sure we're pregnant! Well, Beth is a little skeptical."

Miles dropped the newspaper on the table. "The e.p.t test?"

"Take a look—a bright-blue plus." Mitch held up the stick.

Miles put his arms around Beth and his son, and before the tears spilled, he said, "Some reports say that test is now close to ninety-nine-percent accurate, same as a blood test." Beth couldn't hold back any longer: Her tears came with sobs, and all three clung tightly to one another, sharing the same vision—a child—to hold, to help, to love, to teach, to pick strawberries with, to make memories with.

Chapter 15

They sat in the dining room having tomato-broccoli-cheese omelets and toasted slices of homemade, grainy bread with strawberry preserves. Beth's blood test was positive, the period never showed up, she was now six weeks pregnant, having missed two periods. Euphoric, wanting to shout her news to the paperboy, the UPS man, people walking the country roads for exercise, then settling down to a protective mother-hen behavior and feeling the symptoms of pregnancy—nausea, vomiting, breast tenderness.

They had agreed to keep their emotions and the coming event secret, just within their house, the six of them including Hilde, Lech, and Mosel, until after the divorce. All feared it could be detrimental, perhaps cause loss of sympathy from the judge.

Beth was superstitious about making plans for the baby and forbade them to buy any layette items. Miles and Mitch talked schools, pre-K to prep to college. Beth put both hands over her ears. "I'm not listening!"

Mitch and Beth slept entangled, arms around each other. If she turned her back to him and snuggled to his chest, his hand stayed spread on her stomach, as if to protect their child. *I want to be the first to feel the movement.*

To Mitch's dismay and confusion, Beth continued returning to the B and B mornings, after he left for the Clinic. She spent her time in leisure, a luxury she hadn't known during her ten years of marriage. Each week a different color arrangement of roses was delivered to the B and B for her suite. There was always a card with a message—"Missing you"; another time, "Spa night?" or simply, "I love you." Today, a large card had a handwritten poem:

> *Here is my heart,*
> *I give it to you.*
> *It doesn't want to stay*
> *with me, just keeps*
> *watching for you.*
> *No good for me anymore,*
> *your name scrawled all over.*
> *Keep it in your pocket,*

feel the purr of contentment.

Beth called Mitch's cell. "I didn't know you were a poet."

"Inspiration does strange things."

"It's quite lovely, thank you."

* * * *

The previous night after getting home from the deli, Beth had checked her cell phone for messages. Larry the Lawyer had called, said he would call the next morning at eight. She had brought her cell to breakfast, explained she was expecting a call. Mitch told her to take it in the library, and when the phone rang she excused herself.

Larry's tone was serious-lawyer. "We have a court date two weeks from Wednesday. Come in early on Tuesday so we can go over our strategy. I want to be over-prepared." His voice softened. "Are you up for this, Beth?"

"I'll do whatever you say. I want the divorce."

He hesitated before continuing, dreading what he needed to say. "The detectives have spent many hours with their investigation. I'll go over all that when you come in, but for now I want to tell you a few things. Raymond and Alyssa are having an affair. He often stays nights at her apartment. Also, both are under investigation for the shooting at the Clinic, Alyssa being the number-one suspect. She is under surveillance, mostly to make sure she doesn't get close to you, though we believe they don't know where you are living. Raymond will be arrested for attempted murder in the drug overdose case the day before our divorce court date so we can bring him to court directly from jail. We don't expect to be able to hold him for more than seventy-two hours, because we have no concrete evidence and the case would be his word against yours. Raymond has retained an aggressive attorney for the divorce, who has asked us for your financial information. But our team was prepared for him. This is a tremendous burden to put on you, Beth. I will call the doctors Matthews today and ask them to help you deal with it."

Beth listened carefully, filing the information in her mind. She had become stronger, confident of her backup team, ready to join the battle. "Larry, will you let me know when Raymond is arrested? If he's in jail and there's no chance of running into him, I can go to the townhouse, get my personal stuff, clothes, and some things my mother gave me, also return art and furniture to my parents' house."

"Yes, we'll coordinate that time. I'll notify the detectives and the Clarington Hills Police Department, and, of course, Mosel will be with you."

"Larry, if Raymond will be in jail, are you thinking you need to protect me from Alyssa?"

"I don't want you to be frightened. You know Alyssa can be difficult, so we are being extremely cautious."

Beth thought, *Difficult? If I told about the years that I observed Alyssa's behavior, people would surely think it was gross exaggeration—mean and vindictive, intense hostility, all rolled into her insatiable personality. Difficult? Yes, she's the epitome of difficult.*

The next day Miles and Mitch sat with Beth in the library at the Matthews home. Larry had called to let them know there was strong evidence indicating Alyssa may have been the shooter at The Plum Tree Haven Clinic. They repeated the facts to Beth: It had been discovered that a car was rented on the day of the shooting using the ID of Beth Alexander James. They surmised that Alyssa had access to that ID when Beth had gone to the hospital in an ambulance and her wallet was left at their mother's home. Actually, Alyssa had stolen the wallet from Beth's purse the day of their mother's memorial service. Further investigation found that Alyssa was a topnotch shot with both rifles and pistols and owned several models of both, though they had not been located. There were still some loose ends, but the detectives were working to tie them up. Alyssa was dangerously "on the street," as the detectives said, but they were watching her every move.

The doctors Matthews carefully observed Beth's reaction, facial expressions, signs, then paused to see if she seemed overwhelmed before continuing with more of Larry's information. He had said, "We especially don't want Alyssa to learn about Beth's location. Remember, Raymond has been told she's in a hospital in Michigan, and for now we want both of them to believe that. Alyssa might show up for Raymond's court appearance, since he will be under arrest and they are involved in a sexual relationship, so she'll want to know what's happening. We're not sure how much information he's sharing with her. Try to warn Beth about Alyssa's possible appearance and somehow prepare her for an encounter. I'm leaving this up to you. I need your help."

The Matthews' home library was designed for the art of enjoying a book, immersing oneself in the escaping waters to wherever the words would convey. There was no sofa, just six large, comfortable chairs with ottomans and cozy afghans placed in two semicircles facing each other, then four more of the same chairs tucked into private nooks to sink into the pleasure of aloneness with reading.

Beth and Mitch sat in chairs next to each other, Miles across the ottomans from them. They had repeated Larry's information, slowly, carefully answering her questions about mental illness.

"I'm pregnant," she said in a serious tone. "I'm concerned about genetics. I don't want mental problems to be passed on to my child."

Miles looked at her lovely face, the anxious sense of responsibility in her eyes. "Beth, the truth is we don't know why mental illness one day shows up in the middle of an illness-free family. Studies tell us variations in the genetic blueprint contribute to the illness, also a combination of genetic factors. When there is a lack of feeling, no thought to actions, impulsiveness, something has gone wrong in the brain. The genetics of mental illness may be related to the genetics of brain development. To ease your mind, I would say your parents were mentally healthy, as were their parents. Mitchell's parents and grandparents were mentally healthy. I don't believe you have to worry about our child."

She smiled at the 'our' and took a deep, worried breath.

Mitch reached across the huge arms of the glove-leather-soft upholstered chairs and clasped her hand to show she was not alone. "We can't analyze Alyssa without talking to her, and she would have to be willing to be analyzed, otherwise she wouldn't be truthful. From reading reports about her, I would say she is narcissistic, has an obsessive love of one's self, and is deeply interested in self-gratification. Some descriptions of her lifestyle indicate masochism, pleasure derived from pain. She has proven to have a dangerous and deranged personality, certainly a character disorder. We are telling you all this, Beth, because Larry feels Alyssa may show up at divorce court to support Raymond and possibly to taunt you. Miles and I will be sitting with you and Mosel. The court security will be advised to watch her intently, warned that she could possibly attack you."

The memories of growing up with Alyssa flooded Beth's mind. For years she had tried to keep them dammed up, but now the sinking feeling of a feared confrontation rushed through her body and she shivered at the thought. *Did she really try to kill me?* Beth was five years older, had wanted to cuddle the little sister who would push her away with an irritated expression. She'd tried to play games with her—Uno, wooden puzzles, or color the outlined princesses in fairy-tale coloring books. Alyssa, with dark-brown hair, hated her sister's shiny blond tresses. Once when Beth had colored the princesses' hair yellow, Alyssa screamed at her sister, "You aren't a princess!" Alyssa then went into the kitchen, got the butcher knife from the wooden holder on the counter, came up behind Beth, who was still seated at Alyssa's child-size chair and table set, grabbed a handful of Beth's silky hair, and sliced it off. Kitchen knives were stored away after that. Alyssa had been only six years old then, but menacing threats had continued until Beth left home for college. Now she thought, *Yes, she would try to kill me, and she is mentally and physically capable of carrying out that longing.*

Chapter 16

Saturday morning Mitch told Beth he had just checked with his lead psychiatrist at the Clinic; everything was calm, and he would like to spend the day together. He was trying to relieve her anxiety about the upcoming court date with Raymond and possibly Alyssa.

"First, let's take a walk across the road, down the path along the Andersens' corral. Kathryn will be arriving any minute to be with Prince, and we can watch them play. Then we'll have a tennis match, and if you let me win, I'll take you to Ellie's Fudge Shop."

She rewarded his joke with the laugh he loved. They walked through the kitchen, grabbed windbreakers for the warm fall day from hooks in the mudroom, went out the side door, and across the dirt road.

After Prince had the last of his apple, he trotted in a wide circle. Mitch, watching him, said, "He seems restless, usually he keeps coming back to us, but I believe he knows this is the day Kathryn is coming."

On Saturday mornings, Kathryn's grandfather always opened the corral gate before Kathryn arrived. Prince would see his friend as the car came down the road and turned into the wide, circular driveway. He would trot through the gate and greet her as she jumped out of the car. That had been the weekly reunion plan since Queen B had died only a few weeks after Prince was foaled.

Just as Prince got to the far side of the corral, a white convertible, top down, slowed on the county road along the other side of the corral. Kathryn was standing up in the car, arms waving, yelling her horse's name. He started a gallop, parallel to the road, racing to get to the gate where Kathryn would meet him. Fritz Andersen had not yet opened the gate for Prince. The end of the corral sat back from the large farmhouse with a thick hedge the same height as the split rail fence that ran all across, blocking the corral from the expanse of a grassed backyard. Today, someone had left the large ride-on mower parked next to the hedge on the grass outside the corral.

Mitch and Beth watched the beautiful animal in full stride, galloping, happy his friend was here at last. Mitch grabbed the top rail of the fence, mumbled in a low worried voice, "He isn't stopping, he's going to jump the fence," then yelling, "Stop, Prince, stop!"

Prince was too caught up in his goal, getting to his girl. His long silky mane flying, his muscular haunches working, tightening, his forelegs bent, Prince cleared the fence and hedge, landed on top of the mower, and collapsed. Struggling, he found his way to standing, stood, holding up a broken foreleg that dangled like a loose sock.

Beth and Mitch were running towards the end of the corral, watching Kathryn as she sobbed loudly, hugging her horse's lowered head with both arms.

Fritz Andersen, just coming out the front door to the wrap-around porch, had heard the thundering crash. He instructed Kathryn as she had jumped out of the car, "Stay beside him, don't let him move." He called the veterinarian, begging for quick response. "Bring the hoist to get him in your trailer, come as fast as possible"—the tightening in his throat wouldn't let the rest of his plea be heard—"please, please hurry."

Kathryn, not yet twelve years old, watched her best friend, her confidant, being hoisted into the horse trailer. At this young age, she would have to endure the pain and emptiness of loss. Her grandfather held her in his arms. Mitch looked at his neighbor. "Let her have some closure. Kathryn, tell your friend good-bye." She walked into the trailer, a wide band under Prince's belly was connected to the overhead hoist, holding him stabilized to stand on three legs. She put her hands on his face, his ears, her cheek against the horse's cheek. "I love you, Prince, I will always love you."

As the vet pulled the trailer off the grassy yard, out of the driveway, Kathryn sank to her knees, sobbing, "It's my fault—he was running to meet me."

Mitch knelt in front of her, his eyes as red and teared as hers. "Kathryn, every week I will come to your house in Lake Forest. We'll talk about Prince, and I will explain to you why this is not your fault. Things like this happen, and we have no control over them. Remember, I saw him being born, I named him for you, I love him, also."

The tears streamed down Beth's face. *I am so fortunate to have found this sensitive, loving man.* Feeling the child's loss but not knowing how to help her, Beth admired the consoling way Mitch talked to her.

There was no tennis game or Ellie's fudge. Beth, Mitch, and Miles sat in the screened porch, drank hot tea, talked about the unexpected assaults in life. Miles offered, "Every morning when we get up, we face the day with optimism, but we have no idea what that day holds for us."

* * * *

On Tuesday Beth was scheduled to be in Larry's office. After breakfast, three vehicles caravanned to her Clarington Hills townhouse: Beth and Mitch with Mosel riding in the Mercedes, Lech and Miles in a big Toyota SUV, Hilde and Walter, Lech's friend and outdoors helper, in a large pickup truck.

* * * *

That morning, as Raymond and Alyssa started an early run along Lake Michigan, he had been arrested for attempted murder, for giving his wife an entire prescription of the antidepressant Zoloft. Alyssa tried to intervene, loudly threatening the officers with a lawsuit, reaching for a tree-trunk neck. But an enormous uniformed policeman held up his hand. "Miss, don't do anything you'll regret."

Raymond assured her, "They don't have anything, they're fishing. I'll call you later."

Detective Rice called Mosel while they were on the road. "All clear, one in safekeeping, eyes on the other, proceed with your plans."

Beth asked Hilde to start packing a set of Rosenthal china with matching crystal, given as an anniversary gift by her parents. She pointed out several pieces of art—oil paintings, Chihuly glass bowls, Lladró figurines, and asked Walter to pack them in the cardboard boxes with bubble wrap. Tears welled up in her eyes as she looked at her large but feminine desk, its deep carved floral vines across the front and down the curved legs. Elizabeth had told her, "Every woman needs her own desk," and bought the expensive rosewood secretary for Beth's thirtieth birthday. "The wood actually smells like roses," she had told her mother. "I must take the desk," she said to Lech, who had already started removing framed art from the walls.

She led Mitch and Miles to the bedroom, and as she put armloads of clothes with hangers onto the bed, they carried them out to the open back of the SUV. Mitch felt a pang of jealousy, looking at the charming home where she had lived, slept with another man. *I can't bear to look at the bed where he held her, made love to her, where she cuddled with him like she does with me.*

Beth noticed her jewelry box had been rummaged through, and items were missing. In Raymond's armoire she found his spare shaving kit, loaded with a strange mixture of her jewelry—gold earrings, chains, bracelets, strands of pearls, many items with peridot, her birthstone, small diamond earrings. Carelessly entangled with a fine gold chain was an amethyst brooch that Elizabeth had removed from her own lapel and pinned to Beth's jacket when she saw her daughter wearing a lovely lavender suit. Beth emptied them back into her jewelry box and silently, sadly, put the mirror-covered box in her suitcase. *He intended to sell my jewelry and probably everything in this house he didn't want, thinking I would never be back here. He can have this house and all the depressing memories it contains. I denied the existence of his contempt for me, refused to admit the blatant deceitfulness.*

She started wrapping her beautiful collection of antique crystal perfume bottles, which Elizabeth had started buying and storing away for her when she was in college, replacing the collection Alyssa had maliciously broken years before. She made piles of shoes, boots, jackets, workout sweats, tennis outfits. *I have awakened; the nightmare has ended.* For three suitcases she folded items to take to Wisconsin, then said to Lech, "Please put the boxes, art, and desk in the garage at my mother's house, take the clothes inside and lay them on the bed of the master bedroom. Only these suitcases go to the B and B."

Mitch looked at her, a puzzled expression on his handsome face. "Don't you want to take everything to Wisconsin, put the boxes in our garage, where you can unpack them? They can hang the clothes in your closet, and you can organize them later."

"No, I'll just take the suitcases to the B and B, the rest will be at my mother's until I can decide what I want to keep."

Mitch was disappointed. *What is she thinking? Does she want to move into her mother's house, her house? Larry is keeping her in Wisconsin for her safety, but perhaps she's planning to live in Clarington Hills in the future when circumstances change, when her life is no longer in danger. What about us, our child; are we not going to be a family?*

She gave Lech directions to the Alexander house while Mosel made arrangements with the Clarington Hills Police, who had been parked in the driveway of the townhouse, to open the garage door for them. She called Charles to let him know about the commotion, soon to arrive.

Mosel, Beth, Mitch, and Miles left the townhouse and headed for Larry's office in Chicago. Lech, Hilde, and Walter were still packing and loading the pickup and SUV.

The rest of the day was spent with a team of lawyers and investigators in Larry's conference room. Miles took notes, so he and Mitch could discuss the strategy later, be prepared mentally should the judge ask him, as senior psychiatrist, to testify on Beth's behalf, perhaps about her condition when she arrived at The Plum Tree Haven Clinic. Larry happily let them know their case had been assigned to a female judge who had been on the bench for twenty-five years and did not like to hear about abuse of women. He felt that was a good sign.

Beth, Mitch, and Miles would be staying at the Matthews condominium. Larry put his arms around Beth. "I want you to drink a couple glasses of wine tonight. Everything is under control." To the doctors Matthews he instructed, "Our court call is at ten in the morning, please be in the courtroom by nine."

* * * *

Mosel had picked up Charles, brought him downtown to meet Beth, Mitch, and Miles for dinner at the chic restaurant NoMI, in the Park Hyatt Chicago on Michigan Avenue. Charles took her hand, thinking sadly of how she reminded him of Elizabeth, whom he still mourned. "Tomorrow morning, my dear girl, I will be sitting with you. Larry knows he can call on me as a witness." Then his thoughts carried him to Elizabeth, and he smiled, adding quietly, "I mean, Larry the Lawyer." Beth knew that was how her mother had always referred to Larry and knew Charles was thinking of her.

As the waiter poured deep-ruby Cabernet into three stemmed balloon glasses, a stunningly beautiful woman stopped at their table, being led through the restaurant by the maître d'. "Mitch, what a nice surprise to see you! Hello, Miles. Mitch, you haven't returned my calls, are you avoiding me?" The twinkling eyes, the perfect smile.

Mitch looked up at her without rising. "Melanie Worthington, this is Beth James and Charles Sullivan."

Melanie was wearing a reddish-brown dress, form-fitting from the low scoop in front to just above her knees, the same color as her hair, which hung heavily in dips and waves past her shoulders. She ignored the introduction, stared smiling at Mitch, waiting for an answer.

"I haven't called you, Melanie," he said in a flat, dry, informative tone, "because it was over between us four months ago, we both agreed to that." It was an answer that may have been meant for Beth's information, but certainly informed everyone that whatever had been between them was no more, at least as far as Mitch was concerned.

"Haven't you wanted to check on me?" Her voice was thick and syrupy, overly sweet, too contrived, and she tilted her head in a way unlike her normal straightforward, unsweet self.

"No, Melanie, I'm sure you're fine." Short, clipped, dismissive.

"Nice to see you, Miles," Melanie said, disregarding Mitch as she walked away to her table to join a handsome, gray-haired, well-dressed, older gentleman.

Mitch put his hand on Beth's arm. "I'm sorry, sometimes our past enjoys haunting us."

"She's quite beautiful."

Miles answered for him. "Only on the outside."

* * * *

Larry met them in the courtroom with three lawyers from his office, two private investigators who knew Raymond's every move, and the accountant who kept the Alexander records and paid the bills. Beth sat in the first row next to Mosel, who was in the aisle seat on the opposite side of the room where Raymond would enter. Mitch, Miles, and Charles were seated on Beth's other side. All were wearing conservative dark suits—the men with white shirts and blue ties, Beth in a navy pant suit and pale-yellow silk blouse, the attached oblong scarf tied into a floppy bow.

From the aisle came a mocking voice, "Well, my sister, fresh from the loony bin."

Mosel jumped to his feet, arms and hands up, alert, ready for action. Mitch put his arm across Beth's chest; two security guards had started toward them. Alyssa moved in front of Beth, her top lip curled in a sneer. "He never loved you, he's mine, I branded him." She leaned closer to Beth. She had harassing information too over-flowingly joyous to hold back. It spewed forth even as Mosel's large hands were ready to grab her throat. "He had a vasectomy fifteen years ago. Fifteen years ago!" Alyssa was unaware of, unconcerned about the huge man towering over both of them.

As the guards roughly hauled her out the side door, she threw her head back with a high-pitched laugh that echoed like a coyote howling.

Beth was pale; Mitch could feel her shivering as if a cold wind had engulfed her. She was thinking, *The deceit of it! Letting me think I might be pregnant any month, knowing the whole ten years it was never going to be. He had a vasectomy way before we were married! How could I have been so gullible?*

Mitch slipped his hand inside her jacket, spread his fingers on her stomach, in a voiceless message: *You are pregnant, no matter what has happened before, there is a baby growing inside your body at this moment.* She felt his signal, knew the meaning of his hand on her swelling belly. It calmed her, reset her assurance. She thought, *I'm happy Raymond isn't the father of this child.*

Raymond was brought in the courtroom, handcuffs removed inside the door, wearing a jumpsuit of incarceration gray. He had been arrested for attempted murder, but the gray jumpsuit was premature. "I just follow instructions," the head guard had said. Raymond's attorney, Saul Joseph, was enraged when he saw his client in Chicago Correctional Facility garb, which immediately labeled him a criminal, as Larry's team intended. Mr. Joseph had requested that Raymond wear his own clothes and had dropped off a fresh white shirt, navy blazer, dark-gray slacks, blue-and-gray tie; all had been in Alyssa's closet to be changed into after their run. "There was a misunderstanding, a mix-up," the captain explained to Raymond's attorney. This was Chicago. If one knew the right people, mix-ups could happen.

The judge was announced, entered the courtroom, and immediately got down to business. "I have read the extensive briefs filed by both parties, and I have a few questions. Mr. Joseph, why is there no mention in the disclosure section of an existing investment account in the name of Raymond Frederick James?"

Mr. Joseph hesitated for one second. "Your Honor, could I please have a minute to consult with my client?"

"No, I will ask your client myself. Mr. James, did you inform your attorney that you have a substantial investment—let me look at this statement—worth over three hundred thousand dollars?" Raymond looked at his attorney, who quickly asked, "Your Honor, could I have a few minutes with my client?"

"Mr. Joseph, I have all the information I need right here in front of me, and I have spent hours going over these statements. Mr. James, it looks to me like you faithfully stashed away over two thousand dollars every month for ten years. At least you were faithful about something. Mrs. James, did you know about this account?"

"No, I was not aware of it, Your Honor."

"How could you be aware of it? You aren't even the beneficiary. It's a Candice James, sister, in Champaign, Illinois." The judge paused, stared contemptuously at Raymond and then at his lawyer. "Mr. Joseph, you and your client are negligent in your brief, fraudulent to this court." Another look that said, *How dare you!* She continued, "Mr. James, you are one hell of a lucky guy. Mrs. James is giving you the townhouse her parents gave her as a wedding gift. I see it's only in her name. Apparently they didn't like you enough to make it joint ownership, or maybe they didn't trust you. I sure wouldn't. Mrs. James is asking for no support from you, but you, on the other hand, think you are entitled to her inheritance, even though you have screwed around for all your married life, all carefully documented by private detectives hired by Mrs. James's parents. On top of that, you had the nerve to secretly build a nest egg for yourself. I'm looking at you and asking myself, Why is this guy coming in my courtroom, an accusation of attempted murder hanging over his head, thinking his emotionally abused wife owes him something? What she owes you is a good solid kick out the door, and I'm here to help her do just that. I've searched these documents, and I can't find one positive thing you contributed to this marriage. I am awarding Mrs. James half of your stashed investment, to be paid to her within sixty days. You get the townhouse, because of Mrs. James's generosity, minus her personal belongings and anything in that townhouse she wants to remove. Unbelievably, Mrs. James gives you the BMW you bought while she was in the hospital by selling her jewelry given to her by her mother. You've got guts! Now you're single! This divorce is granted!" She gave him the stern look of an angry school principal to the constantly trouble-causing boy and banged down her gavel.

Raymond was immediately surrounded by four beefy Chicago policemen and hustled out of the courtroom. He scowled at his attorney, looked around for Alyssa, who had been denied return to the courtroom.

Beth stood, Mosel hovering over her like a bear protecting his cub. "Larry, thank you, I know you and your team worked diligently for these great results."

Larry was jubilant. "Let's celebrate—lunch at The Ninety-Fifth."

Beth put her arm on his shoulder. "Larry, I want to go home."

He looked at her beautiful but strained, tired eyes, thinking she had held up well under the heavy load of trauma and knew where she wanted to go. "Beth, you can't go to Clarington Hills yet, we're working on it. Just wait a little longer, I'll keep you posted." He looked up at Mosel, at least a head taller. "Dan Rice will continue to be in touch with you." Mosel knew what that meant. Dan was keeping watch on Alyssa.

* * * *

Mitch called her. It had only been two hours since Mosel had dropped them off at home, then he and Beth had gone to the B and B. She had looked at Mitch as they parked in the Matthews' driveway. "I just want to lie down, can we talk later?"

He'd asked if she would like to have a quiet dinner at the local Italian trattoria. "Just the two of us. I want to hold your hands, look at your face, tell you how much I love you."

She wanted to remove the sadness from his face, but she felt exhausted, too tired to make conversation. Instead of good-bye she asked, "Will you write another love poem for me?"

"Absolutely. I'll include it with roses. The florist and I are on first-name basis, I'm her best customer."

Beth smiled, agreed to meet him at the trattoria.

* * * *

Mitch sat with his dad in their library, feeling like the books had tumbled on top of him, in a strange combination of happiness and sadness he couldn't explain. Perhaps happy she was no longer married, but sad they still had no commitment. "Dad, I need your advice. I have found the woman I want to be with for the rest of my life. I don't want her to feel pressured to move in with us because she's pregnant, and I'm afraid she'll refuse if I propose marriage so soon after her divorce. I remember when I got divorced, I just wanted to spread my wings and fly. Of course, I didn't have the weight of pregnancy on my shoulders. For Beth, the pregnancy is a complex mixture of conflicting feelings—a soaring happiness along with the responsibility that keeps her grounded. I'm struggling like an insecure teenager in love. What is she thinking, Dad? Does she want to be a single mother, independent, raise the child on her own?"

Miles listened to his son. He ached, wanted to solve his boy's problems. "Of course you feel insecure. In the back of your mind is the dark cloud that your mother left you. It's inescapable, it's every child's fear hiding in the back of their mind, for you a reality. Then your wife left you. Well, it was an agreement, but still she left, even little Molly Larsen left you. There are insecurity issues in your psyche."

"Dad, you're not helping me feel better." They both laughed—the child wanting the Band-Aid from his parent.

"I want you to be aware of why you have insecure feelings, so you are prepared, emotionally able, to handle personal problems as they arise. Be ready because just when that self-confidence has a smooth complexion, up pops insecurity like a pimple. I believe Beth is thinking of the child, the father of the child, and a family setting. She's been through some traumatic stuff—her mother's death, proof that a husband didn't love her, probably married her for her money, and the acceptance that her sister has mental problems and has tried to kill her. Also, this pregnancy is a wedge in a door she can't close. Give her some space, some breathing room; she's intelligent, she'll get it all processed. No matter what decisions she makes, how or where she decides to live, you are the child's father. She knows you love her, she won't cut you out of their life."

* * * *

The evening brought a cold wind sweeping across the valley, collecting dried leaves into piles against fences or wherever there was a recessed area. She wore an eggplant-purple wool wrap-coat with a large shawl collar that could be turned up into a hood. Mitch laid it across the back of the empty chair at their table and sat next to her. She thought, *My mother would have approved of this handsome, attentive, elegantly dressed man. She would have liked those wide shoulders, too.* Mitch was wearing an ash-colored V-neck sweater over a blue-and-gray buttoned shirt. The speckled gray in his hair seemed to have been put there to match his outfit. *Those dark-gray eyes are overdoing the coordination, but I love the whole picture.*

There were a few things she wanted to ask him, check them off the list that was in her head and she started talking as they sat down. "Tell me about Melanie. I'm jealous."

* * * *

Mitch smiled to himself, thinking, *I guess this is going to be a no-nonsense conversation night.* "I want to tell you everything, so you know the areas deep inside my mind and all of my life up to the day I found you." He had taken on such a profound manner, it startled her.

"Last year Dad and I were in Chicago to attend an opera at the Lyric. I don't go often, but he has a few friends, ladies and men, that he usually takes turns inviting. For some reason I went with him that time. We stayed overnight in our condo, and the next day decided to shop at Bloomingdale's. Melanie was buying Christmas gifts for the men in her life, asking our opinion. We talked and she gave me her phone number. I saw her a few times in Chicago, not often enough for her, I guess; she started driving to Green Valley without telling me she was coming. Then she would get angry because I didn't leave the Clinic right away to be with her. It didn't go well at home, either. She would make herself comfortable, imposing on Hilde to wait on her and telling Dad about her wealthy parents, summer homes, family vacations in St. Moritz, St. Barts, Tahiti, Lanai. He tried to be hospitable, but I noticed he would make excuses and leave when she was at our house. Our relationship was in a continuous slide downhill, and after a few months we agreed it was over. I don't know why she started calling me again, I wasn't interested in talking to her. Maybe she was bored, between boyfriends."

"Would you have been interested in talking to her if I hadn't come along?"

"No, it was finished before I met you, and I had no interest in starting it up again. We were a mismatch from the beginning."

She thought, *Okay, tonight I have to tell him what is on my mind. It's the right thing, the fair thing to do.*

"Mitch, do you feel resentment because I'm pregnant? Are you stifled, does it tie you down, would you like to see other women?" It all rushed out in a stream, thoughts that had been on her mind.

"Beth, let me explain how I feel. I fell in love with you before you were pregnant. It is a tremendous bonus that we are expecting a child. You alone complete my life; the thought of us having a child makes me think I've won the lottery! And no, I don't want to see other women. I can only handle one relationship at a time. I would get multiple women confused, call them by the wrong names, forget which one I'm supposed to pick up. I'm a one-woman man, and you're the one woman."

She laughed that way he loved, chin tilted back, mouth open, eyes sparkling.

Mitch gazed at her, wanted to hold her in his arms, thought, *What will I do if I can't hear that laughter for the rest of my life?*-

Beth leaned toward him, whispered, "How did I get so lucky?"

It was a slow night for restaurants in downtown Green Valley. Dark and cold outside, perhaps people preferred the coziness of their own living rooms with a warm blaze in the fireplace. Mitch and Beth sat at a back table with no diners near, a private space where they could discuss each other's anxieties.

He clasped both her hands in his, brought them up to his lips, closed his eyes. He knew he shouldn't say it, but the words pushed out of his mouth like water from a faucet. "Beth, I moved you out of your ex-house, but you're still living at the B and B."

It will hurt him, but I must be truthful. "Mitch, I know you want me to move in with you. Let me remind you we sleep together every night." She gave him a smile that transmitted the memories of their nights—arms and legs entwined, kissing, lovemaking. "I love being at your house, with Miles, Hilde, Lech, Mosel. It feels like a family, and now looking forward to a baby with you, the man I love, a reality I've been too afraid to let enter my mind. My darling, I need to think through everything that has happened to me the last few months. I…I need a psychiatrist."

They both laughed. "You have one, my love, you have one right here. I'm happy to talk it out with you, answer your questions, help you."

"You're too close to the subject, too involved, and wonderful Miles would be biased."

"I could recommend someone, a colleague."

"Let me think about that. For now, I want to stay at the B and B. I just need some time alone."

Chapter 17

Alyssa visited Raymond at the correctional facility, where he still had not been formally charged for attempted murder and would probably be released the next day.

He growled at her, "Where the fuck were you? I needed you in that courtroom—I didn't have any backup. This is a nightmare, and now I owe that inept shyster my left arm."

"Don't upset yourself, I'll pay the attorney. Who were those people sitting with my sister?"

"I recognized the doctor from that asylum or whatever it is, and once when I glanced over there he had his arm around her shoulders. Isn't that being a little too friendly for a doctor? Seems unprofessional to me, like there's something going on."

"Sounds to me like you're jealous." Alyssa watched for any positive reaction about Beth from Raymond, which she wouldn't tolerate. The hostility, hate, jealousy ran deep, had been ingrained for years.

* * * *

"I detest her, I don't care who she fucks." He was saying what he knew Alyssa wanted to hear, reassuring her, but thinking, *I hate jealous, unconfident women.* "Larry the Lawyer really screwed me through and through. I think the big black guy is a bodyguard." *She's going to pay the attorney fees, that might make the aggravation from her worth it. She could be useful a little longer, it all depends on how long I can stand being with her. She makes me crazy, like her.* Raymond's thoughts flew in different directions like popcorn out of a hot kettle.

Alyssa became calm, analytical. "If the psychiatrist was with her, that means she is still at that private hospital in Wisconsin, not in Michigan like they told you. Why would they lie about that? I think it means they suspect the victim at that asylum was meant to be Beth in her cute little red jacket, and they're protecting her. How sweet!"

Raymond was worried. He didn't know if he could be indicted for attempted murder or what evidence they had against him. "I should have killed her when I had the opportunity, blew my chance. I would have saved myself all this shit. Call my attorney—I need some answers."

"If you haven't been charged by eight o'clock tomorrow morning, Ray, they have to release you. I don't believe they have a case against you, no proof that you gave her the drugs. She could have taken them herself, it's your word against hers, and they are aware of that. Larry may have arranged the whole scene, had you arrested just so you would look bad in court. Of course, the judge didn't like you after reading the investigator's reports." Then, facetiously: "Wasn't it generous of Beth to give you the townhouse?" Alyssa had read the court reporter's transcript, a matter of public record.

Her comment ruffled up his anger. "That judge told her she can take whatever she wants out of the townhouse. I need to get over there and remove some things I don't want her to take. Will you pick me up with my car tomorrow morning when I get released? I'll drop you at work, then go to the townhouse. If she thinks I'm in custody, she won't hurry to get her stuff, and I need to get there before her."

* * * *

The next morning Raymond was presented with an order of protection to keep him away from Beth, citing her parents' house in Clarington Hills as her address. Then he was released from custody, no fanfare, just, "You're free to go, Mr. James." Alyssa was waiting in his car, which had been parked in her building's garage. He let her out at the Michigan Avenue men's store where she worked. She had already called in sick, and hailed a taxi when he was out of sight and went to the self-storage facility where she maintained a unit. The ten-foot-square, temperature-controlled space contained a gun rack for rifles and scopes, a cabinet for handguns and ammunition, a sturdy square table and chair for cleaning guns, a double chest with drawers filled with whips, knives, massage-type vibrators, several binoculars of different strengths, an assortment of branding irons, and tote bags of various sizes and shapes. Like a professional who was familiar, knowledgeable, up to date on her goods, she picked a rifle fitted with a scope, a box of the right ammunition, and put them in an oblong canvas bag. She stopped before going out the door, as if she had just remembered something else, then went to the chest, opened the drawer containing vibrators, and chose a small black case, put it in the tote. *Oh, yes, he'll like this. It doesn't even hurt—tiny electric shocks, all over the body, and a special wire to put up his ass, a tickling sensation like quick-pecking, a woodpecker nibbling.*

Alyssa took a taxi to a rent-a-car office where they kept cars on the premises, chose a non-attention-getting brown SUV using her sister's driver's license, and headed toward Wisconsin. *If you are at that insane asylum, I will find you. This time I won't be in a hurry. I'll find the right face, whatever you're wearing.*

* * * *

Raymond noticed the blank walls of missing paintings as he walked through the townhouse. *That bitch has already been here. She probably took the good stuff I could have sold.* He checked for the jewelry he had scavenged—gone! A vacant space where her expensive desk had sat upset him because he hadn't gone through all her papers yet, looking for deeds, bank accounts. He stood looking at an empty, etched-glass breakfront. He wasn't sure what it had contained but knew it was something worth money. He had admired the collection of crystal decanters that had filled a large, footed, sterling silver tray on top of the bar. *I might have kept those for myself.* He called Alyssa; who else could he complain to? *She'll like hearing me talk negatively about Beth.* "Your fucking sister has already been here, took everything I wanted!"

Alyssa was on the tollway, headed north to Wisconsin. "Don't worry about stuff. I'll buy whatever you want." That was what he wanted to hear. She continued, "Meet me at Gino's at six o'clock tonight, we'll have a good steak dinner. Then I have a surprise for you."

"I'm not doing any of your pain shit, Alyssa."

"No, no, I'm going to tickle your butt—you'll like it, I promise. You're going to beg for more!"

As Alyssa was talking, Detective Rice was following her in his unmarked black Jeep Cherokee, a plainclothes sharpshooter sitting next to him. They were accompanied by two unmarked Illinois State Police cars with two specially trained marksmen in each car. Dan Rice was in contact with his friends in Wisconsin—Mosel Porter, Beth's bodyguard, and Doug Green of the Sheriff's department, who'd had Inge's B and B and the Matthews home on their drive-by list since Beth had moved out of The Plum Tree Haven Clinic. Detective Green would be waiting on a ramp at the border and enter the highway behind Detective Rice. The plan was to catch Alyssa on the dirt road down the side of the Clinic, the spot from where Meghan had been shot. They hoped she had the same rifle she had used to kill Meghan in that black bag; Rice was sure it was either with her or in the storage unit she had just visited. He would get a search warrant to find out what she kept in there.

Detective Green called the Clinic, set up an emergency conference call with the doctors Matthews, and filled them in on the report from Detective Rice—Alyssa had retrieved a black bag, which they believe contained a weapon, from her storage locker, rented an SUV, and was headed north. The Sheriff's department had been dispatched to patrol roads in the Clinic area. Men from special sharpshooting divisions were following Alyssa's car. Doug Green asked if they would like deputies at their gate and inside the Clinic.

Miles, essentially, put the Clinic on lockdown—removed the gate guard, replaced him with two Wisconsin SWAT team members, locked all doors at the Clinic, and closed the drapes. A deputy in an unmarked car was parked outside the gate, another at the front entrance, two rifle-armed deputies were inside the reception area.

As the State Police and Detective Rice crossed the border into Wisconsin, they were joined by Detective Green and two Wisconsin State Police cars. One drove ahead of Alyssa, then exited before her in case she was aware of being followed. After getting off the highway, it was thirty minutes to the Clinic. So far, she was headed in the expected direction.

Detective Dan Rice was in charge of the operation, had argued with his captain and the State Attorney's office not to arrest Alyssa too soon. He was confident the thorough, detailed investigation would give proof of Alyssa's guilt in the murder of Meghan Walsh. However, even though the weapon had not been found, Dan Rice would not give up—he'd had her apartment and car searched, the river near the Clinic dredged. He promised, "If she still has that rifle, I will find it, and if she threw it away, it will turn up. Everyone on the street where I came from knows I'm looking for it, and I'm willing to pay for it. Please, no premature arrest."

This morning, the round-the-clock watch had finally paid off. Alyssa had unknowingly led them to her storage unit. Even if she didn't retrieve the same weapon used to kill Meghan, they had another good place to look. As she left the car rental agency and headed for the highway, Dan Rice began a carefully planned pursuit with determination for a successful conclusion—arrest as she was poised to kill again. He was sure she was headed to the Clinic with the intention of killing Beth, now that she thought she knew where Beth was staying. With special dispensation for information only, Dan had bugged the visitation area when Alyssa visited Raymond in the correctional facility, listened to the conversation during her visit with Raymond, and heard her surmise that Beth was still in Wisconsin.

Cooperation was extremely important, and as he notified each police and security department head, the details to catch Alyssa in the midst of another murder fell into place. All knew it would be important not to tip her off as to her pursuers.

Alyssa, in the brown SUV, turned onto the dirt road alongside the grounds of The Plum Tree Haven Clinic. There were no patients walking on the path around the circumference of the grounds, no one on the bridge over the stream, no wheelchairs being pushed by the interns, no couples meandering among the bare trees looking for birds that may have stayed north, fluffing their feathers, burying little heads under warm wings. She drove slowly, stopped close to the thick pine hedge, took the ready, scoped-rifle out of the canvas bag, and murmured to herself. *I know you walk every afternoon, wind, rain, or snow, that's your daily dull routine in your dull life. I'll sit on the hood of this car until you come out. I'll be waiting for you. How excited I was when I thought I had finally killed you, only to find out it was someone wearing your cute red jacket! I've been preparing for this moment all my life. I hated the way our stupid mother and father indulged your every whim because you were so precious. The three of you were so annoying. You didn't deserve Raymond, his handsome face, his perfect body, and you didn't know how to treat him, the way he needed to be treated. He's mine now. I will control him with sexual treatments and money. We will never mention your name; your very existence will disappear from Earth. After I kill you, we will have you cremated and thrown to the wind. I'll have that trash-bin house where we grew up demolished, sell the empty lot.*

Alyssa opened the door of the SUV, crawled onto the hood, sat cross-legged clutching the rifle in one hand, binoculars in the other. *This evergreen hedge will hide me, no leaves on the trees to obscure my vision, a perfect view. I'm patient when I go after what I want.*

Within five seconds, the brown SUV was surrounded by six cars, and a black-clad sharpshooter was standing a few feet from the grill aiming a rifle at her face. As she looked around, she saw four more rifles pointed at her. A loud voice from a speaker howled, "Throw your weapon to the ground and raise your hands."

* * * *

Detective Dan Rice called Dr. Mitchell Matthews and related the successful arrest. It had lasted less than three hours but was filled with stress—the update phone calls as Dan and the policemen followed Alyssa on the highway, the slow ticking minutes of the progress north toward Green Valley. At the Clinic—frightening explanations to the staff, trying not to alert the patients to the lockdown. Also, the worry that Beth would leave the health club too soon and need to be told about the exercise going down. The doctors Matthews didn't want her to know until it was over and Larry had related the news. Then they would sit down with her and discuss the dramatic event.

Beth had spent the morning in the health club—a yoga class, walking on the treadmill, a tight-muscle-relieving massage, then sitting in the hot tub relaxing, thinking about her ordeal in court. She had found a one-piece bathing suit that had lots of scrunched gathers across the front. *This hides a multitude of sins until I admit to being pregnant.* Beth would not let Miles and Mitch reveal the pregnancy until well after the three-month date. "Most miscarriages occur before three months, so let's wait a couple more weeks to tell people, just to make sure." She continued to play tennis with Miles and his friends, Jackson and Ivan. They thought he was being the polite gentleman, saying, "I got it" or "Don't run back for that lob, let it go" or "Don't lunge for any balls." Mitch or Miles or both held her arm when they walked together, helped with her coat, watched her diet making sure she ate balanced meals and took her vitamins, drank enough water. She became their charge; her care was their responsibility. She thought, *I love all this attention!*

One Sunday evening Miles had come home after spending the night in Chicago attending a performance of the Chicago Symphony Orchestra and having dinner with a friend. Mitch and Beth had eaten a light dinner at home and were in the library playing Scrabble. She looked up as he came in the dark-paneled room, fireplace blazing. "I'm glad you're home—Mitch is cheating, making up words." With a boyish grin, Miles handed her a

Bloomingdale's shopping bag. From within the layers of tissue, she withdrew and held up three white-with-blue-trim onesies, two soft baby-blue receiving blankets, a knit outfit of footed pants, and a hooded sweater in pale blue.

"Miles, what if it's a girl?"

"In my professional opinion, it's a boy." They all laughed. She just got up and hugged him. "You are a psychiatrist, not a gynecologist, but you are the world's best Papa."

His eyes filled with tears, "Yes, I want to be Papa."

* * * *

Mosel had received the initial call of the departure from Chicago from his friend, Detective Dan Rice, who kept him current throughout the morning. Both hoped Beth would stay in the health club until it was over, so they could let Larry have the burden of releasing the news to her. Mosel was talking to Dan, getting the final message, "Mission achieved, all clear," as Beth came into the reception area.

"Okay, Mosel," she said, "I've been washed, ironed, and hung out to dry. I'm ready to go home."

He let her off at the front porch of the B and B, parked, went inside to eat some roast beef sandwiches Inge had ready for him. Later, they would pick up Mitch and Miles for dinner at André's, the local French restaurant where Mitch had taken her on their first date. Every time they invited him, Miles said, "You two go by yourselves, have some together time without me." Beth always answered, "We have together time after dinner when you are in your own room." The two men would eye each other, one happy, one happy for his son. Then she would put her arms around him and add, "I want you to have dinner with us, I love our family time."

At the B and B, as she hurried up the steps to her suite, her cell chimed. She saw it was Larry the Lawyer calling.

"Beth, please sit down and listen carefully to what I want to tell you." She thought, *This must be important, he's talking to me like a lawyer.* He continued in a calm, but serious voice, almost as though he was nervous about what he had to tell her and forcing himself to slow down. "I have the news you've been waiting for—Alyssa has been arrested for suspicion of the murder of Meghan Walsh at The Plum Tree Haven Clinic. After the divorce hearing, she was permitted to visit Raymond in jail. We had asked them to allow their meeting, hoping to get information, plans, admission of something—anything. Of course, we recorded their conversation. Alyssa asked Raymond if he knew the big black guy with you and they both decided he was a bodyguard. Raymond recognized Mitch from his visit to the Clinic when he delivered clothes to you and told her the doctor from the 'asylum' was sitting next to you, concluding that you were still there. Raymond was quite upset, told her he wished he had killed you when he had the chance, a vague admission of guilt, but we couldn't use it anyway, because it wasn't a legal recording. However, before they released him, we were able to get an order of protection. He is not allowed within five miles of your mother's house—your house, rather—in Clarington Hills. We will still be watching him to make sure he doesn't get near you. Beth, I'm sorry I'm not there telling you all this in person. Do you want me to stop, call you tomorrow?"

She was sitting on her sofa, but had not relaxed into the cushions, sat upright, listening intently, trying to absorb his words, but they were loose, racing around in her head, her own thoughts trying to catch up. "I'm okay, Larry. Is there more?"

"There is more, graver news. Alyssa picked up Raymond in his car at the facility. He dropped her at her workplace, but she didn't go to work. She got a taxi to her storage locker, south of the Loop, came out with an oblong carrying case. She rented a car, drove up to Wisconsin to the Clinic, and was arrested there as she sat on top of the car holding a rifle. One more thing, Beth: We got a search warrant for her storage space. It's full of guns and crazy stuff, whips, knives. The detectives have been accumulating evidence. Alyssa also went to the Clinic by herself when Meghan was killed—a rental car, tire tracks matching that car, shell casings by the tire tracks, the bullets that were fired from that gun. They wouldn't arrest her until there was a good case against her and have been looking for the gun. Beth, are you okay?"

Larry's information felt like a heavy weight on her chest, it labored her breathing.

While growing up, Beth had wanted to love her little sister. She had been perplexed when the child rejected her, but as Alyssa got older and became intimidating, Beth would try to avoid her. It especially upset Beth when Alyssa caused their parents great anguish—the calls from principals about violent behavior of hitting with belts, books, scratching with her fingernails and pencils, attempted strangling, then the rude, enraged yelling and tantrums at home. Elizabeth and Christopher took her to psychiatrists, who recommended another specialist or simply told them she was too uncooperative. Sometimes Alyssa ignored the doctor and read for the entire session; later she simply refused to go.

Beth slumped into the sofa cushions, exhausted from Larry's oppressive news. "Larry, I'm relieved that she's finally been caught. You make me face the reality I have kept hidden, that she's a dangerous person. She never liked me, but now she is angry with me because Raymond is angry with me, he didn't get the money he was after. Even though we're divorced, I believe she may want me totally out of her way, perhaps so she simply won't have to hear my name. I don't want to see her again. I feel guilty saying this, but please don't ask me to testify. I can't keep placing myself in front of her, allowing her to abuse me. When did her arrest occur?"

"It just happened this morning. She was arrested near The Plum Tree Haven Clinic, on the dirt road alongside the grounds, the exact spot from where Meghan was shot. One more thing: The doctors Matthews know all this. It might be helpful for you to discuss it with them, get a little psychiatric advice. This is a heavy load to put on you."

Beth was trying to process Larry's news, putting it together with the first shooting at the Clinic. *So now we know Alyssa did kill Meghan, thinking it was me, then, disappointed in her mistake, she came back to try again. Meghan, sweet girl, I'm so sorry I sent you out that day in my red jacket!*

"Larry, thank you for your protective caring. I know my parents put this burden on you. Now that Alyssa is in custody and there's a restraining order against Raymond, could I go home, move to my mother's house?"

"Yes, but let's keep Mosel until you feel comfortable being alone. Also, Beth, it's your house now. You won't be able to settle in physically or mentally until you accept it as yours. That's what your mother wanted."

* * * *

After Mitch and Miles got the phone call from Dan Rice and then a wrap-up call from Larry, they concentrated on getting the Clinic back to normal. Mentally exhausted, they closed the door to Mitch's office and discussed the information from Larry. On Mitch's mind was the fact that Beth would now be free to leave the B and B, move to Clarington Hills, and would be faced with that decision. Mitch hovered above depression. "She has refused my pleas to move into our house. I believe she thought all along she would move to Clarington Hills when she had the opportunity, after problems with Alyssa and Raymond were solved. If she decides to leave, I can only hope she'll allow me to be an active part of our child's life."

Miles replied, feeling the distress, "Beth loves you, she'll follow her heart. Let's not back her into a corner, Mitch. Give her some room to figure it out. I should let you two go to dinner tonight without me. She may not feel at ease talking about this with me there."

"Dad, you know that isn't true. Whatever she wants to say, she wants to say it to both of us. That's Beth."

* * * *

They saw the headlights of the Mercedes as Mosel pulled into their driveway to pick them up for the reservation at André's. Mitch watched her carefully, trying to read her mind, as he slid onto the backseat. She tilted her head up for his kiss, greeted Miles, who had gotten into the front seat with Mosel. Her voice was bubbly, her hair moving like a heavy drape as she talked.

Beth had not allowed herself wine with dinner since getting the positive confirmation of pregnancy, so Mitch didn't drink, either. Miles ordered a single glass of Cabernet sauvignon for himself.

He opened the subject of Larry's phone call, sensing it was on both Mitch's and Beth's mind, but perhaps each hesitating to start, "Beth, how do you feel about Alyssa's arrest?"

* * * *

All afternoon, since the call, it had been constantly on her mind, especially the thought of how she was going to tell them she wanted to go home to Clarington Hills. Miles had given her the cue she needed. *I must say it now, before I lose my nerve.* Quietly she said, "It's a relief to not watch over my shoulder fearing a sister who would like to end my life." She was finally giving in to the feeling of hate, but along with it came a tinge of guilt—it seemed wrong to hate one's sister. She thought, *My sister and my husband, aren't those the people I'm supposed to love?* She admitted to Mitch and Miles, "I now realize I can only feel free to breathe as long as she's locked up. It's interesting that I have always felt she would change. I just kept thinking the next time I saw her she would hug me, apologize. I guess I got that from our mother, who called Alyssa's behavior a 'stage' that would pass."

Beth took a deep breath, put a hand on each one's arm, sat up straight, willed herself a slow, steady voice. "I love both of you, I'm so grateful that you are in my life, and I want the four of us to spend lots of time together."

Mitch knew what was coming next. He inhaled, stiffened his body against the blow.

She continued. "For now, I would like to go to my home in Clarington Hills. Please don't be upset with me. I want to sit at my mother's desk, read her poems, feel her warmth, remember her advice and her love. I need to clean out some cobwebs in the house and in my head."

* * * *

Miles looked at his son, knowing Mitch was suffering at this moment. Even though they had discussed the possibility of this decision from Beth, his heart would be breaking.

Mitch swallowed and looked like there was bad-tasting medicine going down his throat, yet still managed a slight smile. "Beth, sometimes, in life, even after the roadblocks are removed, there are other obstacles hindering progress. Let me know if you need me; a phone call for my help would get me on the road to Clarington Hills in a split second. I'm here if you just want to talk, and especially to let me know you are okay."

Beth gave a little sigh of relief. She thought, *Okay, I told him and he accepted it like a gentleman. It makes me love him even more.*

Miles was proud of how well his son had handled the disappointing news. Beth returned to the Matthews house with them after dinner. Nobody mentioned the discussion with Larry or the comments at the dinner table. It was understood she would be leaving the next day. She and Mitch made love with an undercurrent of desperation, clinging embraces, holding on to the night, as if a storm was passing through and they were fearful of what damage awaited.

* * * *

As if the next morning was a normal weekday, Beth and Mitch were up early, and had tea and strawberry muffins in the dining room. Miles had already gone to the health club, not wanting to be at home when she and Mosel left for the B and B to pack. Also, he didn't want to be there when Mitch said good-bye and then left for the Clinic.

Beth apologized to Inge for not giving her notice of leaving, told her she would receive a month's additional rent for her suite and Mosel's room. Mosel put their luggage in the trunk and they headed for the highway. Beth rode in a mixed aura of euphoria and sadness. *I've caused Mitch so much sorrow, I hope he'll forgive me. I'm grateful for his love and support, but I can't continue this relationship with my head full of a jumbled mixture of anxiety. I recognize that I've survived a series of dramatic changes. I feel divested of the two people who controlled my mood and my environment. Now I must deprogram in order to live life, not imitate life. I need to sort the laundry, get rid of things too soiled, fold and put away stuff I want to save and find the right space for the new.*

She called Charles, told him she was coming home, would stop at the deli for lunch and bring it over to his house. "Make a pot of chamomile tea, I have a slew to tell you, I'm going to be there for a while."

"Chamomile? I thought you only drank black tea."

"Too much caffeine, I'll explain later."

* * * *

Charles rested his gray, stubbled chin on the knuckles of his graceful, ample hands, elbows on the inlaid oak strips of his breakfast-room table. Beth wanted to take it from the top, couldn't remember how much she had told him of what elements and felt that laying it all out from A to Z would give him the full story so he could advise her. The recap would help her gain some perspective herself. She told him the details of her stay at The Plum Tree Haven Clinic—the two young girls she had met there, Meghan and Lindsey, her state of depression when Meghan was killed while wearing her jacket and the helpful sessions with the doctors Matthews. "During the last few years," she added, "some of my friends had sessions with their 'shrinks,' as they called them, but I had never been to a psychiatrist. Everything that had been buried revealed itself like unwrapped mummies. I no longer have secrets to hide. Well, I do have one."

She smiled at him, but he didn't ask what. He wanted her to talk uninterrupted until she had told him everything.

Beth related the story of Inge and Luke, the dilapidated house Inge had inherited and they remodeled into the B and B where they lived. She described the massive renovated Matthews farmhouse with the many-acred strawberry field where Mitch had grown up, raised by his father. She confided about the mutual sexual attraction, the nights spent with Mitch, which probably began as a yearning to receive the intimate affection from an attentive, intelligent, handsome man, and became love with all its jealousy and possessiveness, and the struggle to tame those wild beasts.

She hesitated and let the smile spread across her face, took a deep breath, and like a sudden gust, she said, "I'm pregnant!"

They both knew Charles was aware that was the announcement she had been wanting to make for years. The actor asked, just to be sure he'd heard right, "With child?"

With laughter, tears, hugs, she gasped as though she could barely believe it herself. "Charles, I'm going to have a baby. I love saying it out loud!"

* * * *

In Beth's house, there were two helper's rooms with a sitting room in back of the kitchen. Elizabeth's housekeeper stayed in one, four days each week, then left to be with her daughter's family on weekends. Mosel took over the other bedroom at night, but stationed himself at an upstairs window during the day when he wasn't walking around the outside of the house and through the back grounds. Beth gave her cell phone to Mosel, who took her calls, mostly from Larry and Mitch, telling them she would call them back in a week or two. Beth had told him, "Mosel, I just need to think." Mitch continued to call several times a day, but Mosel had no message for him. "I just want to make sure she's okay, Mosel. Do you tell her I call? Is she eating? I talk to Charles every day, so I get some news about her from him. Be careful, take care of yourself, also."

Larry called every few days. "Mosel, as long as you are with her, I don't worry. Call me if you see anything suspicious and I'll get more help for you. We don't know if Raymond will try to contact her or sneak into the house to steal something to sell or even hire someone to do his dirty work."

The carpet in her mother's bedroom at the foot of the bed, where she had vomited the night Charles found her unconscious, had been cleaned, but the thick pile still revealed an area of discoloration. She called a designer/decorator, who had done some refreshing in the house over the years, and together they made plans to redecorate the spacious master bedroom, which she now referred to as "my bedroom." The two side-by-side bedrooms, hers and Alyssa's, would be remade into a large guest suite with a sitting/reading/TV area and bedroom. The old guest room would become the nursery, which left two other bedrooms as extras. The dining room table was spread with piles of fabric and carpet samples, pictures of furniture, and paint chips. Lunch, every day, was at Charles's house. Mosel picked up salads from the deli; they would invite him to join them, but he ate at his post, the upstairs window, on lookout. "You two eat in the breakfast room. I'm on duty."

Two of Beth's childhood girlfriends, Daisy and Bobbie, who had visited her in Chicago during the preparation for divorce court, fitted her into their tennis games at the Green Hills of Clarington Country Club. "We need a sub almost every week, or else someone is happy to sit out." She also booked sessions with the tennis pro, just to hit balls and practice her serve, after which she relaxed in the hot tub or sauna. She wore loose-fitting tennis tops over her pleated short tennis skirts. She didn't have a stomach bump, but she noticed her hips had grown wider, the waistline filled in, spreading across her back. Her girlfriends thought she had gained a few pounds. Beth wasn't ready to announce her pregnancy. In the back of her mind sat the old-fashioned stigma—a pregnant unmarried woman. She was still getting acquainted with her situation.

The nausea had continued in the mornings, but it seemed to be tapering off. Still, every morning she was reminded of Mitch. When she'd had the first symptoms of morning sickness, he would get up, go to the kitchen, and bring back plain toast and a gentle herb tea, usually peppermint. Sometimes it would quell the urge to vomit, otherwise it calmed her stomach afterward. She knew he was thinking about her and was worried about their situation. Mosel took his calls, now up to six or eight times daily, reassuring Mitch she was busy with the decorator, playing tennis, and spending time with Charles, who also got calls from Mitch.

Flowers were delivered by the local florist every few days—her favorite thick-stemmed pale-pink roses tucked into bushy baby's breath, white daylilies big as saucers, huge, yellow chrysanthemums, almost the color of his Corvette, which made her laugh, remembering he had told her Miles called it his midlife-crisis-car.

"Charles, I'm four months pregnant—how I love saying that! My house is getting organized, I have vacuumed the fuzz out of my head, and I've processed the life-changing events that have confronted me. Now I want to see the beautiful man who loves me."

Dramatically he answered, his chin lifted, in the way only Charles could say it. "The time has come to call him; he's waiting anxiously to hear from you."

* * * *

Sitting in her living room, away from the chaos of redecorating, Beth felt contentment, as if she had passed the test, was ready for the next challenge. She dialed Mitch's cell phone. He answered, looking at the caller ID, knowing Mosel had her cell phone. "Mosel, is she all right?"

"Yes, darling, all is fine. I'm calling to ask if it would be possible for you to get away from the Clinic for a couple days, starting with dinner here at my house tomorrow night." A soothing calmness came through her voice, like she was talking with a smile on her face.

Mitch was elated that she called. "Yes, yes! I'll be there." Deep inside he was worried, unsure of her intentions. "Dad, do you think she wants to tell me in person that our relationship is over? I call many times a day, maybe she wants me to stop calling. She's busy—planning redecoration on her house, playing tennis, living her life without me. Is she thinking she wants to raise the child by herself, stay in Clarington Hills, and is going to offer me visitation?"

Miles also felt she had reached a conclusion about her relationship with Mitch. "Let's try to think positively. She is a sensitive, intelligent woman, and she'll do what she feels is best for the child. In some way that will include you. Whatever her decision, we must accept it."

Mitch couldn't clear her from his mind. *If I have low expectations, the disappointment won't be as deep.*

In the early afternoon, more flowers were delivered to Beth's home. A gigantic bouquet, big as a bush, containing every yellow bloom the florist could find—Shasta daisies, pale-yellow roses and carnations, golden irises with an enormous yellow ribbon circling the vase as if someone had gathered an armload of flowers and tied them up. She knew the yellow represented their baby, carried within her body. She had told Miles, "Until we know the gender, we think yellow, not blue." An envelope behind the huge bow contained a faxed sheet of paper he had sent to the florist, with a handwritten poem. She sat down to read it.

Who Am I

I am the sunshine, reflecting
amber from your eyes,
the fringed shawl of warmth,
the umbrella for your protection.

I am the soaring hawk
watching your every move,
the warbler singing his song for you,
the child following in your footsteps.

I am the honey in your tea,
your macaroni and cheese,
the salt for your popcorn,
a glass of ruby-red wine.

I am the pulsing heartbeat,
the blood in your veins.
I am the man whispering
of love and promise.

Beth saw the headlights of the yellow Corvette turn in the circular driveway and stop at the wide, curved front steps. She excitedly opened the door before he could ring the doorbell. He was holding an extra-large white-paper-wrapped ribboned box with a small gold sticker in the corner that said "Ellie's Fudge Shop." She held it up to her nose, as if she could smell the fresh fudge through the wrapping. "I hope this is Rocky Road, I've been craving it." She stared at the face that filled her dreams, gave him a quick kiss on his sensuous lips and led him to the kitchen.

Her eyes were too sparkly, lips too perfectly shaped, hair too shiny, breasts too round and full, his heart pounding too fast. He enveloped her with his arms, put his mouth over her top lip, sucked easily. He kissed her forehead, eyelids, nose, cheeks, neck, lingering. She felt his obvious hardness, pulled away, and smiled at him. "I missed you, too." He closed his eyes, took a deep breath, exhaled slowly, a fretting frown across his handsome face.

"It smells like something's cooking," he said, trying to get his mind on a different track.

"I wanted you to know I can cook." She gave him a satisfied-with-herself smile.

"That's good to know, because if I lose my job and have to let Hilde go, I know where I can get a good meal."

She laughed the laugh that made him search for ways to bring it out—a little joke, a clever remark. He wanted to spend the rest of his life listening to it. The roasted capon was in the warming oven with steamed vegetables, a fresh green salad in the refrigerator. On the kitchen counter, perched on a pedestal plate, was an apple cake, which she had baked in a scalloped Bundt pan and sprinkled with powdered sugar. The dining room table was set for two with gold-rimmed Rosenthal china, matching water glasses. "No wine for pregnant ladies," she told him. Tearfully, she had set her mother's fancy International Silver sterling flatware, crystal candle holders, damask napkins, knowing her mother would be happy she was using them.

"Thank you for all the flowers," she said. "When they arrived I took them to Charles's house so he could see how beautiful they were, then brought them back here and enjoyed them every day. He hasn't seen this one—it was too heavy to carry, but I described it to him. He thinks you're very romantic. I've never seen so many different yellow flowers in one bouquet. And I'm impressed with your poetic ability, the poem's quite lovely." The beautiful vase of assorted yellow hues sat on the table, dwarfing the place settings.

He wanted to hold her again, but she continued talking. "I'd like you to see the backyard before it gets too dark." She remembered he had supervised the landscaping at the Clinic, had learned from his father to appreciate the growth of the land, felt a connection to the blooming trees, flowering bushes, fruits and vegetables. She knew he would appreciate the work and love that had gone into the extensive garden and led him out the back door. She walked with him on the flagstone path, pointed out the peach, apple and pear trees her parents had planted, told him the names of the flowers, now all asleep in their mulch beds, then took his hand and guided him into the gazebo.

It was that time of year when one morning could surprise with a light snowy frosting covering the fields of pumpkins, or else delight with a few sun-filled days people liked to call Indian Summer. Today there was a warmth that came with stillness in the air, as though winter had been put on hold, all living things holding their breath.

Beth and Mitch sat on the circular bench inside the graceful, arched structure. He thought she seemed a little edgy and it put him on guard. She spoke softly, slowly, as if she was preplanning, prethinking her words. "Mitch, I've been considering our relationship."

His body stiffened. *She's much too serious. She's going to break up with me, end our involvement. I must stay strong, accept her decision.*

"I know you love me. I'm so appreciative of your tremendous professional help. You rescued me from the depths of confusion, resuscitated me—thank you."

He thought, *And now the "but": But we should live separately. I can't be angry, I love her too much.*

She continued. "Now we are expecting a child, a fulfillment of both our lives…"

…so you can visit us, he thought, anticipating her next words, preparing himself for the bad news, the discouragement, the disappointment.

"I love you, Mitch. I want to spend my life with you and our child. I was wondering if you would marry me?"

Someone was doing a drumroll inside his chest sending a roar to his ears. "What? Did you just ask me to marry you?"

Her eyes twinkled as she smiled at him. "That's an interesting answer, Mitch."

He jumped up, pulled her to him, lifted her up, swung her around, laughing, saying her name over and over. "Yes, yes, yes! I want to marry you. I love you, I love you!"

They sat in the gazebo a while longer, quiet, embracing, thinking about the way their lives had just changed again. Mitch was ecstatic. *Am*

I dreaming? No, she's worked it all out, just like Dad said she would. Have I ever been this happy? She wants us to be a family! Though it had been on his mind, he remembered he hadn't asked how she was feeling. *We have so much to catch up on!*

She led him back to the house. He remained quiet, still trying to process the proposal. She said, "Mitch, I hope it will be okay with you if we spend some of our time here in Clarington Hills, go back and forth from Wisconsin, so our child will know where I grew up, also."

"Of course. Your parents would be happy to know we brought our family here."

She gave him a tour of her home, explaining the rooms being redone. "This is our bedroom." She put her arms around him, whispered, as though someone could be listening, "It's a new bed, we can test it later." Then upstairs: "A new guest suite for Miles, he'll come here with us, won't he? And I think he'll like my dad's den/library. This is the nursery, which is going to be yellow and white." They laughed, remembering that Miles had already bought some blue baby things.

"Beth, I must call Miles. Do you mind?"

"Call him and let me talk to him when you're finished."

Miles answered on the first ring; he said he'd been thinking of them since Mitch had left earlier in the evening, worried, sharing his son's apprehension. "Dad, you're going to need a new suit. Beth has asked me to marry her."

He handed the phone to Beth.

"It took him a while to answer, he kind of stuttered."

"He was just playing hard to get." There was a hesitation, then in a choked voice, "Beth, you are my daughter—I love you." He rushed the words to get them out before his throat tightened, a suppressed emotional silence. She said, "I love you, too, Miles. We'll be home soon."

* * * *

The master bedroom, in the midst of being redecorated, had swatches of fabric lying on chairs, large samples of carpeting end to end on top of the stained area near the foot of the bed. "Want to help me pick the carpet color?"

"No, my love, I will leave that to you. I just want to make love to you."

"I don't know if you're going to like what you find under these slacks—disappearing waist line, puffy stomach."

"I want to see and feel every inch of your body, experience the changes every day and be so much a part of this pregnancy, I won't be sure if it's you or me who is pregnant."

He undressed her, starting with the long-sleeved, loose-hanging, fine-knit lisle sweater, then sat on the bed, pulling her in front of him. "Your breasts are spilling out of this lacy bra. I know they're tender, I'll be careful." He ran his tongue over the fleshy excess, unhooked her bra, gently moved his tongue to her nipples, sucked easily. He removed her slacks, lace panties, and backed her into the cushioned armchair, then knelt on the floor between her legs. He placed her thighs over his shoulders, his mouth between her legs, sucking, arousing her to prolonged, low moaning. She relaxed her head back onto the chair cushion, thinking, *I have never felt such sexual emotion, as if his passion is being transferred electrically through my body.* He took her arms, pulling her up to him, backed her to the wall and lifted one thigh to his hip, leaving her open, ready for his swollen, hard erection. Both of his hands held her buttocks as she clung to him, her arms wrapped tightly around his shoulders. He knew the way her breathing changed, the way her body stiffened just before orgasm. He was ready to release at the same time while calling each other's name, the involuntary, uncontrollable spasms of pleasure.

He turned, gathered her up in his arms, and even though it was only a few steps away, carried her to the kingsized bed and as he braced himself with one knee, he placed her down carefully, like returning fragile crystal to its satin box. Lying together, her arm on his chest, hand reaching up to his face, fingering his ears, his neck, the back of his head, then falling together into a dizzy, spiraling tunnel of sleep.

He awoke slowly, as if from a daze, a reverie, her breath tickling his neck. She felt him stir. "Are you awake, my darling?" It was barely a whisper.

"Beth, did you ask me to marry you last night or was that a dream?"

"I asked and it took you a while to answer," she teased.

Mitch just laughed. "I was too happy to speak. I want to go to that fancy jewelry store on Oak Street and buy my fiancée a diamond ring."

"We can buy wedding bands, but please understand, Mitch, I want to wear my mother's diamond ring. It would be so meaningful to me, and I know she and Dad would like that."

"Could we get our marriage license Monday? I'm ready right now. When we get married, will you call me your husband? Say, 'Yes, my husband,' 'Let's go, my husband.' I want to steep in the husband-water, make a strong sustenance for our family. When I sign that marriage license, it will be a lifetime commitment, that's my promise to you and our child. Are you prepared to accept my pledge, wholly involve yourself, your love?"

There was a required waiting period after a divorce in one state, marriage in another state, but he knew Judge Bradford would help them get it voided.

"Yes, I give you my promise. I will stand beside you for the rest of my life." Teary-eyed, they clung to each other, imagining a child, giggling, running up and down the rows of strawberry plants.

* * * *

After Mitch and Beth had left the Clarington Hills house, and before heading home to Green Valley, they went to Chicago for a day of shopping. She had been hiding her spreading waistline, but by the time they would be on their honeymoon, it would be obvious she would need maternity clothes, and Mitch was happy to share the experience. "I'm sorry you won't have a bikini-clad wife on our honeymoon," she said. "Let's tell people we meet it's our anniversary."

Beth thought back to the first morning she'd experienced morning sickness at the Matthews home. Mitch had said, "I want to be with you every morning, help you through this period, feel the changes in your body, share the information as the baby grows inside you, plan the nursery, and buy maternity clothes with you."

She thought, *I needed this time to solve the equations, work it all out. He only missed a few weeks.*

Chapter 18

The snow fell so softly it seemed like the flakes were suspended in the quiet night sky. A white sparkling blanket lay across the strawberry field, and the winter-bare trees grabbed at the fluff for a covering of their own.

Bundled guests were greeted in the foyer of the Matthews home by Mitch and Beth, hugging, thanking each one for coming. Mitch was wearing a steel-gray suit, silver silk tie, the palest gray shirt with initialed cuffs and diamond cuff links. Beth had had a jeweler make them for him—two block letters—MM. Miles had teased, "Great! I can wear those, too, since they're my initials. See how much money I saved you, Beth? One pair for both of us."

Mitch smiled. "Not a chance, Dad."

Miles, the handsome best man, wore a slightly darker gray suit, the same effervescent smile, the same short haircut. Both men wore a pink rose on their lapel, in honor of Beth's favorite color and favorite flower.

Beth wore a dress and matching jacket of beige velvety kidskin, so soft and supple it seemed to be the same suede as a pair of expensive gloves. The fitted bust of the sleeveless dress was of double-embroidered beige lace, then, attached below her breasts, were gores of the suede flaring out to a swinging skirt just below her knees and dyed-to-match silk high-heeled pumps. The suede jacket fit the contours of her bust, trimmed with the same lace, sewn inside like a lining, extending onto the lapels. She removed the jacket for the ceremony, and wore a large lavender orchid pinned near her shoulder. Sparkling beneath her chin-length swingy, blond-highlighted hair were the surprise earrings Mitch had given her the night before—square diamond studs, three carats each, two-inch platinum chains with two-carat square diamonds on the ends.

There were five tables of ten place settings each, beige damask tablecloths hanging to the floor, and centerpieces that could have come from Monet's garden—purple irises, dark-blue cornflowers, pale-pink roses and peonies and spikes of lavender.

A few club chairs and end tables had been removed to a back bedroom to make room for the tables, scattered through the living room and hall. Hilde had given up her kitchen to the caterers, was invited to sit with Lech, Inge, Luke, Mosel, Dan Rice, Doug Green, Walter, and two housekeepers. Beth's childhood friends, Daisy, wearing a purple silk dress and jacket carrying a bouquet of pink roses, and Bobbie, in a lavender dress and jacket carrying a bouquet of dark-purple roses, were her maids of honor.

Miles's old friend, Ivan Van Camp, tennis player and lifelong musician, had been sitting at the baby grand piano playing love songs since guests started arriving. He stood, dinged a clear note, asked guests to be seated at their assigned places. Another of Miles's old friends, Jackson Bradford, tennis player and retired judge, took his place in front of the fireplace. Mitch held Beth's hand, they walked together to stand in front of Judge Bradford, followed by Miles escorting the two maids of honor. Mitch requested that Ivan play the beautiful love song, "All I Ask of You," from *Phantom of the Opera*. Mitch whispered the words, both of them remembering it was one of the love songs he had played for her at their beginning.

Daisy read the wedding poem, "Through the Seasons of Our Life," the bride's promise, from the love story, *Saving Snowflakes in My Pocket*.

Through the Seasons of Our Life

Your touch is warm Spring on my shoulders
and causes me to blossom like new velvety irises.
I am the May Day Girl
with bridal wreath in my hair,
laughing a dance for you.
The smile in your eyes reflects a heart's promise
of continuous love—
your soul's declaration of trust.

I will join you into the commitment of Summer rain
for nourishment and growth of family.
From the fresh-washed garden
I will pick a deep red rose—
the color will remind us of our blood
flowing through our children.

Storm clouds will not dim the brightness
of our caring nor our protection of each other.

As trees take their rest, slough off Autumn colors
and it bares your senses,
I will lift your spirits with my game,
like the cool swirling wind plays with the leaves.
The warmth of our bodies pressed together
gives us strength to fortify
against the thunder of hurt
and lightning strikes of harm.

When youth leaves us to sing her song
among swaying skirts and prancing feet
and our hair turns silver as Winter snow fields,
let us walk side by side down that new path
like the Gray Wolves who mate for life.
Our candle of love will burn bright
in the window of fate
and we will be grateful for memories.

There will be another Spring—
new-growth on the pine trees,
girls with bridal wreath in their hair,
and cherry branches full of fresh buds
that will blossom like young laughter,
as the blood of our children
flows through their children
and the seasons of life pass by us.

Judge Bradford told about Mitchell Matthews, whom he had known since he was born. His friend, the father of Mitch, a young doctor, raised his son alone from the day the nurse handed the child to him in the delivery room. He told the guests, "Miles brought Mitch to the tennis court, first in an infant carry-seat, then a stroller, then the little boy sat on the bench with puzzles and books. He started tennis lessons, hitting with the pro, and by the time he was a teenager we wouldn't play with him, knowing he would beat us. When he left for college, all of us felt an empty spot in our heart, the boy we loved had grown up. Now, that man brings a lovely woman before me. I have known her for several months. She became the fourth in our twice-weekly tennis game with Miles, Ivan, and me. We argued each time we played about who would get to be her partner; of course, she's the best player. It is with sincere affection I give them my blessing in matrimony, and perform the sacrament of marriage."

Not really hearing Judge Bradford, smiles on both faces, holding hands, looking into each others' eyes, Mitch and Beth waited patiently for their long kiss as husband and wife. Their hearts jumped on a merry-go-round, calliope sounds filling the room.

The caterers served plates of filet mignon with bordelaise sauce, steamed and buttered artichoke hearts, and individual sweet potato soufflés, and poured Miles's favorite Cabernet sauvignon. The wedding cake was two large tiers of carrot cake with thick cream-cheese frosting, decorated with the same flowers as the centerpieces, but made from dyed icing and marzipan. A plate of assorted Ellie's fudge was placed on each table.

* * * *

The day after the wedding, Mosel drove Mitch and Beth to O'Hare Airport to begin their honeymoon, three weeks in Bali and Tahiti. Mosel had collected his clothes, books, laptop, and magazines from his room at the Matthews house, put them in two duffel bags, and moved into a furnished apartment in Chicago. Larry had set up an interview for him with a private security company that provided bodyguards for celebrities performing in or visiting Chicago. Miles was left in charge of The Plum Tree Haven Clinic.

Chapter 19

Alyssa was incarcerated in the Chicago Women's Correctional Facility undergoing psychiatric evaluation. Larry had hired a criminal attorney for her, not giving the choice much thought, not really caring if he was a competent lawyer or even if he was interested in her case. He was one of those lawyers who was most concerned about his fee—first the retainer, then who paid the balance.

As Alyssa's executor, it was Larry's responsibility to oversee her financial support, which obligated him to pay her bills, but he considered it a legal responsibility not a moral one. *How could I possibly put my heart into helping her, especially now, knowing she made two trips to Wisconsin specifically to kill Beth?* The trust from which Larry paid Alyssa's bills did have some limitations—maintenance support, but not an extravagant lifestyle, left to Larry's judgment. It did specify, "Under no circumstances, no financial aid to Raymond James." He happily refused Alyssa's demands to pay Raymond's divorce lawyer or allow him a credit card.

The criminal attorney Larry hired had several meetings with Alyssa, then she fired him. She called her friend Cheri, who contacted Chicago's infamous, shamelessly arrogant criminal attorney Jeremy Rouster, proudly known as "The Rooster." It was a perfect match. Jeremy sent her to his own psychiatrist, Dr. Mack Heller, who had evaluated other clients of Jeremy's and who had testified in court as to his findings—insanity, if that's what Jeremy wanted him to say. Dr. Heller was paid well for his services. For Alyssa's meetings with the prosecutor's psychiatrist, Dr. Heller coached her on the right behavior—the psychotic state to envelop and portray, fictional stories to have ready to tell of emotional abuse. There would be no one to dispute her claims. To Alyssa it was a game, playing the mentally fragmented sufferer, wearing a veil of decency, an actress in her starring role of victim.

Raymond called the facility trying to reach Alyssa. He was told she would call him at her designated phone time. She did call him at her designated phone times, only to get his answering service.

Wanting to keep Alyssa on a string in case he could use her, but happy to not have her tied around his neck, Raymond went on the prowl. He met a Chicago socialite, fourteen years younger, at twenty-one, who spent her days at Pilates or yoga classes, or at a Michigan Avenue day spa for facials, massages, manicures, pedicures, hair wash and blow dry, and shopping on Oak Street. Each evening started at a trendy bar where the Chicago singles crowded six deep, the noise reaching the level of a rock concert and serious negotiating occurring.

Being adept at the singles-bar game, Raymond had acquired a new ploy. He would get to the bar before the crowd accumulated, get a stool, hunch over his gin and tonic, not looking around, not talking, giving no attention to the perfect-teeth smiles, the low-scooped necklines, the swinging lustrous hair. Even with rounded back and sagging head, Raymond was handsome—broad shoulders, full shaggy hair, a custom-tailored cashmere blazer, soft Egyptian-cotton shirt that fit across his muscular chest, and, always, a flashy silk tie. The contrived pose enticed women to peek around him to check out the face. He would look up, revealing a slow smile on his movie-star face to the question, "Are you okay?"

With grave eyes his reply: "I am sadly, newly divorced."

The concerned sweetness: "Oh, I'm sorry." A smile, a thought, *Let me help you with that.* The porcelain complexion, luminous pink lips, sea-glass-blue eyes belonged to Casey Gerber.

He swiveled around to face her. "As in 'Casey at the Bat'?"

She giggled. He wasn't sure she understood his reference, but it wasn't important. The curtain had risen on Act Two. Casey received his full attention, never straying from her face, his eyes taking her in, swallowing her up. She was flattered, giddy, lost in the performance. He took her hands in his and kissed her fingertips. "It's so loud in here, would you like to go someplace quiet to talk? I want to know everything about you." She nodded. He continued, "My townhouse is in Clarington Hills, and I'll take you there another time, it's so far, but I have a friend who's out of town and offers me use of his condo when I'm in the city. He has a well-stocked bar. Shall we go there and talk?"

Raymond parked in the garage, then he and Casey took the elevator to Alyssa's condominium. He opened a bottle of Perrier-Jouët, poured it into two long-stemmed, Baccarat cut-crystal champagne flutes.

"Wow! Champagne! He must be a good friend."

Raymond clinked her glass. "This is a special occasion."

She was impressed with her catch of the night. "What are we celebrating?"

"My happiness." He put his face close to hers, kissed her lips lightly. "I haven't been this happy for such a long time."

They finished the bottle as he listened attentively, asking questions innocently, which gave him information about her parents, vacations, second homes, number of siblings, her own condo in the city, and her allowance. *I love trust-fund babies.* She passed the test, so he held her face in his hands, ever so gently, then kissed her passionately, at which he was an expert—not too much saliva, not a limp lump of a tongue, not a cave mouth. He drew her into his snare. "It was an incredible stroke of good luck, a wonderful pleasure to meet you in that bar tonight."

"I want to give you more pleasure," she answered, as she slid off the sofa to her knees between his thighs, unzipped his pants, and was pleasantly surprised by his large, full erection. He leaned back on the soft cushions as she fondled, squeezed, licked, sucked him to orgasm.

"I have a reward for you, sweetheart." He led her to the bedroom, undressed her, slowly caressing and kissing her smooth, flawless body as he removed each article of clothing. He knew he would find breasts with implants; he had already felt the firmness, but they were a feast to look at and hold, a handful, and her nipples seemed to be sensitive. He separated her legs, knelt on the thick carpet, reached up playfully to her nipples while he sucked hard, his tongue inside her. She was loud when she came. *Yes, so uninhibited—we're going to have lots of fun*, he thought.

"I have more for you, sweetheart." He gave her the longest fuck she'd ever had—from behind as she kneeled on the edge of the bed, then standing, both her legs wrapped around his hips, he grasping, holding her butt, she, arms clinging to his neck, moaning loudly. "We're not finished," he told her, then sat her on the bed, stood between her thighs, pushed her down on the bed, pulled her ankles up to his shoulders, his slick penis finding her throbbing vagina. "Don't come yet," he panted. She gasped, "I want to get on top of you." She climbed on him before he was fully lying on his back and pushed her body onto his wet, pulsing penis. She screamed as both climaxed, and collapsed on top of him.

He stroked her body, kissing her neck, nipples, face, told her his life story—worked twelve-hour days trying to make enough money to meet the outrageous demands of his self-centered wife, her extravagant lifestyle, lost his job because he was too aggressive, taking clients away from the other brokers who couldn't close the deal, had such pressure to make more money. "In the divorce," he told her, "I was able to keep the townhouse and my car, but she got all the money, savings, art, jewelry. Don't worry, sweetheart, I am a worker. I can sell anything. I will get another job, take you to lots of nice places, and soon as I get some money, I will buy whatever your precious heart desires. You give me inspiration; you breathe fire into me."

Raymond didn't find out if her credit card was paid by a family accountant, as he suspected—*These rich people don't pay their own bills*—but he would get that information later and she would get a card for him on her account. Her parents would never know they were helping to support Raymond James's lifestyle.

They slept late. Raymond made two cups of coffee in Alyssa's kitchen, then drove to Casey's apartment. Leaning over to touch her face with his fingers, he gave her a light, sensitive kiss. The building where Raymond dropped Casey off was an innovative, architectural prize-winning, mostly glass building in Chicago's near north 'in-area' exactly where he had planned to move when he sold the townhouse and was awarded the support from Beth's trust. *I will live here as I planned. No one can stop me, I'm too smart for them. I will go around anyone who tries to block my path—I know all the detours.*

On the freeway, driving to his Clarington Hills townhouse, he felt exhilarated. *You still have what it takes, Ray. You were great last night, turned your life around.* His cell chimed; the caller ID showed Lawrence Simon. Anger rose up to his mouth like bitter bile. Raymond answered, "Fuck you!"

* * * *

Larry ignored his greeting. "Raymond, I want to inform you that Alyssa has requested I pay the balance due on your attorney's fees. That is not going to happen." Before Raymond could click off, Larry added, "Also, you cannot use Alyssa's apartment while she is incarcerated. I don't think you want me to tell her you took a young woman there, drank champagne, and had a noisy evening. Do not go back there again or I will have you arrested for trespassing." Larry thought, *It's a full-time job to block his manipulating con jobs. If I don't stay one step ahead of him, he'll sell his townhouse and move into Alyssa's condo.*

* * * *

Of course, that idea had already crossed Raymond's mind.

Larry's threat was just a small setback for Raymond. It gave him the incentive to move forward, put his head down and walk into the storm. It challenged him to find other channels for his plans. *That bastard probably has the place bugged. If he tells Alyssa, I'll convince her I was trying to impress a new client and his wife. I'm on a new road, in the fast lane; Larry can't catch me now.*

Joel Wolfe had set up an interview for Raymond with the biggest competitor of the Lobo Agency. Raymond hadn't seen Joel since he had been fired, but they still occasionally talked. Joel explained Ray's departure from Lobo as being triggered by a "frivolous lawsuit from Ray's wife that ended up in the newspaper, and a complaint from a big client, causing my father to ask Ray to take a leave from the company, which was followed by a messy divorce." But he was careful to add, "Ray wrote a tremendous amount of policies; Dad had to hire two new brokers to take his place." It was a brilliant reference, and the owner hired Raymond on the spot. The Lobo Agency continued to send commission checks to Raymond, from past policies he had written, but that would soon taper off. Without new client commissions, his credit card not being paid by Beth's accountant, paying his own phone bills, taxes, insurance, and utilities, his lifestyle was drastically changing. *I thought I could retire; now I have to start working again! It's my fault: I should have put poison in the chai for that bitch.*

As Ray parked in his garage, his cell chimed again. He now recognized the number, a pay phone at the women's correctional facility. "Sweetheart, I've been worried sick about you. I have a million things to tell you." He knew the inmates were not allowed to call out after eight in the evening. "I waited for your call all night, fell asleep about midnight holding my phone, so I wouldn't miss your call."

She didn't fall for it. "Where the fuck have you been? I called you five times yesterday. I can't call out after eight."

"Oh, I didn't know that. I called the facility, but they wouldn't let me talk to you. I hate this, I need to see you. I just got a call from your executor,

Larry the Louse, who informed me he will not pay my attorney's fees even though you requested it."

* * * *

She didn't trust him or need him, but decided to keep him on her string a while longer. She thought, *I have a good lawyer, but I may need him later.* "Larry said the will specifies that money is for my support only. I have money elsewhere, don't worry, I'll take care of it."

* * * *

Ah, just what I wanted to hear. Pay my bills, sweetheart, and I'll stick around. "Sweetheart, I have a job. I've been interviewing and talking my butt off. I have an appointment today. You know I can sell, but, sweetheart, I need a credit card for business lunches. People with money want a successful-looking broker who takes them to a sophisticated restaurant." *A built-in alibi when you can't reach me.* "Larry canceled my credit card; can you get me one on your account, just until I start making money?"

"Yes, I'll call today and add you to my Amex."

"Thanks, sweetheart. I miss you. Tell your lawyer to call me anytime. I will help any way I can. You know I'll say whatever he wants me to say. I'm here for you, sweetheart."

Raymond could hear women's voices in the background. Alyssa's time was up and they were letting her know it. *Every time I think about her going to Wisconsin with a gun to kill Beth, it sends chills down my spine. She killed that innocent girl, thinking it was Beth. She's a dangerous psychopath—I hope they put her away for good. I have to work on getting some money from her before she goes to trial. Soon as I get that credit card, I'll max it out, in case Larry discovers it. Maybe I'll get a couple months' use. Can I sneak back in her apartment, take out some stuff to sell? I'm sure she'll never live there again.*

His cell chimed again. *I'm popular this morning!* It was Joel Wolfe. "Hey, Ray, guess where your ex-wife is, as we speak? In Tahiti, on her honeymoon—and listen to this, she's pregnant! I guess she's not in a coma, after all." He laughed, like the old days when they shared so many laughs. "How's that for News of the Day?"

Raymond was walking to his bedroom to change into gym clothes for his workout and stopped midstride. "It's the psychiatrist, isn't it? I knew there was something going on when I saw his arm around her shoulders in the courtroom. I can smell sex a mile away." He thought, *Maybe this is gossip.*

"Are you sure? Who told you?"

"Beth's old friend, Daisy Garrett, and her husband, Trip, were at the wedding and he told our buddy, Zack, who called me. The wedding was at the doctor's home in Wisconsin, a fancy country house out in a field, in the middle of nowhere."

Chapter 20

In the Chicago court system, it could take a year or more for a criminal case to get to trial, but there were exceptions—specifically an insanity plea and especially if there was an aggressive lawyer demanding that his client needed to be institutionalized and receiving treatment, for her own safety and, as demonstrated, for the safety of others.

Meghan's parents had given their permission for the case to be tried in the Illinois court system instead of Wisconsin where the States Attorney and law enforcement had pledged full support to the Cook County States Attorney.

Meanwhile, Alyssa was playing her game—remembering that she went to The Plum Tree Haven Clinic the first time with Raymond, but didn't remember not going in the Clinic to visit her sister she loved. She was so sure she had sat and talked with her. Then, recalling parts of the second trip when the patient wearing Beth's red coat was killed, but certainly she did not remember taking a rifle. She only had gone there with Raymond to spend time with her sister. There was no recollection of a third trip to Wisconsin and the arrest. Alyssa submitted to diagnostic tests for mental health, bizarre and criminal behavior, and willingly accepted antipsychotic drugs. *I will take on the persona of a vegetable. A carrot is not conscious of acts or existence or feeling. My mind will be buried underground.*

She didn't tell him, but Alyssa decided to discontinue the phone calls to Ray. *I'll let him figure it out.* Larry the Lawyer, her executor, joyously related to her the news of Raymond's escapade in her apartment. She thought, *So that's why he hasn't answered his phone, he's dicking his way through the bar crowd.* In Ray's last conversation with Alyssa, he'd related the news of Beth—married and pregnant, off on a South Pacific island honeymoon. To Alyssa, there was no longer the amusement of stealing her sister's husband. *Where's the fun if I can't rub her face in it? I'm through with him; he's too heavy around my neck. My lawyer is sure he can get me into a psychiatric hospital for the criminally insane. I'll use my time and energy on the computer, research The Plum Tree Haven Clinic, and find the residence of Dr. Mitchell Matthews. There are ways to get out of every hospital, even prison hospitals. I'll make her watch as I kill that baby. I can't wait to make her suffer, then I'll play some games with Dr. Matthews.*

* * * *

Ray was pacing. He'd made himself available to receive Alyssa's calls, but she didn't call. Larry the Lawyer had called, however, threatening to notify the court if he didn't pay half of his hidden IRA which the judge had awarded to Beth. He also received a daily call from his divorce attorney, Saul Joseph, who had taken the case with only a deposit. He had been so sure he would win big bucks for his client and a big fee for himself from the abundant trust fund. He complained, "Raymond was not truthful, didn't tell me all the facts—the IRA, his infidelities. The judge had all the goods, I didn't have a chance." Also, Ray had not received the credit card Alyssa said she would order for him. *Is she avoiding me, reneging on her promise? I need to go after Casey. With my style, my finesse, my flattery, she'll be stunned, won't know what hit her. I'm the perfect future husband—no baggage of children, no child support, no alimony. I'll be the model son-in-law—handsome, well-dressed, well mannered, intelligent, adoring of their daughter, respectful, kind, hardworking. I'll send the money from my investment account to Larry the Louse. It will be replaced before my custom-made shirts are ready.*

Chapter 21

Beth was two days past her delivery date, with a full, swollen abdomen that caused her to waddle when she walked, side to side like a duck. She caught Mitch and Miles exchanging smiles and reproached them angrily, telling them it was inconsiderate behavior. Both men jumped up, put their arms around her, told her they loved her, were proud of the way she had handled the last difficult month. They explained their smiles were the acknowledgment of the happiness she had brought to their home. Still irritable, she started to cry, revealing the frustration of being past the expected day. "I could have made it to the date I was told, but you miscalculated, Mitch, and now I don't have any patience left. I don't even feel like I'm ready to give birth. I might be like this for another month!"

They helped her into bed, Miles fluffing up pillows, Mitch taking off her shoes, massaging her feet. Smiling, Mitch whispered, "Where's that crooked toe you always try to hide from me?" He had found her only imperfection, and knowing about it had given him a feeling of possessiveness. Miles, thinking she might be self-conscious about her crooked toe, sent a quiet warning to his son. "This is not the time to tease." Miles wanted to smooth her ruffled feathers, make up for their indiscretion. "Would you like a cup of hot tea?" he asked her.

Beth snapped, "I want both of you to leave me alone!"

Mitch continued rubbing her feet and legs, then covered her with a light blanket. Miles picked up a book from her desk, the collected poems of Edna St. Vincent Millay, turned to a page she had tabbed with a pressed rose encased in plastic bookmark, and began reading aloud. She relaxed, fell into a deep dream-filled sleep, replaying her childhood—the excitement of a baby sister that turned to sour disappointment with her tantrums, vicious behavior, mean and spiteful words, often aimed at their parents.

As Beth opened her eyes, she saw that a monitor had been placed on her night table. She knew she only had to utter one word and the two men who loved her would come to the bedroom. She felt guilty for her harsh upbraiding. *I have lost my sense of humor. Why couldn't I have seen the amusement in my pregnant duck-walk? I'm too sensitive, thinking they were laughing at me. I must apologize.*

Her mind wandered to the beautiful wedding only a few months ago and their honeymoon in Bali and Tahiti. In their suite, part of a floor had a see-through section where they could watch fish swimming below. It was an exotic paradise, a perfect honeymoon of just being together. Even though she perceived herself as fat, throughout their honeymoon—no longer a flat, toned stomach, a roundness to her hips, no shapely waistline—she'd felt intensely sexy. She told her new husband, with a little embarrassment, "I'm so passionate."

He responded, "I'm loving every minute." Then like a doctor, he gave her the medical explanation. "There is an energizing blood flow to the pelvis area, and the hormones, progesterone and estrogen, give you the desire for sex. Breasts are bigger, nipples more sensitive, all producing a sexy feeling."

"Science removes the glamour." She smiled at his serious explanation.

"Even with the scientific knowledge, to me you are extremely sexy and quite glamorous."

* * * *

Beth remembered the bustle of activity when she and Mitch had returned from their honeymoon. First, an appointment with the pediatrician, Michael Pearson, whom Mitch had met when both were starting their medical practices in Green Valley; then, through the years, they had met often to play racquetball. Beth also had an appointment with the ob-gyn, Jonathan Stone, before leaving on their honeymoon and had scheduled another appointment and an ultrasound for when they returned—so typical of Beth to wait extra long. "I don't want a mistake about the sex of the baby because of being tested too early."

The three of them were excited, but Miles was uncontrollable. She thought about the day he had come home from a weekend in Chicago with a shopping bag of blue baby clothes shortly after Mitch had told him she was pregnant. There was no question in anyone's mind about whether or not to reveal the sex of the baby. "No one in this house wants a surprise," Beth had said at breakfast on the morning she was scheduled for the ultrasound when Hilde asked Miles, "Will you call us when you find out?"

"Miles," Beth warned, "there is a real possibility that this baby is a girl." *Would he be disappointed?*

"My grandbaby can be male or female, either will be my joy."

"Dad, you won't know what to do with a girl."

"But I will learn and be incredibly happy with the process."

* * * *

Shifting her heavy body to find a comfortable position, looking at her swollen belly, she remembered watching the screen during the ultrasound. Mitch, Miles, Dr. Stone, and the technician were deciphering the projected images. The tech pointed with a ruler. "This is the umbilical cord and this is a penis."

Miles could not contain himself, kissing Beth's hand and her forehead, hugging Mitch, wiping ecstatic tears. "Beth, my daughter, I love you." The tech gave her earphones to listen to her baby's heartbeat. *I have been waiting ten years to hear this little heart!*

After the determination that it was a boy, the big discussion was a name. Mitch and Miles went through the list of names that started with M, joking about money saved by passing down initialed luggage, shirts, cuff links. Beth quietly said, "I would like to name him Christopher."

Mitch smiled at his wife and dad. "Christopher it is, a great name."

* * * *

Now, alone in the big bed, sinking into the pillows, she was thinking about the daily discussions, the plans, the anticipation of having a baby in the house. The movements in her belly had become strong, Mitch always slipping his spread-out hand over her enlarged abdomen to feel a poking elbow or a moving foot. She enjoyed sharing the activity with Miles—standing next to him as he sat at the dining room table, taking his hands and placing them on her belly. He would lean his head toward her, talk to the subtle position changes beneath his hand.

"Chris, this is Papa. I have many stories to tell you, much to teach you about life. We will walk together in the strawberry field and the vegetable garden. I'm waiting for you."

Mitch would look up. "Has that boy started answering you yet?"

"No, but I can tell he hears me. He will recognize my voice when he gets here."

Beth also shared the baby movements with Hilde, whose only child, a girl, at eighteen, had run away with her boyfriend after intense arguments with her parents. Lech and Hilde had wanted their daughter to break up with the boy, ten years older, who had led her into the drug world, Lech threatening to report him to the police. She'd left in the middle of the night, a note on her bed—"I hate both of you, don't try to find me. I'm happier than I have ever been."

* * * *

Beth thought, *When I get up from this overly comfy bed, I must apologize to Mitch and Miles for talking so rudely to them. Hopefully they'll understand under normal circumstances I would never behave like that.* Her body lay idly content, her mind going over her transformed life.

Yesterday had been their Sunday morning ritual, breakfast at The Morning Glory. Mitch and Miles, each holding one of her arms, escorted her to their reserved table in the back corner. The Morning Glory's owner, Thelma Hirsch, was the same age as Miles, seventy-four. He had gone to high school with her and her deceased husband, Tim. The widowed owner ran the breakfast-only restaurant with her two daughters. Her son was in charge of their farm with help from his two sons. Three years ago, excessive rain had ruined crops in the area and caused flooding, which had filled the Hirsch's house with two feet of muddy water. There was no income from the farm that year. Thelma and her son, Joad, borrowed two hundred thousand dollars, using The Morning Glory for security, from a local bank. Thelma made her loan payments conscientiously every month. The problem was that the owner of the small private bank informed Thelma that the three-year contract was up and, as agreed, it was time to renegotiate in order to renew the loan. The bank would now charge one point, plus the interest would be increased.

As Miles sat down, Thelma asked if she could talk to him after breakfast. He stood, pulled a chair up to the table for her. "Thelma, sit here, have coffee with us, and tell me what's on your mind."

Shyly, she related the banker's demands for the loan renewal. Mitch listened also. "Dad, can they impose more interest even though rates have gone down? They want to charge Thelma way over prime."

"It's a private bank and they can legally charge whatever they can get away with. Thelma, I'm glad you told me about this. We aren't going to let this greedy bastard get away with taking advantage of you. How much time do we have?"

"Only two weeks, because I kept putting off calling to ask you for help."

"I'll get back to you, Thelma."

"I love you, Miles Matthews." She got up, went to the kitchen. Miles looked at Mitch. "Order for me, I'm going outside to make a call." On his cell, he found the home number for his old friend, Gordon Boyd, president of United Bank of Wisconsin, Green Valley Branch. "Gordon, sorry to bother you on Sunday morning. I need to see you tomorrow morning in your office."

The young waitress removed his cold cup of coffee, poured a new steaming cupful in a fresh cup. He caught Thelma's eye, signaled her over. "Give me the loan papers, I'm going to the big bank tomorrow. Don't worry, Thelma, these moneyed big shots can't come in and try to take advantage of working people. You get ready to laugh in his face when you go in his fancy office and tear up his proposal."

She leaned down and kissed his cheek. "I knew you would help me."

"Dad, what if you can't convince Gordon to take over her loan?"

"I'll take over the paper and finance it myself. Sometimes life isn't worth living if you can't help your friends."

* * * *

And that's the family I've married and become part of. Beth sank heavily into the down pillows around her, under her tummy, feeling grateful for a devoted husband and caring father-in-law. Both had lifted her from deep despair and put her on a pedestal of love, appreciating the child she carried and anticipating fulfillment of their shared desire.

Mitch walked softly into their bedroom, checking on her, not wanting to wake her if she was still sleeping. "I'm awake, darling," she said. "I apologize for talking so rudely."

He sat on the bed next to her, spread his hand over her stomach, kissed her lips lightly. "Let's have lunch. Hilde made that butternut squash soup for you, and the aroma of fresh-out-of-the-oven wheat bread is announcing itself from the kitchen."

* * * *

The conversation flowed into baby plans, as usual. Both men had attended delivery classes with her, to the amusement of the other pregnant women, watching the father-in-law practice the helpful instructions for breathing. Every day she reminded them, "I want to have natural childbirth, no drugs." Arrangements at the hospital had been made by her gynecologist, Dr. Stone—both husband and father-in-law would be in attendance for delivery.

At the dining room table, Miles reached for Beth's hand. He looked into the dark-blue eyes that changed color like the ocean, dark to pale, depending on her mood, eyes he had become so familiar with, eyes that made him want to put his arms around her and whisper, "My daughter, at last you're here."

She smiled at his serious mood. Quietly he said, "Beth, I would like to put a small crib in my room for Chris. These first couple weeks, I want to get up with him and bring him to you for breast feeding, then take him back to my room. I took care of Mitch, waking with him every four hours. I often remember those significant times, and it refills me with love for him. It would mean so much to me, helping you with my grandson like that. Would you allow me the privilege?"

Beth thought for a moment. Mitch watched for her reaction. Hilde was picking up bowls, lingered, waiting for the answer to the unusual request. *Will Beth consider it an invasion of her new motherhood?*

"It would be my pleasure to have your help, Miles. You do the diaper changing and I'll just do the nursing." He put his hands on both sides of her face, kissed her forehead, postponing the tears.

* * * *

At two that morning, Beth awoke feeling strange tightening pangs in her lower stomach. *I've just found a comfortable position and now this child wants to move around in his cramped space. Can't you wait until morning, Christopher?* She straightened her body, her legs, her back, to give the baby more room, closed her eyes to summon sleep. The next tightening was strong and she acknowledged it as a uterine contraction, relaxed into the pain. *My baby is going to be born today!*

Beth realized she was weeping, not from the pain, but because her mind was filled with thoughts of her mother. They had talked so often about the possible reasons she wasn't able to conceive, but her mother had been so encouraging, so optimistic, believing it would happen at any time. Then came the thought Beth had tried to bury, but still sometimes wedged itself into her mind—the day Alyssa had informed her that Ray had had a vasectomy when he was in college, long before they were married. She was thinking the years of deceit would be unbearable if she hadn't met Mitch. She was glad her mother had not been there to hear the mean satisfaction in Alyssa's voice, her howling laughter.

But now she wanted the warm comfort of her mother. *Oh, how I wish you were here, to be with me at this moment, to share this birth! I miss you so.*

When the next contraction subsided, she put her hand on Mitch's bare shoulder, then to the side of his handsome face, over his ear, her fingers feeling his thick, short hair. He woke, put his hand over hers, moved it to his lips. She remembered the morning she had come out of the bathroom, holding up the e.p.t stick indicating positive. Mitch had wanted to share his excitement with Miles. "Beth and I are ninety-seven-percent sure we are pregnant!" he had said. The memory made her smile.

She let the words slip out of her mouth. "We're going to have a baby today, my husband."

He raised up on his elbows, awake, alert. "Let's go. Are you okay? I'll call Miles."

* * * *

The contractions continued like clockwork on their expected minute, following into a countdown, until she was finally pronounced ready for the delivery room. Mitch paced and tried to stay out of the way; the nurse offered him a chair. Miles sat calmly by Beth's side, holding her hand in both of his. He leaned close to her ear, talking quietly about breathing and relaxing between contractions, repeating Dr. Stone's instructions to push. Then he got the signal and said, "Beth, push a final time, very strong, then open your eyes and look overhead in the mirror." He knew she would want to watch her baby being born. Beth looked up and at that moment she felt the child slide out of her body. She would never forget that powerful mixed feeling—the empty uterus, yet the joy of being Mother.

"Rest now," Miles whispered, as they put her to sleep and finished the after-birth process.

Mitch was cradling in his arms the blue-blanketed baby, who had a soft fine-knit blue cap covering his head and ears, down to his pale eyebrows, his deep-blue eyes wide open. Mitch transferred the bundle to his dad. The three stared at one another as if the same thought was being passed. *Okay, I am here for you.* After the nurse retrieved the baby, Mitch and Miles wrapped their arms around each other, tears running down their faces.

Chapter 22

The *Chicago Tribune* picked up the story of Alyssa's case. The juicy facts had the reporters slurping around Clarington Hills and the Lincoln Park area, craving tidbits about her privileged childhood and her single lifestyle. Students from Alyssa's elementary and high school classes said, "I sort of remember her name, but she wasn't in our clique," or "I don't know who she hung with." The doorman at her building politely answered, "I haven't learned the exact names of the residents yet"—a blatant, elusive lie. "I do recognize them, however": a solemn, wide-eyed truth. Other condo owners who were caught upon exiting the building gasped. "We saw her name in the paper, did she live here?" The staff at The Plum Tree Haven Clinic said they had never heard of her. Dr. Miles Matthews gave them a serious stare. "You know I can't comment on that." Either people didn't want to be involved or they didn't want to be part of the exaggerated gossip published in the newspaper. The reporters couldn't find anyone with information for them.

Alyssa's attorney, Jeremy "The Rooster" Rouster, strutted for the press, wearing his most pretentious silk ties, matching pocket-squares of purple, magenta, orange. He announced, "This case weighs heavy on the heart of every parent. A beautiful young woman from a loving, prosperous home, afflicted with mental illness and acting out with bizarre and criminal behavior." It was a stage-worthy speech, serious, dramatic, sad faced.

"The Rooster" filed a lengthy, detailed brief, accompanied by reports from three psychiatrists—a state-appointed, a court-appointed, and, of course, The Rooster-appointed Mack Heller—all attesting to Alyssa's insanity. The sessions of testing and psychoanalysis had continued daily for over three months. The judge studied, researched, asked for additional information, and after two more months, sentenced Alyssa to involuntary commitment at the Illinois Women's Psychiatric Hospital for the Criminally Insane, for a combination of psychiatric drugs and psychotherapy. "I find Alyssa Alexander not guilty as charged, by reason of insanity."

Meghan's parents cried silently, not comprehending the words *not guilty*, only understanding that their child had been murdered and the murderer not held responsible for the crime. Dejectedly they said to the reporters, "How can she be not guilty? At least she will be locked in a prison hospital."

Alyssa had been escorted into the courtroom, wrists and ankles cuffed. She stood in a slouched position, her chin resting on her chest, seemingly helpless. When the judge gave her verdict, Alyssa didn't look up, didn't flinch; there was no change in her blank facial expression, as though she hadn't heard, or perhaps her mind was in some far-off place. That was only the outward appearance. Her mind was as functional as a well-oiled machine and just as cold and methodical. She was planning her next irresponsible, rash adventure.

* * * *

Communication between Ray and Alyssa had diminished to once every two weeks. She wanted to give the impression of being incapable of thinking well enough to make phone calls and carry on normal conversations. She was keeping Ray on a string in case she needed to reel him in for some personal use, otherwise she would be finished with him. Ray had the same idea. *I might need to use her—if she told Larry the Louse that I was going to live in her apartment, he couldn't stop me, could he? Who knows how long she'll be in that hospital, maybe years. I could sell my townhouse and move into her condo.* He was in the courtroom at her hearing, sitting where she would see him, to prove his support.

Alyssa knew who she could depend on. Her supporter sat alone and unnoticed in back, the last row. Cheri received several calls from Alyssa daily. Alyssa was careful to request a different aide each time to dial the number for her, a show she liked to put on. They talked in code.

Cheri—*"How do you feel?"*

Alyssa—"Like shit." (Great)

Cheri—*"Can I do anything for you?"* (Do you have a plan?)

Alyssa—"I just want to hear your voice." (Yes, stand by, I'll keep you posted.)

Cheri—*"Can I visit you at the hospital?"* (What do you want me to bring?)

Alyssa—"I'll put your name on my visitation list. There's a required form for you to fill out." (I will have a list for you.)

Cheri—*"Just let me know when."*

Alyssa and Cheri had met as freshmen in college, drawn to each other by a powerful magnetism. They shared the same sexual desires, both being challenged by the need for pain, and together they learned a skilled application of pain sensation. Sometimes they had inventive sex with each other, but they also drew others into their exclusive circle by invitation only—girls who joined them for the excitement of a new experience but balked at the whips and knives, boys who were interested in the sexual adventure then retreated. The raunchy, tattooed motorcycle gang joined them with experimental sex that included pain, the giving and receiving. Members came into the circle, a few staying, some in and out quickly, all bound by secrecy, acknowledging to themselves they were participating in unusual acts that could affect their future thoughts about sex and relationships.

Alyssa and Cheri had become each other's protector, shield, personal assistant, and shared each other's secrets. They were mostly restrained and reticent toward classmates.

After college they'd bought separate condominiums in the same building, checked in with each other daily, and were available for emotional support or to assist with sexual experiments. In outward looks, they were total opposites. Alyssa, an exotic version—short, slicked-back dark hair, brown eyes outlined with thick mascaraed lashes and black eyeliner. Cheri was a Barbie doll with bouncy blond curls, dancing blue eyes, and shiny pink lipstick. Alyssa wore form-fitting cashmere sweaters, usually black or charcoal, black jeans or hugging slacks. Cheri always had a ruffle—around her neck, at her hips, or on the bottom of her short skirt, and the colors ranged through purple, violet, fuchsia.

Raymond assumed he had branded Alyssa with his initial. She let him believe that, but Cheri's last name was Romaine, and Cheri knew the R was not for Raymond. Alyssa had let him be part of her branding in order to encourage him to allow her to brand him. Her satisfaction came from administering the pain to him and receiving the pain from Cheri.

Their life, from an outsider's viewpoint, seemed haphazard, containing spur-of-the-moment antics, but their amusement was not a gamble. There was always a game plan comprising procedures, techniques, systematic methods, thoroughly researched. Self-satisfaction was their goal, without a conscience to direct right or wrong. Their pleasure derived from hurting, themselves and others, and that hurting could go as far as killing.

Now, Alyssa was ready to move on to her next game plan, which included the desire to destroy a life. Not only was Beth alive and well, she was married and pregnant. The sister she hated was thriving, and resentment welled up in Alyssa like acid. She thought of the satisfaction she got growing up, making Beth cringe, shrink from her threats. Just holding scissors or a knife and glancing at Beth had caused a wonderful frightened expression. *She was the favorite of our senseless parents with her "lovely hair," "beautiful smile," "flawless manners." "What excellent grades, Beth!" I suffered a meaningless existence with three foolish people. I'll punish her for those miserable years, impose the penalty.*

Chapter 23

Wisconsin had put out the welcome mat for spring, eased away the chill, snow sinking into the thawing earth that slowly sipped the water. Then, as if Mother Nature suddenly remembered the growing season was short and she better get moving, there was a rush of green popping up from the gardens, the fields, branches, vines. Birds joined the celebration with music and vibrant color—the jewel-blue indigo buntings, crayon-yellow and orange orioles, the plump chestnut-red breast of robins, and ruby-throated hummingbirds, luminescent in the sun, darting, hovering at early feeders.

Christopher Matthews, almost four months old, now had thick dark-brown hair covering his head like moss and ink-blue eyes so observant it seemed he was taking in and storing everything for later. He slept through the night, at least eight hours. Beth had discontinued nursing, and everyone in the house, including Hilde and Lech, took turns sitting in a comfortable chair to bottle-feed the child, who smiled at the faces of the people who carried, rocked, talked to him.

Lech drove to Clarington Hills every few weeks to pick up Charles Sullivan. He would stay three, four days, give his parenting advice, complain about the cold winter, and take brandy with Miles nightly. "Our girl, Miles, with her perseverance, has left behind her old self. She soars like a kite in her motherhood."

Beth called Mosel every week. "I miss you. When you have a break between jobs, please come stay with us for a few days." Mosel worked for Protection Security Agency, who booked him as bodyguard for celebrities in town for short stays. Often he said, "I'll come next week and pick up Charles on my way, save Lech a trip." Beth loved the company. "Oh, wonderful, my favorite men in our house, all at one time!"

* * * *

It was late afternoon, and summer had begun with long days filled with sunlight that allowed the field workers more time for their labor. Beth stood at the wide plate-glass window watching her father-in-law carrying his grandson through the strawberry field. She saw that Miles was talking, probably explaining to the child about the cycle of the now-lush plants with barely red fruit peeking out. The child loved the sound of Papa's voice.

The field had been mulched in fall with a thick layer of straw. It was the year to allow the plants to form runners in spring; the runners set roots and grew into new, productive plants. After the runners began fruiting, the old unproductive plants were pulled up. This was done every two to three years. Christopher was to hear, hundreds of times, the explanations, stories of the strawberry field, until he left for university, taking it all with him, part of his being, like his dad.

As Beth watched Miles and Chris, her thoughts went back to bringing a baby boy home from the hospital. On the dining room table had stood an enormous blue bouquet—cornflowers, hyacinths, irises, bluish-purple hydrangeas, all gathered with a blue satin ribbon and a huge bow partially hiding a note. "Thank you for mothering our son." Happily, Miles had received her permission to allow the baby to sleep in his room. Asleep, every four hours she would feel a hand on her shoulder, and as she sat up, Miles would place a backrest behind her, then put the freshly diapered, bundled baby in her arms, the little face turning, searching for his mother's breast. Miles sat in an armchair beside her bed, watching, whispering her greatness. Mitch would wake and she'd tell him to go back to sleep, because "You have to work tomorrow to support the family." Miles would take the drowsy baby, kiss Beth on the forehead, say, "Good night, Mommy, see you in four hours."

* * * *

When Chris started sleeping eight hours, Beth said to Miles, "I know you don't want to hear this, but it is time for Chris to sleep in his own room. You can put the monitor in your room to hear if he wakes up during the night. Remember, he was only supposed to stay with you for a couple weeks."

Miles agreed. "I want to thank you for letting me have the privilege of his company for all these months."

"You are the best Papa in the whole world."

* * * *

Mitch came home from the Clinic, saw his wife standing at the window, stepped behind her and put his arms around her shoulders. "What's so interesting outside?"

"I'm watching Chris and Papa. I'm sure they're discussing the phenomenon of recurring strawberries." Beth was holding two sheets of scalloped-edge, ecru stationery with writing in a flowery script.

Mitch laughed. "I know that discussion well. What are these papers?"

"I was remembering that my mother wrote a poem that Charles read at her memorial service. There's an incredible coincidence in her writing." She picked a few lines and read to him:

> *Let my ashes float free so some small speck of me*
> *may join soil in the valley*
> *and accompany apple blossoms into fruit,*
> *or perhaps nourish a field of sweet strawberries—*
> *my memorial, to soothe your sorrow.*

Beth's eyes filled with tears as Mitch drew her close to him.

"My darling, possibly she knew you would end up here. Who are we to say?"

Chapter 24

At the Illinois Women's Psychiatric Hospital for the Criminally Insane, patients lived in barred-window rooms. They had daily physical therapy, sessions with their assigned psychiatrist, and perhaps, if earned with good behavior, time in a large TV/game room. Approved patients could have meals in a cafeteria and sit at small tables for one or two. Very able-bodied female guards patrolled the aisles and stood around the room. There was no glass or plastic or even cardboard, only soft paper plates and a combination fork/spoon of heavyweight paper. The food varied little—chopped salad, overcooked vegetables, cubed chicken or crumbled ground steak. The coffee was warm; no hot liquid to throw at someone.

One side of the TV room had several small alcoves, each containing a table and one computer with lots of game apps, and a guard. Alyssa's perfect behavior and complete cooperation earned her time in the TV room, where she sat at a computer playing solitaire until the guard became bored and looked out the window between the bars. Alyssa would then send an e-mail to Cheri at an address under a made-up name, received on a different laptop. They had developed a complicated code of communication where random numbers stood for words, but the numbers were interspersed through the messages. To someone reading the email, the message seemed nonsensical, as would be expected from a psychiatric hospital. Today the decoded message read—come get me, week from Monday, rent black car, three complete bags—GCC, doctors' parking lot, south side of building near side entrance, nine at night.

It had taken Alyssa three months to establish a confusing pattern of not being in her room because she was in another room for the physically ill on the south side of the hospital. Nurses would consistently notice that she was missing from her lockup room, check her clipboard, and see the notation that she was back in sick bay. Alyssa had given a convincing story to the doctors and nurses, telling them that for years she had suffered from colitis, an inflammation in the digestive tract, gastroenteritis, gastritis, and other stomach ailments that caused burning abdominal pain, dizziness, vomiting, and diarrhea. It was untrue, of course. She often made herself vomit to get rid of the psychiatric drugs, making sure there were witnesses to the symptoms she staged—piercing cries of pain, grasping her stomach, acts of vomiting. When the doctors prescribed medication for her stomach ailments, she either hid the capsules under her tongue until she could spit them out or made herself vomit again.

After three months of Alyssa sporadically missing from her room at shift change, only to be found in the medical wing, the nurses began assuming if she wasn't in her lockup room she must be in the wing for the physically ill. Late at night, she would persuade the nurses to walk with her through the halls, saying the walking helped relieve her pain.

Alyssa was exploring, finding exits, checking guard stations, getting information—doctors had a private parking lot, private side entrance with a combination to get in. She laughed to herself. *I don't need the combination to get in. I just want to know how to get out.*

Cheri received the e-mail she had been waiting for. She knew exactly what her friend, her soulmate, her lover had asked her to do.

The two women had never been seen together in Chicago. When Cheri had assisted in Raymond's branding rite, they knew he would never relate the incident, never admit he had been duped into being branded. If he had to defend himself, explain, he would turn the occurrence into a drunken-night story.

Many times Alyssa had brought men home, the men happily going along with sex games for three. It was a diversion, an amusing distraction from home, from the wife of twenty-five years.

Alyssa and Cheri had spent much of their lives together. Since college it had been simply a matter of walking out one apartment door and a few steps down the hall to the next apartment. If they'd wanted to go out to dinner, they left separately and joined each other at a back-of-the-restaurant table. These precautions were justified when Alyssa was arrested. Detectives didn't know about the friendship, and Cheri was never contacted.

Cheri memorized Alyssa's e-mail, deleted it, and started fulfilling the instructions. With a phony name that matched a fake ID, she made a reservation for a black sedan rental car that would be less noticeable at night when she would hide in the hospital parking lot. "Three complete bags—GCC" signified guns, clothes, cash. Cheri was also an excellent markswoman, had lost interest in the sport, but because of Alyssa's encouragement, kept a stash of guns in her rental storage locker. To get clothes, she would enter Alyssa's apartment through her back door, from the garbage-chute area. No one would see or hear her going in the apartment. Both women had monthly allowances from trust funds, kept accumulated cash in bank security boxes, and each had a key to the other's box. Cheri planned to empty both security boxes, take the cash with her, along with the other requested items.

* * * *

Off the Washington State coast, over one hundred seventy islands made up the San Juan Islands of Puget Sound. Growing up, Cheri, an only child, and her parents spent summers on their private island until her parents were killed in an automobile accident two years after she graduated from college. Caretakers still lived in the island home, but Cheri hadn't been back. The island would be Cheri and Alyssa's destination after driving from the hospital, north to Wisconsin, then back south to Chicago. Cheri planned to drop off the rental car, get her car, drive to Washington, north on Highway Five to the pier. A small motor boat would be docked, as Cheri had instructed the caretaker.

* * * *

At the hospital, Alyssa opened the door to the doctors' parking lot, at first only enough to poke her head outside and check for the security guard who patrolled the parking lots. Not seeing the lights of his Toyota Land Cruiser, she stepped outside. Headlights of the black sedan in a parking space facing the door immediately turned on and the car rolled slowly to the side door. Alyssa opened the rear door and lay on the backseat as Cheri drove out of the parking lot heading for I-94 into Wisconsin. Once under way, Alyssa changed into jeans, T-shirt, loafers, and a short, curly blond wig. Cheri watched her in the rearview mirror, laughed at her reflection. "Does the new hair all grown in match the wig?"

Alyssa looked back at her in the mirror. "I'll let you find that out for yourself."

They stayed on the highway for two hours, Alyssa eating a turkey sandwich Cheri had gotten at a deli before arriving at the hospital. A tall neon sign with "MOTEL" in red letters stood conspicuous against the night sky. Alyssa said, "Pull off at the next exit. Let's get a room with parking in the rear, just in case someone saw us leave. I'm sure there is a camera on that hospital parking lot. We need to get rid of this car soon as possible."

Cheri nodded. "When we get back to Chicago, I'll drop the car off while you wait for me in a coffee shop. Then I'll pick up my car."

In the motel room, as she locked the door behind them, Alyssa started taking off her clothes, stood naked for Cheri, arms over her head, legs apart, beckoning, enticing, begging, luring. Cheri slowly viewed the familiar body. "You even have hair under your arms and on your legs."

"They don't give waxes or hand out razors at the insane asylum."

Cheri smiled, her right hand hung at her hip. Then, as if a storm struck, a sudden cloud burst, she tensed and, with a circular motion, gaining momentum, her open hand slapped Alyssa's face with burning speed, knocking her off balance. Just as she straightened up, the backhand flew across her other cheek. Alyssa grabbed the comforter off the bed, threw it on the floor. She jumped on Cheri, wrapping her legs around Cheri's waist, both falling to the floor, biting shoulders, arms, nipples, buttocks, thighs. Cheri reached for a large tote bag, unzipped it, and produced a vibrator shaped like a banana. She pulled Alyssa to a sitting position, legs apart, straight out in front of her. She placed the vibrator in her own vagina, half of it sticking out, straddled Alyssa, and pushed the other half of the vibrator into her vagina.

Alyssa growled, "Turn the speed up."

"It's on high."

"Turn your speed up."

Cheri's mouth was on Alyssa's shoulder, her teeth sinking into the flesh, blood coloring her lips, streaming down Alyssa's back.

A moan emanated from deep inside Alyssa. "You're a vampire—you've always liked the taste of blood."

"Especially yours."

They slept on top of the crumpled comforter on the floor. Sometime during the night, Cheri pulled the sheet off the bed, covered them, straddled Alyssa, and collapsed on top of her into a restless, impatient, weary sleep.

Cheri had had a childhood of indulgence, and as the only child she'd never learned to share. As an adult she was selfish, self-obsessed, and practiced self-gratification. She went along with Alyssa's sex games that included other people, but she was becoming more and more possessive of

Alyssa. She had decided she would help with Alyssa's vendetta against her sister, then she would stash her away for safekeeping, for her own, like a possession, a favorite toy.

After a breakfast of Alyssa's yearned-for over-easy eggs, crispy bacon, perfectly toasted bagels, Cheri drove the black sedan back onto the interstate.

Alyssa sat in the passenger seat wearing her blond wig. Cheri had given her some maps and pictures that she had printed from her computer. "I researched The Plum Tree Haven Clinic and the doctors Miles and Mitchell Matthews for you. There are two towns named Green Valley in Wisconsin, but only one with a psychiatric clinic. Both doctors have the same home address. Your sister lives with her husband and her father-in-law, isn't that cozy? When you google an address, you can get an aerial view of the entire area where the house is located. Computers give all the information one needs—a wonderful invention."

Alyssa studied the print-outs. "This is exactly what I wanted to know."

"What are we going to do when we get there?"

"Let's arrive around noon and take the chance that Beth and the baby will be having lunch, together in one room, just for our convenience. It would be a bonus if the husband or father-in-law are home, but if not, there'll be a nice surprise waiting when they get there—lots of blood and no heartbeats. With a house this size, there is probably a live-in housekeeper, unfortunate for her. You are going to follow me into the house with a gun. I will have this trusty long-blade you brought, nice and thin and sharp, exactly what I like. I'll put the other gun in the back of my waistband. Just back me up, shoot when I tell you, and aim for the chest. We'll be in close range."

Cheri was happy at the thought of having Beth out of Alyssa's life. *I don't want to hear anymore grumbling, resentment, complaining about that sister she hates. We'll get rid of her and Alyssa will be more content.* She told Alyssa her plan. "After we're finished in Green Valley, I have everything set for us to live on my private island in the San Juan Islands on Puget Sound. They'll never find you there; no one connects us. That was smart of us to not show our association all these years. When we want money or clothes, I'll be able to go back to Chicago, get money from my account, whatever we need, while you stay at the island."

"The island sounds great and so private. I'm tired of dealing with stupid people."

With Alyssa giving directions, Cheri turned onto the paved county road. "Up ahead there should be a dirt road, and two houses across from each other. We want the big house on the left."

Cheri drove past the Matthews house to the dead end, turned around, and stopped, waiting for instructions. Alyssa quickly devised her plan. "There are five people working in the field. We don't want to park at the end of the house by the garage, they'll be able to see the car. Pull into the circular driveway, go around past the front door and park the car at the other end, facing the road. There is a side door at that end of the house, probably to the kitchen or mudroom. It will be unlocked for the workers—we'll enter there."

The side door was unlocked; the first door on their left was a small apartment. A quick check found it empty. They walked through the kitchen into the dining room, Alyssa leading, holding the knife in front of her, bold, confident, signaling that she knew how to use it. Cheri held the heavy handgun with both hands, pointing it alternately at each person, a serious expression, squinting eyes, her finger on the trigger.

Hilde was at the side buffet, pouring tea from a pitcher into tall glasses filled with ice and a mint leaf. Miles and Beth had finished lunch and were sitting at the dining room table to have another glass of iced tea. Christopher was strapped into a high chair between them. Beth had just given him his bottle; he would be awake another couple of hours before his afternoon nap.

A collective gasp filled the room like someone had turned the volume up on the radio, then silence like it was turned off. Alyssa held the knife in front of Hilde's face, showing it to her, then moved it closer, the tip biting into her check. She froze as she felt blood trickle to her jaw. Alyssa barked, "You—sit down." Cheri stood a few steps to the side, the silent support, holding her gun, playing the aide, waiting for orders.

At Beth, Alyssa sneered, "You—don't talk."

Beth remembered that responding to Alyssa only made her more enraged. It always seemed to please Alyssa when Beth cowered. She lowered her head as if in reverence to a higher force, but she was not giving up. She was shocked and terrified and furious that this evil woman who had brought so much mental suffering to her life just wouldn't quit. Now she was threatening to take what Beth cared about away from her. Also, she was tormented about being the cause of harm to Hilde and Miles. She wanted to throw herself over her son, protect him. Flashes of consciousness fueled the resolve to act. Her mind and eyes swirled around the room looking for a weapon, lighting on the heavy brass candleholders in the middle of the buffet just to her right. *When she's one step closer, I'll grab a candleholder with both hands and swing it at her head.*

Miles was also silently planning an attack. *I'm stronger than Alyssa and when she puts that knife near Beth or Christopher, I'll iron-grip her hand and with all my might punch her in the throat with my fist, then tackle the other woman.*

To Miles, a smiley question: "Where's the other Dr. Matthews?"

He answered calmly. "He's at the Clinic. Alyssa, please—"

"Quiet!" Then the confident, in-charge tone: "Isn't this charming, the family right here at my fingertips?" She looked at Beth, pointed at the child with the sharp blade. "I'm so happy you're here to watch the show I have planned for you." She was taking her time, relishing these few minutes of control, enjoying the helpless, pained expressions on their faces. *Such pathetic people as this don't deserve to live.*

* * * *

At the psychiatric hospital, Helen, the head nurse in the sick bay south-side wing, was making her morning rounds. She was followed by an assistant and a young female guard, who was a gym rat, competed in bodybuilding contests, and worked part-time at the hospital. Helen, efficient, suspicious, serious-mouthed, got to the room that, according to her clipboard of papers, contained Alyssa Alexander. It was empty with an untouched, made-up bed. She asked the assistant, "Why isn't there a notation on Alyssa's chart that she is back in lockup?"

A call to the main desk in lockup brought a quick response. "We'll check on that." It started a bustle of activity, guards and nurses looking in every room, murmuring gossip through the halls. "She always put on a helpless show but I didn't trust her."

The lead psychiatrist called Helen. "Have you searched every corner of sick bay?"

Helen answered in her assured, clipped voice. "Dr. Meyer, Alyssa is not in this wing."

Dr. Meyer's response was full of worry. "We have thoroughly checked this part of the hospital. The guards are now searching the grounds. I'm in my office looking at her file. I'll call the police departments listed here and they'll put out a warning with her picture. I'll tell the sheriff in Green Valley to go to the house and tell her sister in person, offer some patrolling."

The Chicago police had a thick file on Alyssa. The captain received the warning, and as he read the report he saw a name he recognized. Daniel Rice was a detective he liked, who had worked diligently on the case and been responsible for the detailed investigation that led to Alyssa's arrest for murder. The captain called Dan. "Here's something that may interest you." He forwarded the information from the hospital to Dan's computer.

Dan Rice was in his car, on the way to downtown Chicago to check in for work. He pulled off the highway, brought up the hospital report and warning on his laptop. He immediately called his friend, Mosel Porter who had just finished an interview for a new bodyguard job that had been set up for him by his security agency. "Mosel, I am worried about Beth. As we know, that sister is crazy. If she escaped from the hospital, she may try again to kill Beth."

"I have Lech's cell number," Mosel said. "If I can't get him, I'll call the doctors Matthews. If I can't reach them, I will head up there myself."

Dan also called Doug Green with the Sheriff's department in Green Valley. He smiled, remembering he used to tease Doug about the town being named after him. "Doug, please patrol that road to the Matthews' house. I miss you, let's get together. Come down here, we'll go to a Cubs game."

Mosel called Lech's cell phone, thinking, *I don't want to be the one to worry Beth. I'm sure she will get a call from the hospital or some law enforcement.* "Lech, they believe Alyssa has escaped from the psych hospital. Just as a precaution, watch for any cars parked on the road or around your area."

Lech didn't like the news, but was happy to hear from Mosel. "Mosel, come visit us again soon. I want to know who you're guarding. You meet all the celebrities, and stories of your experiences put excitement in our lives. While we're talking, I'm walking to the front of the house to look down the road, put your mind at ease." As Lech got to the side of the house, he stopped and whispered, "Mosel, this might be one of Beth's friends. There is a car in the driveway I've never seen before . . ." Then, frightened, he stepped back, pressed his body flat against the wall like a soldier hiding from the sniper, his breathing fast, shallow, nervous. "Mosel, I just looked in the car. On the front seat is a blond wig and on the floor in the back is an open bag. I think there's a gun in it."

"Lech, do you still have that gun I left with you?"

Mosel heard Lech take a deep breath. "Yes, I do, it's in our apartment."

Slowly, calmly, Mosel said, "Listen carefully. Get the gun, walk in the house. If you confront someone holding a gun or any kind of weapon, aim for their chest and shoot. Lech, shoot the gun."

"I'm scared, Mosel."

"I know you, Lech—you can do it, you have to do it. If Alyssa is in the house, she is there to kill. And, Lech, don't forget to take off the safety."

Lech walked into the dining room gripping Mosel's gun in his left hand, his finger on the trigger, hiding it behind his left thigh. He was holding his right hand, palm out, in front of him.

The blond with the gun coolly asked, "Who the fuck are—" but a bullet tore into her shoulder. The other woman dropped her knife and was reaching behind, but a bullet into her chest splattered blood like a dropped glass of water on tile. Another bullet zinged into the blond's neck. Another bullet joined the oozing wound of the woman lying on the floor.

Miles jumped up, knelt beside the blond to check her neck pulse, but blood was gushing out. Unnecessarily, he checked her wrist pulse.

"Shall I shoot them again, Miles?"

Calmly, Miles put his arms around Lech, who had begun to shake as if frigid air had swept through the house. "No need, Lech, you have saved our lives."

Miles took the gun and led him to a chair next to Hilde, who was sobbing, reaching for him.

The gunfire had frightened Christopher; he was crying. Beth took him out of the highchair, walked out of the dining room. Walked away from the sound and smell of gunshot, away from the sight and smell of blood running, pooling on the oak parquet floor. She was talking quietly to her son, holding back the tears, thinking of her gratefulness to Lech. She felt nauseous at the revolting sights and smells. Deep concern swept over her that her child might be traumatized by the memories. She felt pity for her mentally troubled sister and guilt about being relieved she was dead.

Beth was suddenly aware of Mitch's arms wrapped around her and Chris. He had run out of the Clinic door to his car, barely clicking off the call from Mosel.

"We're safe now, my darling! Let's pack a bag for all of us and go to our home in Clarington Hills. Miles will go to the sheriff's station with Lech and Hilde to give statements. They'll join us later. Tomorrow we'll have breakfast in the gazebo. I wonder if those pears are ripe yet?"

ABOUT THE AUTHOR

Barbara Jean Ruther

Barbara Ruther was a corporate speaker and writer for Trans World Airlines. She wrote destination travel programs and gave presentations and seminars to travel groups. She has lived in New York and Chicago, and is now back home, living in Santa Fe, New Mexico.

Barbara is the author of the novel/love story, *Saving Snowflakes in My Pocket,* and *Dirt Roads and Places They Take You - Poetry and Memoirs.*

*For your reading pleasure,
we invite you to visit our web
bookstore*

TORRID BOOKS

www.torridbooks.com